"You're not making me one *damn bit nervous*, Ranger," Ferry said. His face reddened; he took two short threatening steps forward and stood glaring at the Ranger. "Without your *element of surprise*, you ain't so damn—"

He stopped short as the shotgun butt stabbed him hard in the middle of his chest just below where his ribs met. Breath and spittle flew from his mouth. He jackknifed and stood bowed deep at the waist, his hands clutching his solar plexus. The Ranger sidestepped, reached out and grabbed Ferry's Remington from its holster in one slick professional move and pitched it away. The other two gunmen had already grasped their revolvers, but upon seeing the Ranger toss the Remington into the dirt, they kept themselves in check and stood staring. The Ranger grabbed the back of Ferry's shirt collar and raised and lowered the gasping gunman up and down at the waist as if operating a pump handle.

"That's it, Ferry. Breathe deep," he said calmly.

"Jesus, he walked right into that," said Rudabaugh, giving Ferry a look of contempt.

"I saw it coming," said the other man, unimpressed.

Sam straightened Ferry onto his feet and steadied him a little.

"There, you're doing fine," he said encouragingly. He patted Ferry's bowed back. Ferry gasped and wheezed.

"I'll ki-kill you," he managed to say in a strained, weakened voice.

PAYBACK
AT BIG SILVER

Ralph Cotton

A SIGNET BOOK

SIGNET
Published by New American Library,
an imprint of Penguin Random House LLC
375 Hudson Street, New York, New York 10014

This book is an original publication of New American Library.

First Printing, October 2015

Copyright © Ralph Cotton, 2015
Penguin Random House supports copyright. Copyright fuels creativity, encourages diverse voices, promotes free speech, and creates a vibrant culture. Thank you for buying an authorized edition of this book and for complying with copyright laws by not reproducing, scanning, or distributing any part of it in any form without permission. You are supporting writers and allowing Penguin Random House to continue to publish books for every reader.

Signet and the Signet colophon are registered trademarks of Penguin Random House LLC.

For more information about Penguin Random House, visit penguin.com.

ISBN 978-0-451-47159-8

Printed in the United States of America
10 9 8 7 6 5 4 3 2 1

Penguin
Random
House

For Mary Lynn, of course . . .

Part 1

Part I

Chapter 1

Arizona Territory Ranger Sam Burrack sat waiting mid-trail atop his copper-colored dun. Both man and animal stood perfectly still, statuelike in the crisp silver dawn. Their senses searched the silence along the winding trail leading off and upward along the rocky hills. A sliver of steam curled in the dun's nostrils. The Ranger rested the butt of his Winchester rifle on his thigh, cocked and ready, its barrel pointing skyward. He'd removed his trail gloves and stuck them down behind his gun belt. He held his hand in a firing grip around the small of the rifle stock, his finger outside the trigger guard, resting along the cold metal gun chamber.

When the dun's ears pricked slightly toward the trail, the Ranger gave a trace of a smile and rubbed the horse's withers.

Not much longer. . . .

The men he lay in wait for had robbed a mine payroll the day before—in fact, had robbed two other payrolls over the past week. As the sound of horses' hooves overtook the morning silence, Sam wrapped his reins loosely around the dun's saddle horn, stepped down from the saddle and nudged the dun on its rump. The horse moved away behind the cover of a tall rock as if trained to do so. Sam shifted his rifle to his left hand, drew his Colt and held it cocked down his right side. Looking up along the trail, he counted four horsemen riding down, dust roiling behind their horses' hooves.

Riding into sight, the first horseman swung his horse quarterwise to the Ranger and jerked it to a halt.

"Whoa, boys!" he called out to the others, caught by surprise at seeing the Ranger standing there, alone, armed, looking as if he might have been there all night, waiting.

Sam stood staring calmly, his duster open down the front showing his badge should anyone be interested in seeing it.

"How the hell did you get around us, Ranger?" the first rider, a seasoned Missourian gunman named Bern Able, called out. As he spoke the other three jerked their horses to a halt. They instinctively formed a half circle on the narrow trail.

"Simple," Sam said coolly. "You stopped. I kept riding."

"I'll be damned. . . ." Able gave a stiff grin through a long unattended mustache. He looked all around the hill lines encircling them as if to see what route the Ranger had taken. "And that's all there was to it?" His hand rested on the butt of a Remington conversion strapped across his belly in a cross-draw holster. "I'll have to remember that."

The Ranger stood with his feet spread in a fighting stance, his riding duster spread open down the front, his battered gray sombrero brim tilted down a little on his forehead—Sonora-style—against the glare of rising sunlight in the east.

"I'll be taking that money now, Able," he said with resolve. He nodded at the bulging canvas bag hanging from the saddle horn of Able's pale speckled barb.

"*Taking's* what you'll have to do," said a younger Tex-Mexican outlaw named Brandon Suarez. His right hand rested on a holstered black-handled Colt with an eagle etched on its grip.

Sam only gave him a throwaway glance as if it went without saying that he would *take* the money. Then he looked back at Able, who still sat grinning, yet tensed, poised.

"Hush up, Brandon, we're talking here," Able said sidelong to Suarez without taking his eyes off the Ranger. "But he's right, you know," he said to Sam. "I've never understood why you lawmen think a man will risk his life, get his hands on some hard-earned money and just turn around and give it all up to you." He shook his head in disgust. "I'd like to hear just how you see any fairness in it." He fixed a hard, sharp gaze on the Ranger.

"Yeah, me too," said Suarez.

"It would require a lot of explaining," Sam said quietly, almost patiently. "That's not why I'm here." As he spoke his cocked Colt came up causally in an unthreatening manner and leveled at Able's chest, twenty feet away.

He slid a glance over the other two, a young but well-seasoned Wyoming cattle thief named Freddie Dobbs and a huge saloon bouncer from Maryland named Armand "Boomer" Phipps. He noted that Dobbs kept his hand well away from his holstered sidearm. Boomer Phipps, owing to his massive size, was not known for carrying a gun.

"Well, ain't you slicker than pig piss?" said Able. Rather than looking taken aback at how coolly the Ranger had just gotten the upper hand, Able shrugged it off.

The other three just stared, not understanding why Able had allowed that to happen.

"See, Brandon," he said as if undaunted, "that's his way of telling you to go to hell—that he don't give a damn how hard you work, or what-all you go through to get the money. He figures his job is to take it back, make sure it goes to the squareheads who weren't fit to hang on to it in the first place. Right, Ranger?" He glared at Sam as if enraged by the unfairness of it.

"There you have it," Sam said with resolve. He saw the slightest clasp of Able's gun hand on the butt of the big Remington belly gun—the faintest move of his thumb toward the gun hammer.

Now!

Sam's Colt bucked in his right hand before Able brought his belly gun out and up into play. Able flew backward as his blood splattered on Freddie Dobbs. Dobbs' horse whinnied and reared wildly. Sam fired the Winchester in his left hand, hoping the shot would distract Suarez. It did. The outlaw ducked a little as the rifle shot whistled past him. Before he could straighten and get a shot off, Sam swung his Colt toward him and fired. Suarez fell down the side of his spooked horse, blood spilling from his chest.

Even as his world faded around him, Suarez squeezed off a wild shot. Sam saw the round send Dobbs flying backward out of his saddle. He landed flat on his back. Sam swung the Colt toward Boomer Phipps, who sat unarmed and growling in his saddle like a mad dog.

"Hands in the air, Boomer," Sam called out. But even as he spoke he had to holster his Colt quickly and grab Able's speckled barb by its reins as the animal tried to streak past him. He held on to the spooked horse's reins, his Winchester smoking in his left.

"Who says?" Boomer growled at him. He swung down from his saddle. Moving fast for a man his size, he charged at the Ranger, as if unstoppable. "You're not going to shoot me. I'll break your head off!"

Sam knew he needed to lever a fresh round into the rifle chamber, but he had no time. Boomer Phipps charged hard and fast, a massive and deadly force pounding at him like a crazed grizzly. Sam let go of the barb's reins and drew the rifle far back over his right shoulder with both hands. With all his strength he drove the rifle butt forward into Phipps' broad forehead. Phipps stopped as if he'd run into a brick wall. The impact of the huge out-law sent the Ranger flying backward onto his rump.

Instead of going to the ground like any normal-sized man, Phipps staggered backward two steps, caught himself and stood swaying, dazed but still on his feet. Sam came to his feet, levering a round into his rifle, and stood with his feet braced, ready to fire.

"Stay where you are, Boomer," he warned. "Don't make me kill you."

Phipps batted his eyes; he raised his arms and spread his big hands in a wrestling stance.

"You ain't going to *kill me*, Ranger," he said, still dazed. "I'm going to kill you!" He stalked forward a step, then another.

Sam leveled the cocked rifle and aimed it at the outlaw's broad chest. There was nothing more to say— nothing more to do. Sam started to squeeze the trigger. But before he made the killing shot at a distance of less than thirty feet, Phipps crumbled to his knees, growled aloud and pitched forward onto his chest, finally succumbing to the blow on his forehead. Even still he moaned and slung his big head back and forth, trying to clear it.

Sam lowered the rifle in both hands as Phipps groaned and wallowed in the dirt. Stepping over to the dun, Sam took a pair of handcuffs from his saddlebags and a coil of rope from his saddle horn. Walking back to the downed outlaw, he grabbed the reins to Able's barb again as the horse stepped nervously around on the narrow trail.

"Don't make me hit you again, Boomer," Sam said, stooping down, grabbing the outlaw's left arm and pulling it back behind him before Phipps knew what was happening.

"I dare . . . you to, law dog!" Phipps growled, sounding groggy and thick-tongued. He reached his other hand around behind him and flailed about for the Ranger. Sam managed to grab the big hand long enough to clasp the cuff around the other wrist.

Phipps, still a little dazed, struggled against the cuffs and wallowed until he managed to rise onto his knees.

"I'll twist your limbs off!" he shouted at Sam.

Sam stepped back, opened a loop in the rope and swung it down over the big man's shoulders, drawing it tight around his arms. Before Phipps could react, two more loops swung around him and tightened.

"There, now, Boomer, settle yourself down," Sam said. "You're not going anywhere."

Phipps strained and struggled; Sam heard the rope creak with tension.

"Shoot me, Ranger, I dare you," he continued to taunt. "You won't shoot me. You're afraid to—!"

His words cut short as Sam stepped behind him, placed his right boot between his shoulders and shoved him forward. Phipps landed with a grunt and a solid thud. Sam wrapped three turns of rope around his thick knees and dogged the rope down.

"That ought to do it," he said quietly. Phipps struggled, but Sam could see he was wearing out.

"What about me . . . over here?" Freddie Dobbs called out in a weak voice. Sam saw him sitting up unsteadily on the ground. Blood ran freely from a bullet hole in his upper shoulder.

"I'm coming, Dobbs," Sam called out, dusting dirt from his hands. "Keep breathing in and out."

"That's . . . *real* funny," Dobbs rasped.

Sam helped the big outlaw to his feet and steadied

him for a moment. Phipps' forehead carried a swollen welt the size and shape of the Ranger's rifle butt. Blood trickled down from the welt and dripped from his nose. Sam tugged on the short length of rope in his hand.

"Let's go, Boomer," he said.

The outlaw looked down groggily at his knees with the rope wrapped securely around them. He took a short six-inch step forward, swaying, his huge arms bound against his sides.

"How am I supposed to walk like this?" he asked.

"Real slow," the Ranger replied flatly.

An hour passed as Sam dressed Freddie Dobbs' wounded shoulder with a folded bandanna he took from his saddlebags. He tied the bandanna in place with strips of Dobbs' shirtsleeve he'd torn off and cut into strips. Dobbs sat with his shirt hanging off his left shoulder. He looked down at the improvised bandaging and shook his head.

"That's my last shirt," he said in a sad tone.

"I've got worse news than that for you," Sam said, standing, pouring canteen water onto his cupped hand, then clamping the canteen under his arm and washing his hands together. "The bullet is stuck against a bone inside your shoulder."

"*Jesus*," said Dobbs, "that's why I can't bend my arm?" He tried rounding his shoulder a little but stopped in a sharp surge of pain.

"Most likely that's why," Sam said. "The bullet has to be cut out." He looked all around the barren desert hill country as he spoke.

"Can't you slice right in there, dig it up and pluck it out, Ranger?" Boomer Phipps asked, sitting off to the side listening, his forehead still pounding.

"Slice, dig? *Pluck . . . ?*" said Dobbs. He looked back and forth between the two, sweat pouring down his forehead. "What the hell am I, some kind of roasting animal?"

Phipps just scowled at him.

"I can cut it out," Sam said. "But it would be less painful if we took you into town and got it done." He looked Dobbs up and down. "You decide. But it needs doing quick, keep the fever from setting in."

"Man oh man. . . ." Dobbs looked worried as he considered the matter and touched his hand carefully against the bloody bandage.

Seeing the look on his troubled face, Sam handed the canteen down to him.

"We're a day's ride from Big Silver," he said. "There's a doctor there most times."

"Most times?" said Dobbs, taking the canteen. "I don't like those odds."

"Then you should have picked a different game," Sam said.

Dobbs paused, then said, "Say . . . that's Sheriff Sheppard Stone's town." A slight grin came to his parched lips. "Didn't I hear he's a drunk? Heard he's gone loco, thinks he turns into a wolf or something."

Sam stared at him. It had been a month now since he rode with Sheriff Stone, and the woman sheriff named Kay Deluna. The three of them had fought a band of outlaws bent on holding a railroad baron named Curtis Siedell hostage.

"I heard some rumors like that myself," Sam said. "Last I saw Stone he was sober, doing his job like always. Anyway, Big Silver's where we're going."

"I heard about you and Stone riding down Bo Anson," said Phipps, his hand cupped to his throbbing forehead. "I heard you killed ol' Bo for no good reason."

"I killed Bo Anson because he was holding Curtis Siedell for ransom and wouldn't give him up. There was also a few killings that Bo Anson was not even being charged with."

"King Curtis Siedell, the 'baron of the rails,'" said Phipps with a chuff of contempt. "Bo shoulda killed that carpet-bagging son of a bitch—he ought to have gotten a medal for doing it." He glared at Sam. "But instead, you stopped ol' Bo's clock." He shook his head at the unfairness of it. "There's a lot of ol' boys who still hold that against you, in case you don't know it."

Sam ignored the comment and stepped over to Phipps.

"I'm going to untie your knees so you can ride, Boomer," he said.

"What about these?" Phipps said, wiggling his thick fingers to indicate the handcuffs on his wrists.

"I'm leaving the cuffs on and the rope around your arms," Sam said. "If you try to make a run for it, I'll yank your lead rope and you'll hit the ground."

"Yeah, and?" Phipps said as if not worried about being yanked from atop a running horse.

"And you'll ride into Big Silver sidesaddle," Sam warned.

"*Side*saddle . . . ?" Phipps gave him a look of disgust. "I'd sooner die and be dragged in on a rope."

"Suit yourself," Sam said coolly. "I'm just presenting your choices. How you arrive in Big Silver is up to you." He reached down and started loosening the rope around the big outlaw's knees.

Chapter 2

The Sonora Desert, Mexican badlands

"Hector, more whiskey," Edsel Centrila said over his shoulder to Hector Mendoza. He handed his empty glass back to the middle-aged Mexican house servant.

"*Sí*, right away," Hector Mendoza said. He took the whiskey glass and hurried to the office bar to refill it.

Edsel Centrila stood, cigar in hand, at the window of his office looking out across the cattle ranch he'd acquired in a land grant from the Mexican government ten years earlier. In the northeast beyond a line of blackened jagged hills lay the Mexico–United States border. To the west of his spread lay the Sonora Desert, carpeted by sand flats, occupied in perpetuity by meandering hill range and arid rock lands. Within the wavering heat saguaro cactus, tall and treelike, stared back at him with their spiny arms lifted to the white-hot sky as if held at gunpoint.

"*Gracias*," he said when the Mexican brought the filled whiskey glass to him. "Send Charlie Knapp to me."

"*Sí*, I send him," the Mexican said. He waited for a second anticipating further orders.

"Then go to the barn and bring a couple of turn-around horses while I meet these two at the rail." He nodded at two riders galloping out of the heat and white sunlight less than a hundred yards away. He recognized the two dust-covered men as the Cady brothers, Lyle and Ignacio.

"Shall I prepare room in the empty bunkhouse for them?" Hector asked, already turning toward the door.

"No," said Centrila, "they won't be staying long."

As Hector Mendoza left for the barn, Centrila walked out of his office and stood on the wide stone porch of the hacienda, whiskey glass in hand, awaiting the two riders. When the Cady brothers drew closer and reined their horses down to a walk the last thirty yards, Centrila stepped down from the porch and stood at the hitch rail watching them, his right hand on his hip, close to the bone handle of a tall Colt standing in a tooled slim-jim holster.

"Howdy, Mr. Centrila," said Lyle Cady, raising his hat an inch as he and his brother, Ignacio, stopped their horses ten feet away from the iron hitch rail. The two waited for an invitation before stepping down from their saddles. Their horses sniffed toward a horse trough full of water standing near the hitch rail.

"Howdy," Centrila said with a growl in his voice. He gave a short jerk of his head toward the water trough and stood watching as the two led their horses over and let them drink.

"I'll tell you first thing, Mr. Centrila," said Lyle, letting out a tired breath. "This has been no easy ride for Iggy and me."

"If you're expecting to get more money, forget it," said Centrila. "As long as this has taken, you're lucky I don't shoot the both of you." As he spoke he looked the two up and down, noting the nicks and scars and bruises they had acquired since the last time he saw them. "What the hell happened anyway?" he demanded. "I sent you to get my money back from Sheriff Stone. You come back looking like you've been in a gun battle."

Lyle Cady swallowed a dry knot in his throat when he saw Centrila's hired gunman, Charlie Knapp, appear around the corner of the hacienda.

"The truth is, we have been in a gun battle. But that ain't all that's happened to us," said Lyle. Beside him, Ignacio Cady turned and watched Knapp closely as his brother spoke. "We found Sheriff Stone like we said we would. He was on the trail with Ranger Burrack."

"Sam Burrack." Centrila considered the matter, then said, "All right, go on. Tell me how this caused you to come dragging in here a month late." He took a deep breath and stood tapping his fingers on his gun butt. "Hadn't been for the telegraph you sent last week, I'd have figured you collected my money from Stone and took off with it."

"No, sir, we wouldn't do that," Lyle put in quickly. "Like I said in the telegraph, we didn't get your money. Truth is, Sheriff Stone has gone plumb loco. He gets drunk and thinks he's a wolf—"

"I don't give a damn if he thinks he's the president

of the United Sates," said Centrila, cutting him off. "I gave him money to bribe the judge and keep my son out of prison. Stone crawfished and never gave the money to the judge. My son, Harper, is behind bars, and I want him out." He glared at the Cady brothers.

"It's understandable you being upset," Lyle said meekly. "I only wish I knew some way to—"

"You're going to get Harper out of prison," Centrila said, cutting the nervous Cady brother off again. He jerked his head toward Charlie Knapp, who stood watching and listening with a rifle hanging in his left hand. "Charlie's set it up with some gunmen he knows. You two are going with him."

"Mr. Centrila," said Lyle, shaking his head a little, "there's nothing that would please Iggy and me more than breaking Harper out of prison. But the thing is—"

"Good, I'm glad to hear that," said Centrila, for the third time cutting him off. "I had already told Charlie to shoot you both if you tried to crawfish on me." He gave a cruel grin. "You can understand how I feel about crawfishing after the way Sheriff Stone treated our deal."

Lyle started to offer more on the matter, but Ignacio cut in before he could.

"We understand, sir," he said, stepping over half between his brother and Centrila. "Breaking Harper out is the least we can do, as good as you've treated us. Say the word and we'll kill Sheppard Stone while we're at it, that crawfishing son of a bitch."

"Indeed you *will*," said Centrila, as if he'd planned

everything before their arrival. He raised his cigar, took a deep draw, then blew gray smoke upward in a thin stream.

Lyle and Ignacio looked at each other curiously as Centrila gave them an evil grin and continued.

"Charlie will be riding along with you, to oversee things this time," he said. He turned and looked at Knapp as Hector Mendoza led two fresh horses and Knapp's already saddled black barb around the corner of the hacienda. "Charlie," he said matter-of-factly, "if these two monkeys give you any trouble or try to cut out, I want you to kill them both in whatever manner you see fit."

"My pleasure, boss," said Knapp, touching his gloved fingers to the flat brim of his hat.

Seeing the Mexican house servant start changing their saddles and gear over to the fresh horses, Lyle Cady let out a tired dry breath.

"Mr. Centrila, I don't mean to complain," he said. "But my brother and I are as worn out and thirsty as our horses." He eyed the whiskey glass in Centrila's hand. "If we could get some grub in our bellies, something to drink and some rest—"

Centrila only stared at him. This time it was the sound of Knapp's levering his rifle that cut him off.

Both Cadys turned warily and looked at the gunman as he stepped closer to them, holding his rifle aimed at them with one hand.

"Boys," he said in a mild eerie voice, "let's not get off on the wrong foot here. . . ."

The Mexican stepped back from the hastily saddled

fresh horses. The Cadys' tired horses, now bareback, still stood drinking at the trough.

"Where's my manners?" said Centrila. "Hector, fill these gentlemen's canteens for them." He gestured toward the water trough, then smiled and said, "And bring me another whiskey, *por favor*." He swished the remaining whiskey in his glass, raised the glass to his lips and drank it down.

Lyle and Ignacio Cady stood staring, hungry, thirsty and tired. Knapp reached up with the tip of his rifle barrel and tweaked it back and forth on Lyle's earlobe.

"All right, you *Cady brothers*," he said with a measure of contempt. "Let's not impose on Mr. Centrila's hospitality. You can fill your canteens along the way. Haul up out of here," he demanded. "We're going to ride all day, cover a lot of ground before sundown."

The weary brothers turned to the saddled horses without reply.

Centrila grinned and stood watching as the three mounted and turned their horses toward the trail. He gave Knapp a nod when the gunman looked back over his shoulder at him. Then he spoke sidelong to the Mexican house servant.

"Hector, never mind the whiskey," he said. "Lord Hargrove's cattle buyer is coming today to see about purchasing all my cattle. Let's make him feel welcome."

"*All* of your cattle, *señor*?" Mendoza asked, surprised by the news.

"Every last head," Centrila replied. He lifted his head and let out a stream of cigar smoke. "I've gone into the liquor and gaming business—for a while anyway. This happens to be a good time to sell cattle. I can always buy more when the market is down." He smiled and drew on the cigar.

"Señor Centrila, I don't know what to say. . . ." Mendoza gave a puzzled shrug.

"Don't worry, Hector. Your job is safe," the cattleman assured him. "The English only want the beef. They're not interested in the land. I'm still the big bull here." He looked at the Mexican and saw relief in his dark eyes. "Anyway, the deal is done. I've already purchased a saloon. I've got men taking possession until I get there." He gazed off in reflection and smiled to himself in satisfaction.

Big Silver, Arizona Badlands

In the late afternoon, Sheriff Sheppard Stone stood on the boardwalk out in front of his office and watched workers take down the faded wooden sign atop the facade of the old Roi-Tan Saloon. He had not had a drink of whiskey or any other kind of hard liquor for a month. *Not even a single sip of frothy beer,* he reminded himself. Coincidently that was how long it had been since he rode with Sheriff Kay Deluna and the Ranger in pursuit of Bo Anson and his outlaws who had taken rail baron Curtis Siedell hostage. Being sober for a full month was certainly cause for celebration.

Don't you think . . . ? a devilish voice asked inside him. He recognized that voice and knew full well where that question would take him if he weakened enough to follow it. *Son of a bitch. . . .* He let out a tight breath and raised his coffee cup to his lips, not sure if he was cursing the tormenting inner voice, or himself, or the sight of the bright new wooden sign being erected atop the saloon's facade. The new sign read CENTRILA'S SILVER PALACE.

Yesterday, a faded wooden sign had been lowered from above the doors of Sergio Manuel's cantina. Boards had been nailed up over the windows. Shortly after selling his business to Edsel Centrila, Sergio Manuel had vanished, money and all. The only drinking establishments left in town were Centrila's Silver Palace and a run-down cantina, Mama Belleza's, run by an elderly Mexican woman.

All right. . . . Stone let out another tight breath and sipped from his cup of coffee—this being his third full pot of the day, meaning he'd drunk—*how many cups, ten, eleven since noon?* Not to mention how much he'd drunk earlier during the day.

That's a lot of coffee.

To hell with it. He'd been drinking more and more coffee. *So what?* He took another, larger sip and watched the workers nail and bolt the new sign into place. His fingers trembled a little as he dug down into his shirt pocket, inside a stiff little paper box, and fished out a cherry-flavored cough drop and stuck it inside his mouth.

More candy? again the devilish voice asked, taunting him.

No, it's not candy, he countered.

Still, he smoothed down his shirt pocket and looked around as if making sure he hadn't been seen. Since sobering up he'd gone around sucking on candy, hard rock, horehound, sugar plum sticks, anything he could get his hands on, like some spoiled schoolkid. Luckily two weeks ago the mercantile owner had set up a jar of loose Smith Brothers cough drops on the counter. Along with the jar of loose drops, he'd ordered some of the new stiff paper boxes like the one in his pocket— twenty pieces per box. He realized he was on his third box of the day. But he was sober, he reminded himself; that was the main thing.

He adjusted the big Colt standing holstered on his hip and looked away from the workers at the new Silver Palace Saloon and out at the three riders who had been galloping toward town from out across the sand flats for the past hour. At first all he'd seen was the distant rise of trail dust. Now that they'd drawn closer, riding up onto the main street, he recognized the Ranger's big copper dun and the pearl-gray sombrero atop his head.

Figured I'd see you again before long, Ranger, he said to himself. A thin sliver of a smile came to his lips. He felt his pulse quicken a little. Even though he'd just then adjusted his Colt in its holster, he caught himself adjusting it again as he set his coffee cup on the window ledge and stepped down onto the dirt street, where he stood until the Ranger and his two prisoners slowed their horses to a walk and stopped ten feet from him. With a nod from Stone, the two handcuffed prisoners stepped their horses to the hitch rail.

Sheriff Stone eyed the two men in their saddles. He

recognized them both as he walked past them to where Sam sat atop the dun with his rifle across his lap. He noted the blood on Freddie Dobbs' shoulder, the missing shirtsleeve.

"Howdy, Ranger," Stone said. He took the Ranger's dun by its bridle and held it as Sam swung down from his saddle. "Where'd you run into these two sidewinders?"

"They were riding with Bern Able, robbing mine payrolls," said Sam. He nodded at the canvas bag of money tied down atop his saddlebags. "There's one bag from yesterday. There's a smaller one inside it from the other day."

Stone looked at the two prisoners again, then back at Sam.

"I'm going to guess that Bern Able didn't take kindly to going to jail?" he queried.

"Yep, that's true," Sam said. "Neither did Suarez. They're back there along the hill trail. I drug them off a ways."

"Which one of the Suarez twins?" Stone asked, interested.

"Brandon, as far as I know," Sam said. "That's what Able called him. But it could be Sanford. I can't tell the two apart."

Stone nodded and looked around at the prisoners as if deciding whether or not Sanford "Sandy" Suarez would ride with these two.

"Sandy being a noted gunman, he might hold himself above the likes of this crowbait."

"Take these cuffs off me, you drunken pig," Boomer Phipps growled. "I'll show you *crowbait*." He jerked and strained his thick wrists against the handcuffs.

"That's enough of that, Boomer," Sam said. "Both of you get down and get inside." He looked at Stone. "Freddie's got a bullet in him that needs to be cut out."

Stone gave him a look.

"I didn't shoot him," Sam said. "Suarez's gun went off and nailed him before he died."

"Just my luck I caught the bullet with my shoulder," Dobbs said in a bitter tone. He and Boomer stepped down and stood beside their horses at the hitch rail.

"My offer still stands, Sheriff *Whiskey-head*," Boomer Phipps taunted. "Take these cuffs off and I'll clean this street with your hide." He rattled the cuffs on his wrists.

Sam saw Stone start to take a step toward the big outlaw. But the seasoned lawman caught himself and took a deep breath.

"I'll send for the doctor," Stone said quietly, ignoring Boomer's threat. He raised a hand and waved in a young man as the two prisoners stood looking the town over. Townsfolk had started looking toward the sheriff's office curiously.

When Stone had sent the young boy hurrying off to the doctor's residence, he and Sam ushered the two prisoners inside the sheriff's office.

"How've you been, Sheriff?" Sam asked, seeing a sour look come over Stone's face as he gazed off through the window at the new saloon sign.

"Have I been staying sober, is what you're wanting to ask me, Ranger?" Stone said.

"If I wanted to ask you that, I would have," Sam said. He looked Stone up and down. "Something bothering you, Sheriff?" he asked, his tone no less bristly than the sheriff's.

Stone let out a breath.

"Pay me no mind, Ranger," he said. "I've been high-strung as a tomcat all day." He gestured out the front window in the direction of the saloon. "We get these yahoos locked up, I'll tell you all about it."

Chapter 3

In a cell inside the sheriff's office, a former army surgeon named Dr. Morris Tierney had laid out his surgical instruments on a small table the sheriff brought in and set up for him beside Dobbs' bunk. Dobbs swallowed a lump in his throat and kept quiet, looking at the sharp cutting tools. After a quick inventory of his instruments the doctor poured a few drops of chloroform onto a folded cloth and pressed it over Freddie Dobbs' nose and mouth. Boomer Phipps watched closely from an adjoining cell. Sheriff Stone and the Ranger watched from outside the cell until they were certain Dobbs was unconscious. As the doctor picked up and inspected the edge and point on a thin scalpel, Stone nodded toward the boardwalk and the two lawmen turned and walked out the front door. Noting the tremor in Stone's hands, Sam looked him up and down as the sheriff fished a bag of tobacco from his shirt pocket and begin to roll himself a smoke.

"It's nothing, Ranger," Stone said, his hands settling a little as he smoothed a rolling paper and formed it in his fingers. "I'm used to pulling a cork after jailing a couple of hard cases. Riding dry takes some getting used to." He bit the edge of the cloth drawstring tobacco pouch and pulled it open. "I'd be lying if I said I don't miss it."

"I understand," Sam said, still checking the steadiness of Stone's hands, especially his right—his gun hand. He watched Stone sprinkle tobacco back and forth along the white paper cradle.

"But I'm done with it," Stone said, glancing up at him. He bit one of the strings atop the pouch, drew the pouch shut and dropped it back into his pocket. "It made a fool of me long enough. It ain't so much the whiskey that's got me shaky," he added. "Seems like I'm living on strong coffee and rock candy." He paused and ran his tongue along the edge of the cigarette paper. "But this will all pass. . . ."

"I'm glad it's going good for you, Sheriff," Sam said. "What about that other thing you were having trouble with?"

"What? Oh, you mean thinking I was turning into a wolf?" Stone said.

"Yeah, that," Sam said.

Stone shrugged; he ran the cigarette in and out of his mouth and gave either end a slight twist.

"I'm done with that too," he said. "I don't know what come over me, but it's over now. The more sober I get, the more loco all that sounds."

Sam just looked at him, a little skeptical.

"Trust me—it's over, Ranger," Stone said with a tired grin. He held out a hand. "Want to shake my paw on it?"

Sam still stared, stoically.

"Easy, Ranger, I'm just joshing. Don't laugh yourself into madness," said Stone. He stuck the cigarette in his mouth and searched himself for a match.

Sam gave a trace of a smile.

"I thought it might be a joke," he said. He watched Stone light the cigarette, take a draw and blow it out. "What about the situation with the judge?"

"It's all clear," said Stone. "I explained everything that's been going on—told him about the twenty thousand dollars Centrila passed along for me to give to him. He believes I wasn't going to keep it. Had me send the bribe money to him by rail express, soon as I got back here from Yuma. He's investigating the matter, seeing if he can charge Centrila with attempted bribery and make it stick."

"I wouldn't let my hopes get too high, Sheriff," Sam cautioned him. "It's getting to where rich men don't go to jail, they go to lawyers."

"I know that," Stone said. "I just did my part. The rest is up to the judge. At least Centrila didn't get his son, Harper, out of prison. That shows that the law still works, *some* anyway."

"That's the only way we can look at it," Sam offered.

"Speaking of Centrila," Stone said, nodding toward the new sign above the saloon. "He now owns two of Silver's *three* drinking and gambling establishments."

"Gave up the cattle business for gambling establishments?" Sam speculated, taking in the new sign, seeing the men gathered out in front of the Silver Palace.

"He's not fooling me," Stone said. "He ain't giving up cattle, not for long anyway. He's got an ax to grind with me. I figure he's going to wait his chance and have me killed. He's got the gunmen to do it, and there's no better place to get a lawman shot down than in a crowded saloon." He inspected the front of the Silver Palace as if seeing the place where his fate would some-day unfold.

"Say the word," said Sam. "We'll both go jerk a knot in his tail. Maybe he'll back off."

"Ha," said Stone. "He's nowhere around. We both know that a snake like Edsel Centrila wouldn't be caught within a hundred miles of a man he had killed." He nodded at three well-dressed horsemen moving up to the Palace's hitch rail at a walk. "You ever heard of Silas Rudabaugh?"

Sam gazed at the three riders, seeing them stare back at him and Stone.

"Rudabaugh the stock detective," Sam said, calling upon his memory for the gunman. "Heard of him, never had cause to meet him." He watched as a short, frail-looking Mexican woman walked purposefully toward the three gunmen, cursing them as they stepped down from their horses.

"You're getting ready to," Stone said, "unless you prefer to watch from here."

"Watch what?" the Ranger asked.

"This!" said Stone. As he spoke, he and Sam both saw the Mexican woman swing a shotgun up from under her black shawl and aim it at the three gunmen.

"No, Mama Belleza!" Stone shouted loudly as he broke forward in a run, his hand on his holstered Colt. "Lower that scattergun *right now!*"

Sam ran alongside him. He sensed that Stone's concern was more for the woman than the three men.

The woman swung toward Stone and the Ranger as the three gunmen stood facing her from fifty feet. Seeing the sheriff, the woman lowered the shotgun just as she pulled both the triggers and sent an upsurge of dirt exploding into the air ten feet in front of her. The impact of both barrels firing sent her staggering backward. But she managed to catch herself and stay on her feet. She threw her bony hands up in surrender. The shotgun fell to the ground. The three gunmen laughed aloud. One of them lowered a shiny Remington back down into its holster.

"I do not shoot at you, Sheriff!" she shouted in a tearful voice. "I shoot at this pig." She jerked her head toward the middle gunman, who stood watching with a stylish charcoal gray coachman's hat cocked jauntily to one side of his head. He clenched a thin cigar in his teeth. A long gold watch chain looped down from his vest pocket.

"Easy does it," he whispered to the other two gunmen. "She's not worth a bullet." His black-gloved hand rested on the butt of a big Colt standing in a cross-draw holster, the lapel of his black riding duster pulled open behind it.

Stone slid to a halt and took both the old Mexican woman's hands in his and held her.

"You can't be doing this, Mama Belleza," he said,

keeping his voice lowered. "You're lucky they didn't kill you."

The elderly woman paid no attention to his warning. "Who is this one?" she asked, eying the Ranger.

"He's Ranger Sam Burrack, Mama," Stone said quickly. "He's here on business." He turned toward Sam with her. The three gunmen watched, wearing smug grins. "Ranger, this is Mama Belleza. She owns the Hermosa Cantina."

"Pleased, ma'am," Sam said. He kept watch on the three gunmen as he touched the brim of his sombrero toward the frail elderly woman.

"Let's get you out of the street, Mama," Sheriff Stone said. Slipping an arm around her thin waist, he started to usher her toward her run-down cantina a block away. The Ranger walked over and picked up the smoking shotgun lying in the dirt. He broke the gun open and hung it over his forearm.

"Whoa there, Sheriff, what's your hurry?" the man in the coachman's hat called out. "Aren't you going to ask if I want this woman arrested? She *did* come here to kill me."

"I'm taking her home, Rudabaugh. Come to my office if you want to bring charges," Stone said. He turned and walked away with the frail woman against his side. Sam stood in the street facing the three men, covering the sheriff's back.

"What's this? *Ranger Burrack* must think we're all three back-shooters," said one of the gunmen. This one wore a black bowler and long matching duster.

The Ranger looked closer at the man speaking.

"*Dirty* Donald Ferry . . . ," he said, recognizing the man.

The man spread his arms and gave a stiff smile.

"Maybe then, but do I look *dirty* now, Ranger?" he said.

"The name always lent itself more to your character than your personal hygiene, Donald," Sam replied. As he spoke he raised the empty shotgun from over his forearm, snapped it shut and started walking forward. "Who are your pals?" He looked the other two men up and down.

"See what the Ranger's doing right now?" said Ferry instead of answering Sam. "He's getting in close with that shotgun so's he can crack somebody in the jaw with the butt of it." He grinned. "But it ain't going to happen this time like it did before."

Sam stopped two steps farther back than he'd intended to and looked down at the shotgun in his hand as if he hadn't realized he was carrying it.

"You feel better if I stop back here, Donald?" he said. "I don't want to make you turn pale and nervous."

"You're not making me one *damn bit nervous*, Ranger," Ferry said. His face reddened; he took two short threatening steps forward and stood glaring at the Ranger. "Without your *element of surprise*, you ain't so damn—"

He stopped short as the shotgun butt stabbed him hard in the middle of his chest just below where his ribs met. Breath and spittle flew from his mouth. He jackknifed and stood bowed deep at the waist, his hands clutching his solar plexus. The Ranger sidestepped, reached out and grabbed Ferry's Remington from its holster in one slick professional move and pitched it away. The other two gunmen had already grasped their revolvers, but upon seeing the Ranger toss the Remington into the dirt, they kept themselves in check and stood staring. The Ranger grabbed the back of Ferry's shirt collar and raised the gasping gunman up and down at the waist as if operating a pump handle.

"That's it, Ferry. Breathe deep," he said calmly.

"Jesus, he walked right into that," said Rudabaugh, giving Ferry a look of contempt.

"I saw it coming," said the other man, unimpressed.

Sam straightened Ferry onto his feet and steadied him a little.

"There, you're doing fine," he said encouragingly. He patted Ferry's bowed back. Ferry gasped and wheezed.

"I'll ki-kill you," he managed to say in a strained, weakened voice.

"Let it go, Ferry, he got you," Rudabaugh cut in sharply. He said to the Ranger, "I'm Silas Rudabaugh, Ranger." He raised his hand from the butt of his Colt and gestured it toward the third man, a stout man with a thin mustache who wore a wide-brimmed hat with a flat crown. "This is Clayton Boyle. We've both heard of you." With that he let his hand fall to his side, away from his holstered Colt. "You wield a wicked shotgun." He nodded at the bowed gunman with a string of spittle hanging down from his lips. "I'll remind Donald that you could have done much worse, had you a mind to."

"I know Dirty Donald," Sam said. "He was stoking himself into pulling that Remmy on me. I figured it better to stop him before he went too far." As he spoke he picked up the shiny gun, wiped it off and handed it to Clayton Boyle. The serious-looking gunman stuck it down into his waist.

"Are you here to back the sheriff's play?" Boyle asked in a blunt tone.

Sam stared at him.

"What *play* is that?" he asked coolly, with a fixed stare.

"Typical lawman," Rudabaugh cut in quickly as if to change the subject. "No offense, but do all you lawmen answer a question with a *question*?"

"Do we?" Sam said flatly. Hearing Donald Ferry breathing a little steadier beside him, he touched the brim of his sombrero and took a step back. He caught a glimpse of Stone walking out into the street, facing his direction, a raised rifle in hand.

"We're not out to break any laws here," Rudabaugh called out.

"We're here overseeing things—making sure things go smooth for Edsel Centrila with his new businesses," Boyle added. Beside them, Donald Ferry straightened some more and wiped a sleeve across his mouth. He reached out toward Boyle, one hand still clasped to his aching chest.

"Give me . . . my gun . . . I'll kill him," he rasped.

"Lower your hand, *Dirty* Donald," said Boyle, "or I'll kill you myself."

Stone turned on the street and walked alongside the Ranger to the faded, run-down Hermosa Cantina. In-

side the cantina the Ranger handed the empty shotgun sidelong to an elderly bartender, who broke the
gun open and walked it behind an ornate but faded
tile bar. Stone tapped his fingers nervously on the rifle
in his hand and adjusted a sweet cough drop in his
mouth.

"You sure put a dent in Dirty Donald's apparatus,"
he said with a slight grin. "I expect he won't be singing
in any choirs for a good long while."

"He was working himself into a lather, Sheriff," Sam
said. "If I'd waited any longer, I would have had to kill
him." He paused, then said, "How's the woman?"

"Mama Belleza's all right," said Stone. "One of her
granddaughters is with her back there, settling her
down." He gestured toward the living quarters behind
the cantina. "That was close. Had one of those gunmen
shot her, it would have been self-defense."

"I know it," Sam said. "She's lucky you saw it and
stopped it when you did."

Stone stood silent for a moment.

"Can I tell you something, Ranger, and you won't
call me crazy for saying it?" he said finally.

The Ranger looked him up and down.

"I didn't call you crazy when you said you were a
wolf," Sam said. "What else have you got for me?"

Stone looked a little embarrassed.

"All right, I admit, turning myself into a wolf was
just the ramblings of a fool," he said. "But this is different. There's times when I see myself involved in things
before they happen. It's like I see the future." He stared
at the Ranger for a response.

See the future . . . ?

Sam stared back at him, letting it sink in. The smell of stale rye and mescal loomed about them. Noting it, and realizing Stone's struggle with liquor, he nodded toward the open door before the hesitant sheriff could speak. Behind the bar, the bartender raised a shot glass of amber rye to his lips.

"Let's get out of here—get ourselves some fresh air," Sam said quietly.

Stone looked over at the bartender.

"Being around it doesn't bother me none, if that's what you're thinking, Ranger," Stone said, the two of them turning, walking out of the whiskey-scented cantina.

"I understand," Sam replied. "Tell me about seeing the future, Sheriff." He stepped out off the boardwalk and looked down the empty street at the new sign atop the Silver Palace. Stone walked alongside him.

"I shouldn't have said anything," Stone said.

"Maybe not," Sam replied, "but you did, so go on with it. Whatever you say is between us."

"I'm glad to know that." Stone nodded. "Maybe I shouldn't call it seeing the future. There are times when things happen, and I know I've seen it all and heard it all before, the whole situation, every detail, every word spoken." He scratched his jaw. "Maybe instead of calling it *seeing the future* I should call it seeing things I know have happened before?" He squeezed his eyes shut in confusion.

Sam considered it and shook his head.

"I'd stick with *seeing the future* if I were you," he said quietly. "It might be easier to explain—"

"That's it, poke fun," Stone said, cutting him off. "I should've kept it to myself, same as I should about changing into a wolf."

"I wasn't poking fun," Sam said somberly. He gave it a second, then asked, "Is this something you were already doing, or did you just start after you quit drinking?"

"I did it some before," Stone said. "But it seems like I began doing it more once I started riding dry."

"Any chance that's got something to do with it?" Sam ventured.

"No," said Stone. "Whether I'm drunk or sober has nothing to do with it. It happened out there today— Mama Belleza and her shotgun—and I haven't drunk a drop of rye in over a month."

Sam looked off toward the Silver Palace, watching customers hitch their horses to the hitch rail or park their wagons and walk into the saloon.

"Tell me all about it, Sheriff," he said.

"It's hard to explain," Stone said. "Sometimes I'll be doing something, saying something to somebody, and I'll know what they were going to say before they said it. Then I'll say something back and know it's all the same way it happened before—same words, same person saying them, everything. It's eerie."

Sam just stared at him.

"No," Sam said, "I mean, tell me what happened out there today that you thought happened before."

Stone sucked on his cough drop in earnest and eyed the Ranger closely for a moment.

"Forget it," he said after consideration. "You think I'm being foolish." He turned toward his office a block away and said over his shoulder, "Let's go see how the doctor's doing cutting out Dobbs' bullet."

Chapter 4

Inside the sheriff's office, the two lawmen stood watching from outside the cell as Dr. Tierney inventoried his surgical instruments, wiped them with an alcohol-dampened cloth and placed them back in a leather pouch. Dobbs was still sleeping under the dose of powerful chloroform.

The Ranger gazed straight ahead through the open cell door and spoke sidelong to Stone.

"I don't think you were being foolish, Sheriff," he said, reviving the conversation that Stone had cut short only moments earlier. "I'm still curious what you were thinking out there when the woman swung the shotgun up."

"Why are you so curious?" Stone asked.

"Because I saw how fast you acted," Sam said. "It was almost like you *did* know what was coming next."

"The way you saw what was coming when you butted Dirty Donald before he talked himself into trying to kill you?" Stone asked.

"Huh-uh, that was different," Sam said. "I know

what Ferry was apt to do if I didn't stop him. But I didn't think it was something that had happened before."

Sheriff Stone paused and looked away in contemplation for a moment. Then he adjusted the cough drop in his mouth and let out a breath.

"It started the minute I asked if you ever heard of Silas Rudabaugh. You said you'd heard of him, but never had cause to meet him." He looked at Sam and continued. "When you said that, I knew exactly what was going to happen next—right up to running to stop Mama Belleza, and the shotgun going off. Everything that happened seemed like it had happened before—"

"Déjà vu, they call it," Dr. Tierney said, walking out of the cell rolling his shirtsleeves down, his surgical pouch over his shoulder. "It means you've 'already seen' it." He gave a tired smile to the staring lawmen. "It's a condition of a confused or overstimulated brain. A person sees something, hears something, even though it just happened, his brain thinks it happened in the past instead of the present. So it comes into mind as a memory instead of a current event."

"A confused brain . . . ?" Stone said skeptically. "I know I've done a powerful lot of drinking, Doc. But that's over now—I'm sober as a Mormon."

"I'm glad you're sober, Sheriff," the doctor said. "But this happens to people who've never had a drop in their lives." He gave a shrug. "We don't know much about it, but there's a doctor from Algeria studying the condition."

"You're saying there's nothing spooky about it?" Stone asked.

"Only if you believe, as the spiritualists do, that it's a clairvoyant experience, or a memory from a past life." He picked up his suit coat, draped it over his forearm and nodded toward Dobbs' cell. "He'll sleep awhile longer. I'll be back to check on him tomorrow afternoon."

"Obliged, Doctor," said Sam, both he and Stone touching their hat brims as the doctor opened the door and walked out.

"So there you have it," Sam said to Stone as the door closed behind Dr. Tierney. He looked him up and down. "Nothing eerie about thinking something has happened before."

Stone said, "The doctor is a good hand at cutting out bullets and tending the sick. But I wouldn't put much store in what he said about a *confused or overstimulated brain*. He said much the same thing about me turning into a wolf."

Sam gave him a dubious look.

"Did he, then?" he said.

Stone's face reddened. He sucked on the cough drop and fished the bag of tobacco from his shirt pocket with shaky fingertips.

"All right, I know what you're thinking," he said.

"So now you're *mind reading* too?" Sam said.

"Dang it, no," Stone said, getting agitated. "I don't mean it like that. I mean, I know it sounds like everything he said makes me look june bug crazy. But I saw more out there today that I didn't mention—something that's got nothing to do with me having a *confused mind*."

"Oh?" said Sam.

"That's right," said Stone. He lowered his tone of voice, giving a cautious look at Boomer Phipps, who lay snoring on his bunk with his forearm over his face. "While I was running out to Mama Belleza, I pictured her falling dead on the ground. When I got to her the shotgun was gone. There was a smoking revolver lying beside her."

Stone watched the Ranger for a reaction.

"That is strange," Sam said, seeing how the sheriff was getting more and more edgy talking about it.

"Yes, it is," said Stone. "So how would Doc Tierney explain that?"

"I don't know," Sam said. "You'll have to ask him. He sounds like he knows what he's talking about. Maybe it's just going to take more time away from the drinking—get your nerves back in shape. Gunplay can take a lot out of a man."

Stone didn't seem to hear his reply. He appeared lost in deep puzzled thought.

"Did I change the outcome someway, keep her from getting killed, running out and shouting at her like I did?" he said. He rubbed his forehead. "The more I think about all this, the stranger it all gets. I used to think *getting* sober was hard. Now I think the hardest part is *staying* that way."

"Put it all out your mind for a while, Sheriff," Sam said. "Having these gunmen working for Edsel Centrila around is enough to keep you busy for now."

"I'm not worried about Centrila's flunkies," Stone said, sucking on the cough drop while he steadied his fingers and started rolling a smoke.

"I know you're not worried about them," said Sam. "I'm just saying ease down a little. Staying sober looks like it requires some work."

"Yeah, it does," said Stone. "Not only am I not worried about Centrila and his gun monkeys, get right down to it, I'm not really too worried about all this other stuff either." He gave another shrug. "I'm just curious mostly." He crunched the remnant of the cough drop and swallowed it.

"I understand," Sam said. He observed Stone's demeanor start winding down more.

The sheriff opened the tobacco bag with his teeth and shook out some loose tobacco onto the cigarette paper. He grinned and tightened the bag's drawstring with his teeth.

"Anyway, I shouldn't have brought none of this up," he said. "I should have learned my lesson by now, going around telling folks what I think. Half the young'uns in this town still call me the *wolf-man*." He chuckled a little and shook his head. "Maybe the doctor's right. Maybe it's all—"

His words stopped as three gunshots ripped along the street from the direction of the Silver Palace. Dropping the cigarette fixings, he hurried out the door, the Ranger right behind him. Heads of clerks and store owners stuck out of doorways along the boardwalks on either side of the streets. As they ran toward the Palace, they saw the body lying out front near the hitch rail. At the open doorway of the big saloon, they saw drinkers already gathered around Donald Ferry. The gunman stood slumped against the front of the building. He held a hand pressed to his lower side.

"Oh no," Stone said in a hushed tone, slowing to a halt as he neared the body lying in the street. "It's Mama Belleza." He shook his head in regret and lowered his drawn Colt back into its holster. Sam stopped four feet back, his Colt still out, still cocked. He scanned the men gathered out in front of the Palace.

"Draw your horns in, Ranger. It was self-defense," Clayton Boyle said. "She shot him by surprise when we walked out the door. Started to shoot him again—"

"That's right, Ranger. I shot her," Ferry called out in a pained voice. "She gave me no choice."

Sam looked back and forth quickly at the faces of onlooking townsfolk.

"It's the truth, Ranger," the town blacksmith called out. "As bad as I hate it, if he hadn't stopped her, Mama would have emptied her pocket gun into them."

"I saw it too," a woman's voice said brokenly. "Mama must've lost her mind."

Sam eased his Colt down, uncocked it and let it hang in his hand. He looked at Stone, who had kneeled down beside the dead woman. Stone stared almost in disbelief at the smoking pocket-sized Colt revolver lying in the dirt beside her. When he turned his eyes back up to Sam, neither of them spoke; neither of them had to. Sam stepped aside as Dr. Tierney hurried in, kneeled beside the elderly dead woman and pressed his fingers to the side of her throat.

"She's dead," he confirmed with regret. He examined a bullet hole high up in the corner shoulder of her dress. Then he shook his head, stood up and dusted the knee of his trousers. Stone picked up the smoking pocket revolver and stood up beside him. He stuck the warm barrel of the gun down into his waist. The doctor gestured a couple of townsmen in and nodded down at Mama Belleza. "Please carry her to my office, gentlemen," he said quietly.

As the two townsmen stooped down to the dead woman, the doctor turned and walked toward the wounded gunman.

Stone and the Ranger also walked toward the boardwalk of the Silver Palace. They kept six feet between them.

Seeing the two lawmen coming, Clayton Boyle and Silas Rudabaugh sidestepped in between them and Donald Ferry. Stone and the Ranger stopped ten feet away. Sam held his cocked Colt down his side.

"Everybody here is calling it self-defense, Sheriff," Boyle said in a firm tone.

"Out of my way," Stone said in a cool, even tone, "or we'll see what they call it when I blow your skull through that glass window."

Hearing the sheriff's calm deliberate tone, onlooking townsmen slipped sidelong out of the way. Rudabaugh's gun hand poised instinctively. Sam stood firm, ready. He noted the difference in Stone's whole demeanor. There was no hesitancy, no confusion of mind, no shakiness of either hand or voice.

"Ranger," said Boyle, not taking his eyes off Stone, "you heard them call it self-defense. What do you say?"

"I'm backing the *sheriff's play*, remember?" Sam said. "Get out of the way." He looked from Boyle to Rudabaugh and cocked his big Colt.

Rudabaugh studied the situation, the Ranger's Colt already drawn, and now cocked and ready.

"Do as he says, Clayton," he cautioned quietly. "Let these lawman through to do their job." He raised his gun hand slowly and touched the brim of his tilted coachman's hat. "We don't want any more bloodshed at the Silver Palace the same day Mr. Centrila takes over." He gave a stiff smile and moved away a step, letting the two lawmen past him.

Dr. Tierney, having been allowed past the two gunmen to attend Donald Ferry's wound, was already pressing a bandage to the deep slash along the gunman's side as Stone and the Ranger stepped in closer.

"What's it like, Doc?" Stone asked, eying the bloody bandage pressed over the wound.

"It's pretty deep," the doctor replied. "It'll need some stitches."

"I swear to God, Ranger," said Ferry, not even looking at Sheriff Stone, "I didn't want to kill that old woman. She just kept shooting! What else could I do?"

"This is my town, Ferry. Look at me when you talk," Stone demanded sharply.

"All right, Sheriff," Ferry said. He turned his eyes away from the Ranger, pain showing on his face. "All the same, I didn't mean to kill her."

"Could've fooled me," Stone said, giving a jerk of his head back toward the thin body being carried off the street. Before Ferry knew what he was doing, Stone reached out and slipped the shiny Remington from Ferry's holster and held it down his side. "I'll be holding on to your gun."

"For how long?" Ferry asked, ashamed in front of Rudabaugh and Boyle for not having seen Stone's move coming and offering resistance.

"Until I talk to everybody one at a time, *alone*. See what they say about you killing her—"

"I don't think he killed her, Sheriff," Dr. Tierney cut in, looking up from where he stood stooped, pressing the bandage against Ferry's side.

Stone and the Ranger just looked at him for a moment.

"What's that supposed to mean—*he didn't kill her*?" Stone asked, a little put out by the doctor adding his opinion to what was as plain as any gun-down Stone had ever seen.

"I'll have to take a closer look to be certain, of course," the doctor said, "but it appears the bullet missed her, or may have only grazed her, at worst."

Stone looked puzzled; so did Ferry and the two other gunmen. The Ranger watched and listened, keeping an eye on Rudabaugh and Boyle.

"Then what killed her?" Stone asked pointedly.

"I think she might have been—" The doctor tried to speak, but Ferry interrupted him.

"Yeah, what else *could* have killed her?" Ferry asked, as if his marksmanship had been somehow brought into question. He saw how both lawmen stared at him and said quickly, "I mean . . . I didn't want to kill her, didn't mean to kill her, but Jesus . . ."

"Why don't you shut your stupid mouth, *Dirty* Donald?" Boyle said. "Let the doctor talk. Maybe you'll be holstering that Remmy and drinking at the bar quicker than you think."

"Keep running your mouth," Rudabaugh cautioned, "you'll likely end up hanging yourself."

Ferry fell quiet.

"What I'm suggesting, Sheriff," the doctor said, limiting his information to the lawman he knew to be in charge, "is that perhaps this fellow's shot missed, and Mama Belleza simply died from all the excitement."

Missed . . . ?

Sam and the sheriff gave each other a look, then stared at the doctor.

"*Missed . . . ?*" Ferry gave a smug, sarcastic chuff. "Like hell I missed," he said. "She's dead because I *nailed her*, one shot, under fire, bang! That was all. She went down, *graveyard dead*." He looked back and forth between Rudabaugh and Boyle, trying to appear cool and calm. Yet he couldn't mask the shame on his reddened face.

"Yeah, you *nailed her*, huh?" Stone said without hiding his contempt.

"Wait, Sheriff. Listen," Ferry said, "that's not how I mean it. I mean I killed her, yes, but in self-defense like everybody said—"

"Why *won't* you shut up?" Boyle demanded.

"You missed," Rudabaugh said flatly.

"I didn't miss," Ferry shouted. "This doctor is lying!"

Tierney cut in, "As I said, I'll need to examine Mama

Belleza closer to make certain what killed her. But she was a very old woman. Close to a hundred, I've heard. She very easily could have died from all the excitement."

"There he goes again," Ferry said. He shook his head in disgust with the doctor and pounded himself on the chest. "I killed her, damn it!"

"You damn fool, shut up!" Boyle snapped.

The Ranger watched and listened. Stone was still doing his job, working his end of the law.

"You admit to it, then," he said to Ferry. "That you shot and killed a hundred-year-old woman?"

"Yes," said Ferry, "but in self-defense—"

"No, he did not shoot a hundred-year-old woman," said Boyle, cutting him off. He glared coldly at Donald Ferry and added, "He *tried* to, but he *fucking* missed—missed, at a distance of thirty feet. . . ."

Rudabaugh only stared at Ferry, his expression blank and indiscernible.

"Gentlemen," the doctor said, "all of this idle speculation is getting us nowhere."

"Hear, hear," Rudabaugh said flatly.

"Follow us to my office," the doctor said. "I'll determine exactly what killed Mama Belleza as soon as I get this man treated properly." He looped Ferry's arm over his shoulders and turned toward his big clapboard house down the street.

The Ranger and Stone walked along beside the doctor.

"You're not getting out of my sight until we get this settled, Ferry," Sheriff Stone said.

"But it *was* self-defense," Ferry reasoned, "no matter how it all *settles*." He looked back again at Rudabaugh and Boyle. They made no effort to follow the doctor.

"Go on with the sheriff, Donald," said Rudabaugh. "We'll be waiting inside the Silver Palace." He turned and started to walk back into the saloon, the townsfolk moving aside to form a path in front of him.

"Why are we waiting anywhere for this dunder-headed fool?" Boyle asked in a secretive tone as he fell in beside Rudabaugh.

"We'll talk about it in private, Clayton," Rudabaugh said quietly as they stepped onto the boardwalk toward the saloon doors.

Chapter 5

Inside the Silver Palace, Rudabaugh and Boyle sat at a corner table that faced the street through six wavy windowpanes. Boyle had pulled back a pair of striped curtains to provide a view in the direction of the doctor's office. A bottle of rye and two shot glasses stood atop the table between them. Across the wide stone-tiled floor, drinkers lined the crowded bar. Three bartenders in white collarless shirts and black sleeve garters busily poured whiskey and slung frothy mugs of beer. Cigar smoke loomed thick and low from the ceiling.

"I'd say ol' Edsel has cut himself one luscious sweet piece of pie here," said Clayton Boyle. He raised his shot glass as if to toast their good fortune in working for a man like Centrila.

Rudabaugh raised his glass as well.

"It's *Mr. Centrila* to you, Clay," he said with a wry half smile.

The two tossed back half the amber rye and set the glasses down with their fists around them. They each let out a whiskey hiss.

"I'll *Mr. Centrila* him all day long from both ends to the middle," said Boyle, "so long as our pay keeps showing up on time."

"And it will," Rudabaugh said. "We can count on it." He turned loose of his glass and poured them both another shot. "Besides, I look for Centrila to come showing up here most any time now."

Boyle raised the shot glass and gazed into the settling rye as if pondering its purpose on earth.

"I hope he does," he said. "The quicker he tells us to kill this sheriff, the better. I hate planning something and keep putting it off." He took a sip of the rye, this time a short sip, and rubbed his lips together, savoring it.

"Ordinarily I'm the same way," said Rudabaugh. "But this time I figure, what's the hurry? There's worse places to be than waiting for a man who owns the only drinking establishments in town—not to mention the only covey of doves in fifty miles."

"That is the good side to it," Boyle said. He let out a breath. "I need to relax more." He paused, then said, "All right, we come in here to talk about what to do with this *Dirty* Donald idiot. Should I take him off somewhere and head-pop him? He's not worth anything to us."

"No, leave him be for now," said Rudabaugh. "Hiring him was a mistake, but it was Centrila's mistake, not ours."

"Where did Centrila come up with the likes of him?" Boyle asked.

Rudabaugh grinned a little and shook his head.

"Ferry's one of Harper Centrila's pals, as I understand it," he said. "I think the two of them managed to rob a couple of banks together without shooting themselves or each other." He gave a slight shrug. "Now that Centrila's hired him, he thinks he's turned bull of the walk. So let's play him along."

"He's a damn fool," Boyle said.

"Yep, so let's make him *our* fool," Rudabaugh said. He leaned forward a little. "Once Stone is dead, if anybody gets their neck stretched for killing him, let it be Dirty Donald instead of us."

Boyle considered it for a moment, then gave a shrug himself.

"Whatever you say, Silas," he replied. "Who knows? We come across any more hundred-year-old women we need killed, Ferry's the man for the job."

Rudabaugh chuckled.

"Yes, except he can't hit nothing," he said.

Boyle took a sidelong glance out through the wavy window glass.

"Speak of a fool and he sticks his head up," he said. He nodded out the window at Ferry, who walked along the edge of the street from the doctor's office toward the saloon.

"All right," said Rudabaugh, "when he gets here let's make him feel welcome." He raised a hand toward the busy bar and summoned one of the bartenders over to the table. When the tall bald-headed man arrived, Rudabaugh said, "Phil, bring us three cigars, a clean shot glass and a tall mug of beer."

"Yes, sir, Mr. Rudabaugh," said the bartender. He turned and hurried away.

"Hear that, Clayton?" said Rudabaugh. "It's *Mr. Rudabaugh* while we're here on Centrila's payroll. You know, he made me sort of manager of this place—said look after his interest for the time being." He gave his half smile again. "I tell you, I could get used to this."

"I see you can," Boyle observed.

The bartender returned in only seconds with the beer, the shot glass and black cigars in hand. Laying the items on the table, he handed each of them a cigar and produced a long match. He stood expectantly while they sniffed the cigars and stuck them into their mouths.

Rudabaugh gave Boyle a look as the match flared to life and the bartender lit their cigars in turn.

"Anything else, gentlemen?" the bartender asked.

"That's all, Phil," Rudabaugh said, letting out a stream of smoke. He looked at Boyle as the bartender walked away. "See what I'm saying? This ain't no bad job, waiting for ol' Edsel to show up and take over first-hand."

Boyle nodded.

"You're right," he said, "I just need to ease up and enjoy the wait."

"That's the spirit," said Rudabaugh. He nodded toward Donald Ferry as Ferry limped into the saloon, a hand held loosely against the bandaged wound in his side. "Now let's show this boy how much we *like* him."

"You first, Silas," Boyle said under his breath as Ferry walked over to their table.

"Fair enough, watch this," Rudabaugh said, also under his breath. He swung around in his chair, facing Ferry with as much of a smile as he could manufacture.

"How's the side, Donald?" he asked.

"Sore," Ferry said, "but it's not a bad wound."

"What happened over there, Ferry?" Rudabaugh said with interest. "Did the doctor clear you? We were starting to get concerned. Figuring we might have to come break you out." He gestured for Ferry to sit down in an empty chair where an empty shot glass stood as if waiting for him. He quickly reached out with the bottle of rye and filled the glass.

Ferry looked confused, taken aback by this sudden change in attitude toward him. But he eased down into the chair and wrapped his free hand around the shot glass.

"Well," said Boyle, looking Ferry up and down, "are you going to tell us what happened with the doctor, or not?"

"Hey, take it easy, Clayton," said Rudabaugh. "Give the man time to wet his whistle." He held on to the bottle as if ready to pour again as soon as Ferry's glass needed filling. The two stared at Ferry in rapt anticipation. Ferry raised the glass to his lips and took a short sip.

"Well," he said almost hesitantly, "the doctor says my shot grazed the old woman's shoulder, but he concluded it didn't kill her. Stone had to let me go, bad as he hated to." He looked back and forth between the two gunmen as if expecting their scorn. "It *was* self-defense, like we all knew it was."

Boyle sat watching quietly, curious as to how Rudabaugh would handle this. Rudabaugh nodded as if giving the matter serious consideration. Finally he raised a finger for emphasis and gave Ferry a sly grin.

"That was some damn quick thinking on your part," he said. "Not to mention, some *damn fine* shooting."

Ferry looked bewildered.

"*Huh?*" Boyle said. "Quick *thinking* . . . fine *shooting?*" He looked equally puzzled by Rudabaugh's words. "Did I miss something there?" He stared at Ferry as if demanding an explanation. But Rudabaugh held up a hand as if to stop Ferry from explaining his actions.

"Allow me, Donald," Rudabaugh said. He turned to Boyle and continued. "He pulled his shot, Clayton. Aimed high left instead of dead center. It took some cool-handed confidence, the way I see it."

Boyle sat staring, picking up on Rudabaugh's game.

"Imagine the black cloud we could have hung over Centrila's new saloons if Donald had splattered that old crow's heart all over the street, *self-defense* or not," Rudabaugh continued.

Boyle eased back in consideration.

"All right, Silas, I'll give you that," he said. He gave Ferry a nod and studied him as if starting to see him in a little different light. "You figured all that, Donald? That quick?" He snapped his fingers to show how quick. "You figured to fire high, wing her instead of—"

"Of course he did," Rudabaugh cut in before Boyle could even finish his question. "It's a damn good thing too. That old woman's wild bullets could have hit any one of us." He smiled admirably and topped off Ferry's whiskey glass with the bottle of rye. "Drink up, pard. You've earned your seat at *this* table." He tipped the raised bottle as if in a toast and turned his eyes to Boyle for support.

Boyle raised his shot glass, indulging Rudabaugh without showing his disdain for Ferry.

"I'll go along with that," he said coolly.

The Ranger and Stone stood out in front of the sheriff's office to keep their conversation from being overheard by Boomer Phipps and Freddie Dobbs. They saw townsmen flock from all over town to the Silver Palace to drink and talk about the shooting. A tinny piano rattled above street. Farther down the street, Mama Belleza's cantina sat empty, its doors closed, the little adobe structure looking bleak and shadowy in the fading evening sunlight.

"That poor ol' woman didn't deserve to die like this," Stone commented with unveiled bitterness. He sucked on a cough drop; his fingertips rapped sharply on the butt of his big Colt.

"No, she didn't," the Ranger said, "but we both know it was self-defense, whether we like it or not."

"Whose side are you on?" Stone asked, turning a cold eye to the Ranger.

"Whose side do you *think*?" the Ranger said, coming back just as cold.

Stone eased down and looked off along the street.

"I'm on the side of the law," Sam said in an even tone. "I know you are too, else I wouldn't be standing here with you."

Stone nodded and eased down some more.

"Being *lawful* don't always make a thing right," the sheriff said. "Mama Belleza should have died in her bed with family around, not out in the street. She didn't deserve this."

"I understand," Sam said. "We both know the law isn't about what folks deserve. Folks get what the situation bequeaths them. Trim away all the circumstances, she came at a man shooting and he shot back—even took a bullet from her."

"So you're telling me Dirty Donald Ferry had *a right* to stand his ground, Ranger?" Stone said, turning back to him. "Against a woman going on a hundred years old?"

"No, I'm not going to tell you he had the right," Sam said firmly. "But I want to hear *you tell me* that he didn't."

Stone feel silent and looking away again.

"Somebody has to stand up for Mama Belleza," Stone said.

"You've been standing up for folks like her since the day you pinned on a badge, Sheriff," Sam said. "It's not right what happened to her. But once you trim the circumstances down to the bone, the law says she was in the wrong. Those three are no-account outlaws and killers, but Donald Ferry was within his rights. The law owes him the same diligence it owed Mama Belleza—bad as I hate to say it."

"This was all Edsel Centrila's fault," Stone said, refusing to give in on the matter. He gestured toward the Silver Palace. "Him and his dang big fancy saloon . . . driving an old woman like Mama out of business. Causing her to do some fool thing like this." He shook his head. "All just to get back at me for turning him in to the judge."

"You really figure he did all this—bought out this

big saloon, just to get back at you, Sheriff?" Sam asked quietly.

Stone fished a fresh cough drop from his shirt pocket and stuck it into his mouth with shaky fingers.

"I know that's not the only reason he bought it," he said. "But I know him to be a spiteful man, and I have no doubt it played into him buying it. Any time I walk through the Palace doors, I'm going to expect the worst."

"That's not a bad idea any time you walk into a saloon wearing a badge," Sam said. "All this other, maybe you want to give it some more thought."

Stone let his hands fall to his sides.

"All right," he said with resolve, "I know you think I'm being suspicious and crazy, so I'm going to quit talking about it." He took a deep breath and changed the subject. "You know I saw all this coming, don't you?"

"It appeared that you did, I have to admit," said the Ranger.

"Awfully weird incident, huh," said Stone, "how I saw her lying there dead before it happened?"

"Either an *awfully weird* incident or one *awfully* peculiar coincidence," Sam said.

"*Coincidence?*" said Stone. "You saw it, you heard it. Are you now going to say I didn't see it coming?"

"Sheriff, I don't know what to make of you seeing her lying there dead," said Sam. "I might be saying 'coincidence' because I don't know what else to call it. All those other things you talked about seeing before, I believe the doctor might be right. The fact is I just don't know."

Stone thought about it and nodded.

"Obliged that you're honest enough to admit you don't know," he said. "I don't think the doctor knows either, but being a doctor he can't admit it like the rest of us can." He sucked on the cough drop and readjusted it in his mouth. His fingertips went back to tapping his gun butt. "I need some coffee. What about you?"

The Ranger looked him up and down.

"Obliged, but I'm good," he said. "Are you going to be all right here, with Centrila's men in town?"

"All right, how?" said Stone. "I'm getting over the whiskey shakes a little more every day. I'm drawn tighter than a fiddle, but I'm holding myself together." He gave a stiff grin. "I'm not turning into a wolf—"

"I can stay a day or two longer," Sam said, cutting him off, seeing how high-strung and shaky he'd become. "My prisoners wouldn't mind waiting a couple of days before I turn them in."

"I'm obliged for your offer, but you take your prisoners on in, Ranger," Stone said. "I'm all right here." He gazed away, off across the evening shadows along the distant hill lines. "Nobody made me drink. I got into this shape on my own. I'll get through it on my own."

Sam nodded.

"All right," he said. "I needed to make the offer. That done, I'm turning in. I want to head out before daylight."

"Obliged," Stone said, still staring away across the late-evening sky. "You can have the cot in the back room. I'll be at my desk tonight."

"Trouble sleeping?" Sam asked.

"No," said Stone, "trouble dreaming, is all. I can get to sleep, but my dreams wake me up." He gave a slight shrug. "I know it's just the whiskey trying to hang on. It'll pass." He looked away again as if not wanting to talk about it. "Night, Ranger," he said without looking around.

"Night, Sheriff," Sam said, touching the brim of his sombrero.

Chapter 6

Before the first ray of dawn mantled the horizon, Sheriff Stone sat slumped in his chair, his head bowed over his desk like a man deep in prayer. A mug of cold coffee sat at his right hand; loose cough drops lay strewn atop a stack of wanted posters. He snored quietly, deeper in sleep than he had been for the past week. The Ranger had slept on a cot in the back room. When he awakened, he dressed and pulled on his boots and walked out the rear door, rifle and saddlebags in hand, careful not to disturb the sheriff's much-needed rest. He eased the rear door closed behind himself.

While he walked to the livery barn to ready his dun and the prisoners' horses for the trail, inside his cell Boomer Phipps stood up from his bunk and looked through the darkness at the sleeping sheriff as he stepped over to the back wall. In the cell next to him, Dobbs also stood up and watched the big outlaw. Sensing something afoot, Dobbs eased his arm out of the sling the doctor had placed around his neck and walked to the door of his cell. The two prisoners nodded at each other in the laddered moonlight lying slantwise through the rear barred windows.

Quietly Boomer reached up, gripped the window bars in his giant hands and walked three steps straight up the wall until he squatted across the window frame like some ape caged in a public zoo. Dobbs watched, barely daring to breathe, as the big man planted and pushed his feet against the wall with all his massive strength. The iron bars creaked in Boomer's viselike grip.

"*Good God!*" Dobbs whispered, hearing a long muffled groan build and begin to erupt from Boomer's broad chest. At the same time he heard a cracking of rock and hard mortar where the window bars began giving way to the enormous pressure pulling against them.

Glancing toward the sleeping sheriff, Dobbs noted that the snoring had stopped suddenly. He started to whisper something to Boomer, caution him against the deep rumbling sound he was making. But before he could say a thing, he saw the barred window break free of its frame and launch the big outlaw across the cell as if he'd been fired from a circus cannon.

Dobbs ducked down as Boomer hit the front of his cell so hard the entire building shuddered with the impact. Boomer fell to the floor with the bent window bars atop him. At his desk, the terrible racket caused Sheriff Stone to jerk his bowed head up and leap to his feet. He grabbed his holstered Colt instinctively. As he hurried to the front of the two cells to see what had happened, he saw Boomer sling the window bars aside and rise to his feet.

"Hold it right there, *big man*," Stone shouted. "I'll

shoot." He stuck his Colt out arm's length toward the huge outlaw.

"No, you won't, law dog," Boomer shouted in reply. "Nobody's going to shoot me." He started to turn toward the torn-open window. Stone cocked the outstretched Colt and hurried closer, aiming carefully between the bars. But before he pulled the trigger, Dobbs sprang upright, reached through and grabbed the sheriff by his forearm and yanked him forward. Stone's forehead struck the iron bars with the muffled sound of a church bell. He crumbled down onto his knees. His gun flew from his hand and skidded away across the floor.

"Boomer, wait, I got him!" Dobbs shouted.

Boomer jerked to a halt and looked at the sheriff wobbling unsteadily on his knees, his gun gone.

"So you did, Freddie boy," the big outlaw said. He hurried forward as Dobbs grappled through the bars with the knocked-out sheriff, searching him for the cell key.

"Here," Boomer said. He jerked Stone forward against the bars, turned him around and yanked the long key from his rear trouser pocket. When Stone moaned and tried to stop him, Boomer yanked his head against the bars again and let out a laugh at the muffled ring of iron against skull bone. "Told you, you won't shoot me," he said to the limp sheriff lying on the floor.

Huddled at the front of their cells where a partition of bars separated the two, Dobbs stood and hurried to his cell door as Boomer stood up with the key, unlocked his own cell door and stepped out.

"Jesus, hurry, Boomer!" Dobbs said, even as the big

outlaw stuck the key in and turned it. On the floor, Stone groaned and tried to settle the spinning world around him. As the door swung open, Dobbs said, "What the hell? Were you going to leave me behind?" He stepped out of the cell and clasped his wounded shoulder.

"I didn't, though, did I?" said Boomer firmly. He grabbed Dobbs and pulled him toward the cell with the missing window instead of letting him go for the front door. "This way, Freddie. Nobody will see us."

The two hurried inside Boomer's open cell, across chunks of broken rock, over to the open window frame. Boomer picked Dobbs up by the scruff of his neck and hoisted him out of the window. Dobbs hit the ground and looked up, seeing Boomer's big hands reach through and grab the frame edges and pull himself up and out.

"Hurry, Boomer!" he said.

Boomer's big arms and the upper half of his torso squeezed out of the window frame as if the building were struggling to give him birth. But then he stopped and wiggled back and forth vigorously.

"I'm stuck, Freddie," he said, trying to keep his big voice lowered, knowing that behind him the sheriff would come to any minute.

"Push, push hard, Boomer!" Dobbs said. "I can't reach you from down here. You've got to push yourself through!"

"I'm trying, Freddie," Boomer said. He put his hands back flat against the wall on either side and pushed hard. He strained and grunted and twisted back and forth, gaining freedom an inch at a time.

Behind him, Stone shook his head and batted his bleary eyes. He saw the back half of Boomer Phipps struggling in the window. Looking all around for his Colt, he saw it lying on the floor under the edge of his desk and scrambled over and grabbed it.

Pulling himself up the side of his desk, the awakening sheriff saw Boomer give a final push and fall out of sight into the alley behind the building. Colt in hand, Stone collected himself quickly. He ran out the front door and around the corner of the alley beside his office. He arrived at the rear of the building in time to see Boomer push himself up from the ground, Dobbs pulling him by his arm.

"Hold it, both of you!" Stone shouted. He fired a warning shot over their heads, hoping it would hold them in place. But it didn't.

"Run, Freddie!" Boomer shouted, giving the smaller outlaw a shove to get him going. Yet, as Dobbs turned and ran, instead of running himself, Boomer started stalking toward the sheriff with his big arms spread like a standing grizzly.

"You can't shoot me, Sheriff! I'm unarmed," he shouted. He started coming forward quicker, forcing his huge body into a powerful run.

You're wrong, Boomer, Stone said to himself, standing his ground, his smoking Colt cocked out at arm's length toward the large charging man.

The sheriff's first shot hit Boomer in his broad chest, yet the impact only staggered him. Boomer kept coming. Stone fired again; this time the shot hit Boomer in his right shoulder, and again Boomer staggered. But he still wouldn't be stopped. He roared in pain and rage and kept coming.

Stone stood firm, but he knew if Boomer didn't fall soon the big man would be upon him. He fired again—*fourth shot,* he reminded himself as the Colt bucked and belched fire into the grainy darkness. The bullet only grazed Boomer on the inside of his upper arm. But the sting of the four bullets was catching up to the big man. He stopped and swayed in place, feeling warm blood spread down his chest, his arm. He bellowed like an enraged bull; he lowered his head and lurched forward again. There was now no more than fifteen feet between them. Stone stood firm, cocked the pistol and fired.

Shot five, he told himself. He saw Boomer's lowered head lift up with a jolt as the bullet struck it dead center. In the moonlight he caught a glimpse of Dobbs on his knees farther along the alley.

"Don't *shoot*!" Dobbs shouted in a shaky voice, seeing Boomer fall at Stone's feet like a downed buffalo. "I give up! It wasn't me. It was all his idea!"

One bullet left. . . .

Stone glanced down at Boomer, then back at Dobbs. Smoke curled and rose from the barrel of his Colt. He noted the steadiness of his hand as he raised the big warm gun and cocked it in Dobbs' direction. The Colt in his hand felt *right*—he felt *right*, he told himself. Balanced, steady, everything aligned. . . . He eyed down the barrel sights at Freddie Dobbs, who held his hands over his head in surrender. *There it is,* Stone told himself, his aim locked in, his finger tightened on the trigger.

"Don't shoot, Sheriff," the Ranger said, sliding to a halt behind him, his Colt out and cocked, as it had been since he heard the first shot resound along the alleyway to the livery barn. "Ease it down," he added, realizing he'd found Stone on that last split second before bullet hit bone. "You can do it."

Stone waited a second longer; then he lowered the Colt until it was pointed straight down before laying his thumb over the hammer and uncocking it.

"That was close, Ranger," he said in a quiet, steady tone. Along the alley they both saw townsmen appear out of the darkness. Lowering his voice, he said, "He wouldn't stop. He just kept coming at me. I couldn't turn and run."

"I know, Sheriff," the Ranger replied quietly. "A man that size, you did the only thing you could. Reload your Colt and holster it. I'll get Dobbs and put him back in his cell." He looked up at the ripped-out window frame, then down at Boomer's body. He shook his head in regret.

"Boomer Phipps got too big for everything around him," he said.

It was midmorning when the Ranger stepped atop his dun, a lead rope to Dobbs and Boomer Phipps' horses in hand. Boomer's big body lay wrapped in canvas, tied down over his horse's bare back; Dobbs sat slumped, his arm back in the sling, his free hand cuffed to his saddle horn. Sheriff Stone stood on the boardwalk out in front of his office, a warm coffee mug in his left hand, a cigarette pressed between his lips. The bowed mis-

shapen window bars leaned against the building awaiting the town blacksmith. On the boardwalk lay a short
pile of broken rock and mortar cement from around the
window frame.

Stone parked a cough drop in his cheek and took the
cigarette from his mouth.

"Hard to believe any one man could rip out a cell
window that way," he said, toeing the rubble as he
spoke. He looked out at the huge body of the outlaw,
and the horse standing beneath it.

"You had to see it," Sam agreed, also looking at the
broken rock and bent window bars. Freddie Dobbs sat
listening with a sore smirk on his face.

"Sure you don't want to bury that big rascal here?"
Stone nodded toward Boomer's horse. "I bet his cayuse
would be well obliged to you. I'll give you an affidavit
that he died here, attempted jailbreak."

"I'd sooner turn him in at Fort Hamlin, let them do
all the paperwork," Sam replied. "Like you said, it's
hard to believe it happened, let alone trying to put it all
down in writing."

Stone nodded and sucked on the cough drop as if
considering the matter.

"Yeah," he said, "that's true. I best let everybody get
used to me not being a wolf awhile longer, before I go
making any wild-sounding statements."

"You shot him down in cold blood, is what I plan on
telling anybody who'll listen," Dobbs said, straightening in his saddle. He looked back and forth between the
two lawmen as they just stared at him. "That's right, I
will," he continued. "I saw the whole damn thing. I'll

tell them he was unarmed, hands in the air, trying to surrender—"

"That's enough out of you, Freddie Dobbs," Sam warned. "We've already talked about this. Anything else you've *got* to say, tell it to the judge in court. Anything else you *feel* like saying, you stop first and ask yourself how you'd enjoy a pistol barrel across your jaw."

"You better think about this, Sheriff," Dobbs warned, undaunted, ignoring the Ranger. "Tell this Ranger to let me go. Once we ride away, it'll be too late. Anybody wants to hear what happened to Boomer Phipps, I'll give them a whole earful. You all but emptied your gun in him—him only trying to give himself up. Lie about it all you want, Sheriff, I'll set things straight, is what I'll do!"

Sam and Stone looked at each other.

"Every word I said is true, Ranger," Stone said. "He come at me and kept coming—"

Sam raised a gloved hand, stopping him.

"You needn't explain yourself again, Sheriff," he said in a quiet tone. "Boomer tried buffaloing me the same way when I arrested him. Luckily he went down before he got close enough to do any damage."

"That's it, stick together," Dobbs said. "That's what you law dogs always do."

"Let's go, Freddie," said Sam. He gave a sharp yank on the lead rope, causing Dobbs' horse to jerk sideways almost out from under the outlaw.

"There was no cause for you doing that," Dobbs said sorely, readjusting himself in his saddle. "Whatever happened to free speech in this country? I see a miscarriage of justice, I ain't allowed to speak out about it?"

"You've got a right to speak out," Sam replied. "I've got a right not to listen." He looked at Stone and shook his head, indicating that this was what he had to look forward to all the way to Fort Hamlin.

"Have a good trip to Fort Hamlin, Ranger," Stone said with a wry, knowing grin.

Sam backed his dun a step, drawing the two other horses along with him.

"I'll see you on my way back, Sheriff," he said to Stone.

Stone shook his head. His cigarette back in his mouth, he tapped nervous fingers on his gun butt.

"You don't have to come back on my account, Ranger," he said. "I told you I'm all right here without being checked on."

"I know you're all right, Sheriff," Sam said, touching the brim of his sombrero. "I'll be passing through here anyway. Can I stop and water my horse if I've a mind to?" He eyed Stone closely.

Stone stopped tapping his fingers and let out a breath. He touched his hat brim in return.

"Begging your pardon, Ranger," he said. "I might still be a little jumpy. You're always welcome here. I'll see you on your way back."

The Ranger nodded and backed the horses some more. Turning the animals, he rode at an easy gallop along the dirt street, Dobbs and Boomer's body riding right beside him. As he passed the front of the Silver Palace Saloon, Silas Rudabaugh, Clayton Boyle and

Donald Ferry looked out through the wavy window glass beside their table.

"I always say it's a good day when you see a lawman ride out of town," said Boyle. "Especially one who's dead, or soon will be." He tipped his raised glass toward the other two gunmen. "You can start to feel the wide doors of opportunity swing open toward you." He grinned as Ferry nodded eagerly and raised his glass high. Rudabaugh only gave the slightest tip of his glass and a wry smile.

"To dead lawmen, then," he said.

The three tossed back their whiskey. Ferry picked up his frothy beer mug, took a long drink and set it down. The other two watched him wipe foam from above his lip.

"What makes you think Burrack is soon to be dead?" he asked under his breath.

Boyle leaned in above the tabletop, a little whiskey bent, and spoke in an equally lowered voice.

"What makes you think he's *not*?" he asked.

Ferry just looked at him.

"Do you know something I don't?" he asked.

"I know a hell of a lot that you don't know, Ferry," Boyle said slyly. "For instance, I know it's a dangerous trail from here to Fort Hamlin."

"Stick that beer mug in your mouth, Clayton," Rudabaugh said in a harsh warning tone.

"I never said nothing, did I, Silas?" Boyle said.

"No, but you're getting too damn close to it," Rudabaugh replied. He finished his whiskey and set the glass down with a strong bump on the tabletop.

"Hey, pards," said Ferry, "I'm one of us, remember? Is there something I need to know here?"

"No," said Rudabaugh, without taking his hard glare off Boyle. "Clayton here just likes to talk when he drinks. I warn him all the time, it's something that'll get him killed if he ain't careful." He turned his gaze to Ferry. "You're riding with the big guns now, Donald. You'll find sometimes it's best to keep your mouth shut and watch what's coming around."

Part 2

Chapter 7

Charlie Knapp sat beside the small cook fire watching with detached interest as Seamus Gore backhanded Ignacio Cady backward—for what, the fourth or fifth time? *Maybe more*, Knapp calculated to himself. Both Iggy's Colt and his rifle lay in the dirt. So did Lyle Cady, for trying to jump in and help his brother moments ago when Gore first started smacking Iggy around. Two gunmen, Coco Bour and Tulsa Jake Testa, stood over Lyle with their guns drawn. They watched the one-sided fight with flat expressions, glancing at Knapp now and then, checking his reaction to Iggy's getting his face battered by Gore's big rawboned knuckles.

Knapp gave them no reaction. Instead he eyed the spare horses the three men had brought with them and sipped from a battered whiskey flask as he watched. He had to admit he was a little amazed that Iggy was still on his feet, given the beating the big brawler was putting on him.

Folks will fool you sometimes, he told himself.

He capped the flask and let it hang in his hand. Iggy, trying to get a lick of his own in, swung a weak and careless roundhouse at Gore. All the brawler had to do was sidestep a little and let the missed swing drop the staggering Iggy to the dirt.

"And that's that. He's had enough," Knapp said just loud enough to be heard.

Gore and the other two gunmen turned their full attention to Knapp. Gore wiped the back on his hand on his trousers as Iggy crawled away in the dirt.

"I'll say when it's enough," Gore called out in a New York Irish accent. He walked toward Knapp; Coco Bour and Jake Testa followed, giving no regard to the Cady brothers, or to their guns lying on the ground. "Careful, old boyo. I might be giving you a bit of the same." He stopped ten feet from Knapp and stood with his big fists balled at his sides. Bour and Testa walked in closer and flanked him, their gun hands poised at their holsters.

Knapp only stared at him.

Seamus continued. "Now I'll tell you the same thing as I told that one. We don't break this fellow out of the prison wagon until we first see some money cross our palms." He held his hand up flat toward Knapp and wiggled his big fingers expectantly.

Knowing Coco Bour to be the leader of these three, Knapp looked at him as if Gore and Testa weren't there.

"I was told you'd get paid when the job's done," he said. As he spoke he examined the flask and shook it a little, gauging its contents. "If that doesn't suit you, ride away," he said flatly, then turned his dark eyes back to Gore. "I can do this without you."

"Oh?" said Gore, stepping forward. "It looks like I will have to knock this one around some."

Knapp raised a hand as if asking for a second. Gore stopped in his tracks. Without another word, Knapp slipped the flask inside his duster as if to protect it. When his hand came back from inside the duster lapel, he held a big revolver he'd drawn from a shoulder rig.

"*Hey—!*" Gore shouted in protest. But his words cut short as the big revolver bucked once in Knapp's hand. The gunman hit the ground with a fountain of blood spewing straight up from his chest. Before Bour and Testa could respond, Knapp's revolver turned, re-cocked and aimed at Bour's chest. Knapp stood silent, braced ready, nothing else to say.

"Whoa, now," Bour said in a low even tone, seeing that he and Testa had been caught off guard. "I should have said something sooner. Gore can be a little pig-headed at times. *Obstinate*, I'll go so far as to say." He nodded and looked at Testa. "Am I right, Jake?"

"Oh *yes*," Testa agreed, "*obstinate* to a fault, I have always said." They looked at the dead man lying with his mouth wide-open, the fountain of blood having fallen to a trickle on his chest.

"Seems cured enough," Knapp said in an unread-able tone. He kept the revolver pointed, smoke curling up from the tip of the barrel.

"Shoot the son of a bitch again!" Iggy said, he and his brother staggering to their feet. He picked his Colt up, cocked it and sauntered unsteadily over the body in the dirt. His face was raw, red and swelling on either cheek. Blood seeped from his nose down his upper lip. Lyle and the other two watched as he fired two shots into Gore's head. The dead man's head bounced with each shot. Lyle stepped in and laid his hand down atop Iggy's Colt, stopping him from firing again.

"Let it go, brother," he said. "He's as dead now as he'll ever be."

Bour and Testa stood easier as Iggy uncocked his Colt and shoved it down into his holster, easier still as Knapp lowered his revolver and kept it in hand.

"All right, then," said Bour, turning from the Cadys back to Knapp, "all this being settled, maybe we ought to get down to the job at hand."

"Are we square on when you get paid?" Knapp asked, eying the two closely.

"We're square as a knot," said Bour. "Right, Jake?" He looked at Testa for support.

"We are for sure," Testa said. "Point us at that prison rig and watch what we do. Edsel Centrila wants his boy out of jail, we'll get him out."

Knapp uncocked the gun hanging at his side.

"Glad we could work it all out," he said. He looked at the Cadys and gestured down at Gore's body in the bloody dirt. "Drag him off somewhere. We're making camp here. I don't want critters toting his guts back and forth all night."

The Cadys looked at each other, not liking the idea of them having to drag the dead man away. But they resolved to keep their mouths shut.

"Let's go, then," Lyle said. "You get one arm, I'll get the other."

"This son of a bitch," Iggy said under his breath. He looked at the wide-open mouth as he bent and grabbed Gore's limp wrist.

As the two dragged the dead man off into a nearby stand of rock and sand, Bour and Testa turned to Knapp.

"No offense," Bour said, "but are these two the best you could come up with on short notice? I could have brought along a couple of my *nieces* had I known."

"You know the Cadys?" Knapp said.

"I expect everybody knows the Cadys," Testa said. He shook his head in disgust.

"When I saw them," said Bour, "I started to turn my horse around and head to Abilene, truth be told."

"Mr. Centrila said bring them, so I brought them," Knapp said. He eased his revolver inside his duster lapel and pulled out the tin whiskey flask. "I figured the more guns the better if we get into a scrap." He took a sip of rye and passed the flask to Coco Bour. "Although I don't look for that to happen. I'm looking for an easy go of it. Kill a couple of guards, shoot the lock off the wagon door—ride out of here."

"That's our thinking too," Bour said. He took a sip of rye and passed the flask to Testa. "When does all this happen?"

"First thing come morning," Knapp said. He reached for the flask as Testa lowered it from his lips. "So this is all of the drinking until it's over. I'm keeping one of you watching this trail the rest of the day and all through the night, in case the wagon comes by sooner."

"You got it, Charlie Knapp," Bour said. He wiped his hand across his lips and looked all around at the brush and the rock cover they stood in on the broad cliff above the trail. "We'll get Centrila's boy broke out real quick. The way it looks, this place was made for an ambush."

Walking back from where they dragged Gore's body, Lyle and Ignacio saw the shiny tin flask as Bour handed it back to Knapp.

"Don't we get a drink too?" Lyle said when they stopped a few feet away.

"No," said Knapp. "You should have been here when it was offered." He patted the lapel of his riding jacket where he'd pocketed the flask, then turned and walked away. Coco Bour and Jake Testa gave the Cadys a look and walked away behind him.

"I guess he showed us where we stand, brother," Lyle said under his breath. "Far as I'm concerned we can cut out of here any time you're ready."

"Let's keep biding our time," Iggy replied. "Soon as we ride away without getting into Knapp's rifle sights, I'm as ready to quit Edsel Centrila as fast as you are." He looked at his brother closely. "I just don't want us to get killed doing it."

Shortly after daylight the barred four-horse Studebaker prisoner transport wagon rolled onto a stretch of trail running through a deep valley of stone. Seated beside the driver, the wagon guard looked up into the morning sunlight to his right and searched along a flat cliff line looming fifty feet overhead. The diver slowed the four horses almost to a walk when the forward guard on horseback stopped his mount thirty yards ahead of them, turned his horse sideways in the middle of the trail and sat staring with his rifle across his lap.

"What the blazes is he doing, Ernest?" the driver said sidelong to the guard. "This is no place to be stopping. My guts pucker every time I get to this stretch of trail."

"Mine too," said the guard, an elderly former Ranger named Ernest Shule. "Bennie's just green. He'll be all right." He stood up from his wooden seat, rifle in hand, and called out to the forward guard, a young Kansan named Bennie Eads.

"Bennie, what are you stopping here for?" he called out. "We need to keep this rig moving."

Eads didn't answer; he sat staring back at the two lawmen and their cargo of four cuffed and shackled prisoners. The four stood up and pressed their faces against the warm side bars, trying to get a view of the trail ahead of them.

"I say he's lost his mind," said the driver, a former army scout named Curly Ed Townsend. "He wouldn't be the first I've seen do it out here."

"Sit still here, Curly," said Shule. "I'll see what's got into him." He swung down from his seat and walked forward on the rocky trail, looking up along the cliff line as he went. "Dang it all, Bennie, you couldn't picked us a worse place to stop this rig if you tried," he said. "You're giving Curly the willies . . . me too, far as that goes—"

He stopped and fell silent as he neared the guard. He watched as Bennie turned his horse and rode off farther along the trail and stopped and looked back again.

"What are you doing, Bennie?" he called out, hurrying his pace up a little. "Sit still. I don't aim to walk all the way to . . ." His words trailed to a halt. A dark reasoning swept into his mind, and his eyes cut back up along the cliff line. He looked back at Eads and saw the mounted guard turn his horse again and ride away farther.

Oh no!

Shule turned and broke into a full, hard run toward the wagon, waving his rifle at the driver.

"Back them horses out of here, Curly!" he shouted. "It's a trap!"

"Holy Joseph!" said Curly Ed, drawing back hard on the sets of reins in his hands. Yet, before the big wagon horses could even respond to his hand commands, he heard rifle shots along the cliff and saw Shule fall to the rocky ground in a hail of bullets. "I'm coming, Ernest! Hang on!" he shouted, slapping the reins hard against the horses' backs.

As the wagon jolted forward, one of the prisoners held tight on to the bars with one hand and grabbed Harper Centrila to keep him from losing his footing.

"Obliged, Lon," said Centrila, rounding away from the man's hand on his shoulder. Along the cliff line rifle shots resounded steadily; bullets thumped on the wooden part of the wagon framing and kicked up dirt and rock on the trail.

"Yee-*hiii*!" shouted an outlaw named Bill Seadon. "I love a shooting!" He stamped his shackled bare feet on the wagon bed in a crazy dance and shook his cuffed hands wildly. "When Harper here says he's got a plan in the works, he ain't fooling around!"

Shots sliced through the air around the wagon with the sound of canvas being ripped apart. The other three prisoners hunkered down at the front of the barred rig where a thick wall of wooden planking stood between the driver compartment and the deep wagon bed. But Seadon continued to dance and laugh and hoot aloud. Lon Bartow, the prisoner who had grabbed Harper's arm to keep him from falling, started to reach out and pull Seadon down out of the gunfire. But Harper gave him a look and shook his head, stopping him.

"Let the fool dance," he said. "Maybe he'll catch a stray bullet instead of us."

As the prisoners huddled, the wagon rolled on, the four horses picking up speed as Curly tried to get to his fallen pal lying bloody in the trail amid heavy gunfire. As the wagon neared Shule, Curly Ed swerved the horses just enough to stop the rig between Shule and the riflemen above them. With the bared wagon in their gun sights, the riflemen slowed their firing. Up on the cliff, Knapp raised a hand toward Lyle and Ignacio Cady.

"Watch your shooting, Cady brothers," he said. "We don't want to kill him breaking him out." He looked down and saw the driver leap down from the rig, grab the fallen guard and help him climb back aboard.

Back in the wagon seat, Ernest Shule bleeding on the seat beside him, Curly Ed slapped the reins to the horses' backs and put them forward. Behind the two guards the prisoners cursed and complained while Bill Seadon continued to dance wildly and sing with the utter abandon of a lunatic.

"They're here for somebody!" Curly Ed shouted to Shule amid the reduced rifle fire and the sound of the prisoners. "Else they'd still be shooting us to pieces."

"Keep us rolling! Get us out from between these cliffs!" shouted the wounded guard in reply. Wrapping a bandanna around his bleeding forearm, he drew it tight with his teeth. Bullets still ripped through the air, but less wildly now. Curly Ed slapped the reins and kept the rig moving forward until he half rose from his seat, seeing the two figures standing in the trail ahead of them, rifles to their shoulders.

"Uh-oh! Hold on tight and lie low, ol' pard," he said to Ernest Shule. "They've thought of everything!" He slapped the reins even harder. "We're not stopping until we've plowed through them!"

Bullets sliced past them from straight ahead as the two riflemen on the trail opened fire.

"Like hell I'll lie low!" Shule shouted, raising his rifle, returning fire. "I'm near dead anyway. I'm shooting *somebody*, long as I'm fit to do it!"

"Me too!" shouted Curly Ed as he drove the bouncing wagon forward into the rifle fire. He took the reins in one firm hand and reached down and drew his Colt from its holster and returned fire. "Let's go out fighting!"

Chapter 8

Standing midtrail, Coco Bour and Jake Testa fired repeatedly at the oncoming prison transport wagon. They held their ground even as the gunshots from the driver and the guard zipped past them and kicked up dirt around their feet. In the roiling dust behind the wagon, they could see the Cady brothers and Charlie Knapp riding hard, having mounted and ridden down a thin steep path to give chase. In the wagon behind the driver and guard, the prisoners had stopped whooping and catcalling and now pleaded with the driver to bring the wagon to a stop. The wagon had raced out from between the cliffs. On the right a steep rocky hillside fell away hundreds of feet, much of it straight down.

"We'll stop when hell says we have to!" Shule shouted down to them, firing steadily as the wagon rocked back and forth violently.

The prisoners saw the tops of stone peaks and pines streaking past them a hundred feet below as the wagon rocked dangerously close to the trail's edge. Bill Seadon still stood balanced against the side bars and reached his cuffed hands out and let the dust from the wheels spray out off his palms.

"Crazy as a goose flying sideways!" said Lon Bartow. He shook his head. "I never met a Seadon who wasn't." He stared at Seadon as the wagon rocked wildly. Huddled with them, a Southern gunman from New Orleans named "Three-toed" Delbert Swank bounced against the barred side wall and landed back beside Bartow.

"Are you sure they're here to break you out, Harper," he shouted at Harper Centrila, "or to kill you before you get to Yuma?"

"Go to hell, Delbert," Harper shouted wryly. "This is the best ride you ever had—"

Harper's words finished short as the speeding rig's right wheels hit a sunken rock the size of a large melon and flipped the rig high onto its left wheels. Rolling on, it stayed cocked high and dangerous, as if in defiance of gravity. Curly Ed wrestled with the reins and leaned far right to counterbalance the weight and bring the rig back onto four wheels. Beside him Ernest Shule, wounded and bleeding badly, swung his weight as far right as he could and held on. Even the four horses' weight swayed against the risen wagon. But all to no avail.

"Look *at this!*" said Coco Bour; he and Testa both ceased firing. The two lowered their rifles an inch from their shoulders and stood staring in the cloud of burnt powder hanging about them. Still fifty yards away, the barred wagon snaked and veered and slid in billowing dust. Yet somehow the wagon managed to stay tilted high on its two left wheels and speed forward, its four horses struggling to keep the rig and themselves from being flipped over the edge of the trail.

As the two ambushers stared, the wagon broke loose from the four horses. The animals ran swaying to the left, the wagon to the right. Atop the rig, both driver and guard flew from the wooden seat and landed thirty feet away, rolling in the dusty trail. The rig went off the edge of the trail and tumbled downward. On the trail behind it, Charlie Knapp and the Cady brothers slid their horses to a halt and sat watching, stunned, mesmerized.

"What the living hell is this?" Knapp said under his breath in amazement.

The big wagon rolled and flipped and tumbled and bounced, plunging boulder to boulder farther down the steep hillside. Wooden wheels and frame creaked and broke and flew apart; iron twisted and clanged; bars flew away and twirled through the air. In its fall, the big rig spat out the prisoners one at a time every few yards.

The last one, Bill Seadon, landed atop a flat-topped rock just before the wagon ran out of hillside and fell spiraling the last thirty yards, crashing on a wide cliff below.

"That was one powerful run," Knapp said to the Cadys in the rising dust as the silence fell along the trail and hillside. He stepped down from his saddle; Lyle and Ignacio did the same.

"There's Harper. He's alive!" Lyle said, pointing down the hillside.

"I see him," said Knapp. "You two flounce on down the rocks and help him up here." As he spoke, he drew a Colt from his holster and walked toward the driver and guard lying in the middle of the trail.

Flounce . . . ?

The Cadys looked at each other with shared rancor. But they hurried over the trail edge and climbed down to where Harper had risen and stood with his cuffed hands cupping his forehead. A few yards farther down, Lon Bartow rose and staggered and looked all around in wonderment. Farther down still, Three-toed Delbert Swank shoved a section of plank off himself and sat up rubbing his jaw. Bill Seadon had stood up and already started scrambling upward, laughing loudly, his cuffed hands pulling him over rock after rock.

Reaching the driver and guard in the middle of the trail, Knapp aimed his Colt down at Ernest Shule, who lay bleeding, breathing heavily.

"The keys, right now," Knapp said. He wiggled the Colt in his hand.

Shule eyed him with hatred as he reached inside his rawhide vest and brought out two sets of keys to the shackles and cuffs.

"My pard's dead," he said, gesturing his eyes toward Curly Ed Townsend, who lay with his head at a sharply twisted angle, staring up blankly.

"Tough knuckles," said Knapp. "Give me the keys."

"Go get them, *son of a bitch*," said Shule. He drew back and hurled the iron keys out over the edge of the trail. The keys bounced down out of sight among the rocks.

Knapp took a deep breath and shot the guard though the head.

"Now you're dead too," he said. He turned and walked to the trail edge and looked down. As he stood there, Coco Bour and Jake Testa walked up, leading their horses and the spare horses they had brought along for Harper and his fellow prisoners.

"Don't tell me that was the keys that just went flying out," Bour said, the two stopping beside Knapp and looking down with him.

Knapp cursed low under his breath.

"Yes, it was the keys," he said. He looked over at the Cadys, who were helping Harper up the rocky hillside. The other prisoners came tagging up behind them.

"Both of you hurry up," he said to the brothers. "Get him up here, then get over in the rocks and start searching." He gestured his smoking gun barrel in the direction the dying guard had thrown the two keys.

The Cadys looked at each other again. This time Ignacio couldn't keep his mouth shut.

"Any chance Bour and Testa can give us a hand?" he called out in a sarcastic voice.

"No," Knapp said flatly, "these two didn't throw the keys, he did." He gestured toward the dead guard.

Ignacio said to his brother under his breath, "That doesn't even make sense."

"He knows it doesn't Iggy," said Lyle. "He's just pushing us around."

As the two brothers spoke they saw the other forward trail guard walk up to Knapp and the others, leading his horse.

"What the hell are you doing here?" Knapp asked gruffly, eying him up and down.

"Says he wants his money," Bour cut in. "I told him he'd have to see you about it."

"That's right," Bennie Eads said boldly. "I did my job leading them in. I want what's coming to me."

"You'll get what's *coming to you* soon as Harper has his cuffs off," said Knapp, nodding down the steep hillside. "Now get down there and help find the keys. We've been here too damn long as it is."

Eads gave Bour and Testa a look as if wondering why they weren't searching for the keys. But the two returned his look with an unfriendly gaze. Bour snatched the reins to Eads' horse from his hand.

"You heard the man," he said to Eads. "Get down there and find the key. Everybody does their part around here."

For the next half hour Knapp, Bour and Testa watched the Cadys and the guard search among the rocks with no results.

"Damn it all," Charlie Knapp said. He paced back and forth impatiently, rifle cradled in his arm, and took note of the sun reaching higher into the midmorning sky. Harper and the other three barefoot prisoners had climbed the hillside and sat on the edge of the trail sipping water from a canteen and cleaning their cuts and welts with a wet bandanna they'd retrieved from the dead driver and guard.

"This ain't worth a damn," Knapp growled aloud to himself. He turned to Bour and Testa and reached out a hand toward the sets of horses' reins in Testa's gloved hand. "Give me the horses," he said. "Both of you go down and help those phildoodles, else we never will get out of here."

Handing him the reins, Testa followed Bour down onto the rocky hillside. Yet after another unsuccessful half hour of searching had passed, Knapp stood up from where he'd sat down on the trail's edge and dusted his seat with his free hand.

"All of you dog it off. We're not homesteading here," he called down to the searchers. "There's a village, Mejores Amigos, right over the border, less than twenty miles. We'll get shed of the cuffs there."

"Mejores Amigos means Best Friends," Ignacio Cady offered absently.

Harper gave him a scorching stare, then looked up the hillside at Knapp.

"Best Friends my ass, Charlie," he shouted up at Knapp. "How the hell do you think we're going to ride with shackles on our ankles?"

Knapp bristled at the angry tone in the younger outlaw's voice. But he kept himself in check, turned away and led the horses a few steps away without reply.

"Let's get going, then," he finally called back over his shoulder. "We'll deal with this the best we can."

"I don't like the sound of that," Lon Bartow said sidelong to Harper Centrila as the men all started climbing up out of the rocks.

In the waning afternoon, two Mexican men and a middle-aged dove named Dafne, who'd retired from the brothels in El Paso, stood up in the shade of a canvas overhang out in front of a crumbling three-sided adobe. The three squinted and stared as ten riders emerged from the veil of heat hanging over the stretch of white sand between the small village and the distant border hills.

"This is not good," said the older of the two Mexican men, noting the handcuffs, the shackles on four of the men who rode barefoot, bareheaded. Two of the barefoot riders, Bill Seadon and Three-toed Delbert Swank, sat sidesaddle, ladylike. The other two rode with their knees bent deep, chains up behind them across their saddle cantles. They squatted like squirrels, or some strange racing jockeys.

"No, not good *at all*," the other, younger Mexican murmured, staring curiously. "Dafne," he said quietly to the woman standing beside him, "go to your uncle Renaldo until they are gone. I think they see your markings."

The dove, whose weathered face bore exotic and deeply etched Mayan tattoos, reached back and pulled the upper edge of her shawl down, shadowing her cheeks and forehead. She turned without a word and slipped along the side of the adobe and out of sight. But she failed to go unnoticed. As soon as the riders stopped within fifteen feet of the Mexicans, Crazy Bill Seadon craned his neck and looked back and forth in the rubble and alleyways.

"I saw a woman with a whore's face," he said to no one in particular. His chained ankles hung down his horse's side, his knees slightly crossed.

Ignoring him, Knapp respectfully touched his hat brim to the two Mexicans.

"*Buenos tardes,*" he said. He gestured a hand toward the men stopping alongside him. "We need these chains removed. I have gold coins." He had already taken out a few coins and held them in his hand. He jingled them in his fist. "*Comprende?*"

The Mexicans looked at each other. From amid the rubble and crumbling adobes in the village streets behind them, heads appeared at corners and edges of buildings; dark eyes watched the strangers.

"*Sí*, we understand," said the younger Mexican, letting Knapp know they spoke English. "I am Felipe. This one is Paco."

The older Mexican nodded and stepped forward. He inspected the chains dangling from Seadon's dirty bare ankles. "An ax perhaps?" he said to the younger Mexican.

The younger man nodded.

"An ax and also an iron wedge, Paco," he said. He looked up at Knapp. "We have the tools of both an iron-monger and a woodcrafter. I will get them, and we will get rid of the chains." He started to turn away.

But Seadon nudged his horse a step forward.

"Not so fast, hoss," he said. "I saw a woman. She had some markings."

"Yes . . . ?" said the younger Mexican. He gave a slight shrug and waited.

"I knew I saw her," Seadon said with satisfaction. "Where is she? Why'd she leave?"

"She has much to do, *señor*," the old Mexican put in.

"She is gone by now." He waved a hand as if dismissing the woman.

"Like hell she is," said Seadon. "Get her and bring her here, pronto. I want to make friends with her."

"Jesus, Crazy Bill," said Harper, staring hard at Seadon. "Let's get these chains off. Then you can start making friends."

Seadon ignored Harper and stared down at the younger Mexican.

"Felipe," he said. "I want that woman, right now." He looked all around at the few gathering villagers who ventured in closer. "Who manages her—who speaks for her?" he called out. "Who the hell do I talk to to get her on her back?"

"Let it go, Seadon," said Lon Bartow in a firm tone.

Instead of Felipe, the older Mexican stepped forward. He gestured for the younger Mexican to go fetch the needed tools. Felipe turned and hurried away.

"*Señor*, no one manages her, but I will speak for her," said Paco. "She has markings, but she is a tired and aging woman. She no longer has use for a man."

"Yeah, but she could have, huh?" Seadon grinned. Then his grin fell away. "Now, how much for her, soon as I get myself freed up here?" he insisted.

This stupid bastard. . . . Knapp eyed the crazy gunman and let his hand fall onto the rifle across his lap.

"You mistake her, *señor*. She is not a *puta*," the old man said to Seadon, shaking his head. "She is no longer a *puta*. She only lies down with one man—her uncle, Renaldo . . . who spits and suffers with a terrible cough."

"Bloody coughing don't scare me none at all, ol' hoss," said Seadon. "Do you realize how long I've been without a woman?" He stared down at the old man.

The old Mexican looked him up and down, Seadon perched sidesaddle atop his horse.

"From the way you ride, it has been a long, *long* time, *señor*," he said with a flat stare. The riders shared a short laugh; Seadon's face burned red.

"All right, that's it," he said. "I've got to kill this ol' turd. Somebody give me a gun!" He started to slide down his horse's side. But Harper grabbed the horse's reins, stopping him.

"Stay where you are, Crazy Bill," he demanded. "We've got iron we need to get shed of—or have you forgot why we're here?"

"I won't *need a gun!*" Seadon said, unheeding Harper's words. Out of control, he slid down to the ground and lunged forward in his shackles at the old Mexican, his cuffed hands out to choke him.

Paco stepped backward, nimbly staying out of reach. Yet instead of avoiding Seadon's outstretched hands, he grabbed the short chain between the cuffs and rolled down onto his back with Seadon in tow.

Uh-oh!

Harper watched transfixed; so did the others as Seadon fell forward, his stomach on the balls of Paco's sandaled feet, Paco with a firm grip on the chain. Rolling backward quickly, Seadon on top, the Mexican shot his legs straight up and sent Seadon flipping over him, landing flat on his back. The ground jarred; dust billowed. Paco still held the handcuff chain.

Jumping to his feet in a crouch, Paco somersaulted over the prone gunman, his head in Seadon's chest. Seadon, limp and defenseless, rolled with him. This time Paco twisted the handcuff chain as he rolled. When Seadon flipped high in midair and turned over, Paco let go of the chain and stepped out from under the falling gunman.

"*Gawd Almighty!*" Knapp whispered in disgust as Seadon smacked the ground hard, facedown, his cuffed hands stretched out in front of him. The impact of the fall caused the horses to take a step back. "Did he say he wouldn't *need a gun*?"

Paco stood staring down humbly at the knocked-out gunman. Running up, having seen Seadon hit the ground, Felipe tossed an ax and some other tools onto the dirt. He looked at Seadon and up at Harper and Knapp.

"We should begin, *sí*?" he said to them, hoping to divert any retaliatory violence. He quickly stooped down to take Seadon's shackles in hand.

"Huh-uh," said Harper. "Save that fool till last. I'm in no hurry to have him running unfettered."

"Where'd you learn such shenanigans as that?" Knapp asked Paco, seeing him in a different light.

Paco didn't reply.

"He was once a *luchador*," said Felipe, "a wrestler. As a young man he wrestled for both the French and the Mexican circus."

"You don't say so," said Knapp. He shook the gold coins in his hand and smiled. "How much you charge to show us that again—?"

"Whoa, now, Charlie," said Harper. "Let's get these chains off and get the hell out of here." He looked at the other men and saw the disappointment in their eyes. Then he looked down at Seadon and at Paco and shrugged.

"All right," he said. "One more time won't hurt nothing, I don't suppose. After he wakes up good, of course," he added.

"Why not just as *soon as he wakes up*?" Knapp grinned.

Harper looked back down at Seadon, considering it.

"We'll see how it goes," he said. He pushed himself atop his saddle onto his chained feet, like a frog, hopped down to the ground and walked forward, holding his cuffed hands out to Felipe and Paco for his freedom. "Me first," he said.

Chapter 9

On the high hill trails to the prisoner relay cells at Fort Hamlin, the Ranger kept Freddie Dobbs in front of him at all times. He kept the horse carrying the canvas-wrapped body of Boomer Phipps tagging behind him on a ten-foot lead rope. A dark cloud of suspecting blue flies circled and snarled above the seasoning corpse. As the three horses rode along at a walk in the noon heat, Dobbs half turned in the saddle and looked back as if checking the body.

"He's still there," the Ranger said flatly, knowing that Dobbs was in fact checking on him, looking for any chance to make a run for it, in spite of his shoulder wound and cuffed hands.

Dobbs only nodded at Boomer's corpse and its countless flies, and stayed turned in his saddle.

"Ever notice no matter where you go, if something's dead, a million flies show up out of nowhere?"

"Seems I have noticed it," Sam said wryly, willing to go along with a certain amount of conversation. "Why?" he asked.

"Nothing, it's just something that I always wonder. Where are all the flies the rest of the time?"

Sam stared at him as the horses clopped along at a slow, swaying pace.

Dobbs shrugged and said, "I mean, they've got to come from somewhere. Were they just sitting somewhere waiting? I'd like to know more about it."

The Ranger took a breath and let it out slowly, adjusting his rifle across his lap, making sure Dobbs saw him do it.

"Maybe you'll find a discussion group on such matters when you get to Yuma," he said.

"A discussion group. . . ." Dobbs appeared to consider it as he turned forward in his saddle. "If there's not, maybe I'll start one," he added.

"There's a thought," Sam said flatly, his eyes searching along the cliffs and sparse stands of pine on the steep hillside to their right. For the past couple of hours he'd felt the mildly cautioning sensation of being watched from up there. He had learned to never dismiss such inner warnings out of hand. Sometimes they were real, sometimes not. Today they were strong—those innate senses he considered commonplace to man, as well as to all animals who trekked the wilds alone.

"Hold up, Dobbs," he said as he searched the upper cliffs ahead of them and caught a glint of sunlight reflect off a rifle barrel. As Dobbs stopped his horse and looked around, Sam gestured him over to the inside edge of the trail, out of sight from the forward cliff lines.

"What's wrong?" Dobbs asked quietly.

"Somebody's up there," the Ranger said. "Friends of yours, maybe?" He glanced at Dobbs, then shifted his gaze back up along the high cliffs ahead of them.

"Never can tell," Dobbs said, deciding to play it crafty. Sam looked at him and decided he was bluffing.

"Whoever it is has been with us for a while," Sam said, looking back up. "We're going to sit tight here. See if there's an ambush waiting for us—"

"Yiii!" Dobbs shouted suddenly, nailing his heels to his horse's sides, sending it bolting forward into a hard run.

"Wait—" the Ranger said. In reflex he started to give pursuit. So did his dun. But Sam held both himself and the horse back, even drawing the lead rope taught to keep Boomer's horse from bolting off behind Dobbs.

Big mistake, Freddie.

As Dobbs' horse raced out of sight around the protruding wall of stone, Sam heard the sound of rifles bark from the cliff lines overhead. From his view he saw puffs of smoke streak out and drift along the jagged rocks. He had no chance of returning fire from here. Whoever was up there had good cover, he told himself. In spite of Dobbs taking advantage and making a getaway, he hoped he'd made it through to safety.

No sooner had he thought it than he heard the hard clacking of hooves and saw Dobbs' frightened horse go streaking back past him in the opposite direction, its saddle empty and saddle horn missing. As the rifle fire ceased, he heard Dobbs call out to him from farther along the trail.

"Ranger . . . I'm hit," Dobbs cried out. "I'm hit bad. Please, for God's sakes. . . ."

Sam sat still, watching the cliff line ahead of him. Boomer's horse had moved up closer beside him in the fury of gunfire, and at the sound of Dobbs' voice pricked its ears and tried to step forward. Sam drew it back firm-handedly. He looked closely at the animal and its cloud of flies for a moment. Then he took a long breath and stepped down from his saddle.

He needed a better position—*that's all there is to it*, he told himself. He looked all around for a place to tie the dun's reins. *Hang on, Freddie. . . .* He looked back along the trail, hearing the diminishing clack of hoofbeats as Dobbs' fleeing horse moved farther away.

Atop a flat stretch of cliff high up above the trail, a paid killer named Marlin Oakley sighted down his rifle barrel at Dobbs, who lay barely moving in the middle of the trail below. After a few more pleas for the Ranger's help, the prisoner had fallen quiet. The sling was gone that had supported his forearm beneath his shoulder wound. His arms lay spread-eagle over a pool of blood. His left wrist lay cuffed to the broken saddle horn.

"One more time, Monk," said Oakley to the gunman Monk Barber lying on his right. "This time I'll pop his head open like a red ripe melon." He chuckled darkly, envisioning his plan.

Barber looked down at the trail through an outstretched telescope.

"No, hold up," he said to Oakley. "Long as he's alive

there's a chance he'll draw the Ranger to him." He grinned behind the telescope. "That's how the Rebs did it at Falls Church, or one of them damn places."

Oakley let his aim relax and looked over at Barber.

"The Ranger ain't fool enough to stick his nose out in the open for us," he said. "He's most likely heard of that old tactic himself."

"He'll come," Barber said with confidence. "Just hold up and watch. Be ready when he gets out there."

"Wanna bet?" Marlin Oakley said.

"How much?" said Barber.

"I've got five Mexican pesos says the Ranger won't show," said Oakley. "I say the Ranger cuts back and skins out of here."

"I'll take that bet," said Barber, pushing back from the edge, dusting himself off. He stuck the telescope into his belt and reached behind him for a canteen sitting on a ledge.

Oakley pushed back a little, but only rose onto his knees, staying ready to drop down and fire should he need to. The two waited and watched. The hillside below them lay in silence except for Dobbs letting out a pain-filled plea every now and then. Ten minutes passed, then twenty.

"How long are we talking about?" Oakley asked after a while. "I figure he's already turned tail."

Looking back along the trail at the quiet clack of a horse's hooves walking forward from around the stone wall, Barber grinned and nodded toward the sound.

"The waiting's over, Marlin. Here he comes. You owe me five pesos." He stepped over and stood against a rock, leveling his rifle over the top of it. "Let's blast him and the prisoner at the same time."

"Not so fast," Oakley said, rising onto his knee. "What's coming here?"

On the trail below they saw the horse carrying the canvas-wrapped body step into sight and walk to where Dobbs lay on the trail.

"Ha," said Oakley, "I was right after all. The Ranger cut out of here so fast he left his dead prisoner behind." He pushed to his feet and stared down at the trail. "Let's go. We'll have to chase him down to kill him."

Barber stepped over beside him. The two looked down at the badly wounded Dobbs, and at the horse carrying the body.

"I'm disappointed in the Ranger," said Barber. "I expected better from him—never figured him to cut and run."

"He saw we had him," said Oakley. "He'd been a fool to ride into two rifles." As he spoke he dusted his trouser knee. The two started walking down the steep rocky hillside.

"So now he knows we're dogging him, and we still have to kill him, if we don't want Silas Rudabaugh down our shirts, thinking we let him down."

"We'll get the Ranger, don't you worry," said Oakley. "We've got him on the run. We'll pin him down."

The two stopped on a bald, open cliff farther down the hillside. Oakley raised his rifle to his shoulder and aimed down at Dobbs.

"Hold it, Marlin," Barber said, staring with suspicion at the body across the horse's back. They were down close enough now to hear and see the swirl of flies. "Something ain't right down there. I can feel it."

Oakley looked him up and down, but eased his finger off the trigger and lowered his rifle a little.

"Yeah?" he said. "I think maybe you're sour over losing five pesos." He started to aim again at Dobbs.

"No, wait up," said Barber, staring at the body across the horse's back. "This is a trick! That's not the dead prisoner. That's the Ranger under the canvas. I think I just saw something move."

"You're loco, Monk," said Oakley with a dark chuckle. "No lawman would lie in a swarm of blowflies." He shook his head, started to aim again.

"It's him! This is all a trick, I tell you!" Barber shouted, his voice getting shaky as he raised his rifle toward the canvas-wrapped body.

Before he could fire, the sound of the rifle beside him caused him to flinch. He saw the dirt canvas puff slightly on the big body below as the bullet sliced through it. The horse only jerked, but settled instantly beneath the weight of Boomer's body.

"There, you see?" said Oakley. He chuckled, levering a fresh round into his smoking rifle chamber. The shot echoed out across the hill lines. "If that was a trick, I bet he wishes he'd thought it out better."

Barber looked embarrassed.

"I coulda sworn . . . ," he said. Oakley's rifle exploded again. The canvas puffed on the body; the horse tensed, then settled.

"Just in case you still wondered," Oakley said with a thin smile. He levered another round. "Satisfied?"

"Yeah," Barber said stiffly. He nodded at Dobbs. "Finish that one off and let's go. We've still got to run the Ranger down."

"Whatever you say." Oakley gave him a smug look, shrugged and raised his rifle again. He aimed down at Dobbs in the trail as Dobbs tried to crawl away.

This time when the rifle shot resounded, it sounded different somehow, less loud—*less close?*

Hearing Oakley let out a grunt, Barber looked around quickly, in time to see Oakley's rifle fall from his hands as he clutched his bloody abdomen.

"I'm sho-*ot?*" Oakley asked, a strange surprised look on his face. He toppled forward and bounced and tumbled down the hillside.

Realization set in just as Barber heard a rifle levering not too far behind him. He swung around toward it, cocking his rifle, raising it to fire. He saw the Ranger standing behind a waist-high rock thirty feet away— saw him just in time to see the blue-orange fire streak from his rifle barrel.

"*Holy—!*" His words broke away as the bullet thumped into his forehead and sent him spilling backward beneath a red mist of blood and brain matter.

The Ranger stepped around the rock levering a fresh round into his rifle chamber. He looked down at Barber and kept walking, seeing no more of a problem there. He walked on, picking his steps down the rocky hillside until he stood over the badly wounded ambusher.

"Marlin Oakley," he said, recognizing the twisted, pain-filled face staring up at him. "Imagine meeting you here."

"You . . . go to . . . hell, Ranger!" Oakley snarled, clutching his abdomen with both hands.

The Ranger only nodded. He stepped in closer and raised the wounded outlaw enough to lean him back against a rock. Oakley lay trembling, sweat pouring. He tilted his head and looked down his chest at his bloody shirt pocket as the Ranger pulled a thin cigar from it. He watched the Ranger light the cigar and hold it down to his mouth. Oakley took the cigar between his teeth, bit down on it and settled a little, puffing on it.

"I ain't . . . thanking you . . . you killing son of a bitch," he groaned, and coughed.

"You weren't out to kill Freddie Dobbs, so it must have been me," Sam said quietly, ignoring the insult. He sat down on a rock facing the dying man, his rifle across his lap. He knew he had to get down the hill and help Dobbs, but he also needed to know who was behind this.

"Yeah . . . it was you," said Oakley. "I've nothing . . . agin Dobbs." He settled a little more, puffing on what he knew to be his last cigar. "Would have . . . got you too, had it not . . . been for—"

"Who sent you?" the Ranger asked, cutting him off, knowing he wasn't going to last much longer.

"I said, go . . . to hell," Oakley said.

"Don't make me take back the cigar and stand on your belly," the Ranger said in the same quiet tone.

Oakley stared up at him and puffed some more, weighing whether or not he would do it. He believed he would.

"Silas Rudabaugh," he said finally.

"Meaning Edsel Centrila," Sam said, "since Rudabaugh is his top hired gun."

"Um-hmm . . . Centrila wants you dead." He puffed on the cigar. "But it might . . . have been anybody. Nobody likes you . . . much."

"Rudabaugh say why Centrila wanted me killed?" the Ranger asked.

"No . . . I just figured . . . all these paybacks going around . . . one just got stuck to you." He coughed and wheezed and clutched his abdomen tighter. "Seems everybody's . . . got a mad-on at somebody, wants them killed these days." He sighed, wistful. "I shoulda made a fortune at it. . . ."

The Ranger watched him gasp and relax, staring up blankly at the sky. Reaching down, he took the sagging cigar from Oakley's lips and crushed it under his boot.

Paybacks. . . .

Oakley was right. There were powerful men like Edsel Centrila around, rich men who spent big money to avenge themselves of wrongs committed against them, both real and imagined. It wasn't just Sheriff Stone's whiskey-tangled nerves making him edgy and suspicious. Not only did Centrila want Stone dead; he wanted the Ranger dead too.

Why? he asked himself. *Vengeance by association?* He stood up, rifle in hand, looked all around and headed back to the thin path he'd followed up the steep hillside. It really didn't matter *why*, he told himself. Centrila's paid gunman, Silas Rudabaugh, sent men to kill him. *So be it*.

Leaving the two ambushers where they were in the

rocks, the Ranger picked his footing down the hill path back onto the trail. He stooped down beside Freddie Dobbs and rolled him onto his back.

"I screwed up, Ranger . . . ," Dobbs gasped through bloody lips.

"Take it easy, Freddie," the Ranger said. He cradled his head on his knee and looked him over, seeing blood seeping through his clothing from three different wounds.

Freddie saw the grim look on the Ranger's face. He tried to give a dark chuckle, but it stuck in his shattered chest.

"I suppose I shouldn't . . . make any plans, huh?" he said.

The Ranger let out a breath. "Lie still. I'll get you some water," he said.

"Naw, I don't . . . need any," Freddie said, gripping the Ranger's forearm. His voce fell to a raspy whisper. "But do me a favor?"

"The man who shot you is already dead if that's what you're going to ask me," Sam said.

Dobbs shook his head a little.

"Naw, I never was . . . vengeful," he whispered. "Will you . . . keep them flies off me?" He half grinned; his eyes had already started to drift aimlessly.

"I'll do my best, Freddie," said the Ranger, watching him slip on away. He brushed a fly from Dobbs' pale bloody cheek, picked his hat up from the ground and laid it over his face. Then he stood up and walked back toward his dun, seeing Freddie's bay had returned from its fleeing frenzy and stood calmly near the edge of the trail with its head lowered.

"Glad you could make it," he said wryly to the sweaty horse. He picked up its reins and led it over to the dun. He swung up into his saddle, shoved his rifle into its boot and rode forward, leading the bay beside him.

Chapter 10

Merchants and townsfolk in Fort Hamlin stood watching as the Ranger rode into town leading two horses carrying the bodies of Freddie Dobbs and Boomer Phipps across their backs. The manager of the prisoner relay facility, Oscar White, stepped down off the boardwalk out in front of his heavily barred office and met the Ranger. He took the lead rope to the two horses from his hand with a "Howdy, Ranger" and led the animals to the hitch rail. Sam touched the brim of his sombrero toward him.

"Howdy, Oscar," he replied, hearing the scorched dryness in his own voice.

White looked at Boomer Phipps' huge body as he wrapped the lead rope round the rail.

"Glad I'm not having to feed this one," he commented. "My budget is in a strain as it is." He gave a grin through a tangled gray beard. "I'll receipt you for them and get them under the ground right away."

"Obliged," said the Ranger. He swung down from his saddle and stretched his back. "This one is Freddie

Dobbs and this big fellow is Armand Phipps—went by the name *Boomer*."

White took a small pad of paper and a pencil stub from his shirt pocket and officiously wrote the two names down. As he wrote he spoke idly.

"Tried to escape, did they?" he said.

"Yes," Sam said. "Boomer tried to escape from jail over in Big Silver. Freddie Dobbs tried to escape from me and some ambushers shot him. I'll write it all up this evening."

"Tell me the particulars and I'll write it up for you, Ranger," White said. "I know you've no fondness for paperwork."

"Obliged," Sam said. He eyed White curiously. "When you offer to do my paperwork, I figure you want something in return?"

White grinned and struck the pencil and pad back in his shirt pocket.

"Can't fool you, Ranger," he said. "The fact is I've got a jail wagon that hasn't shown up. It should have pulled in here early yesterday—the wagon your prisoners would have rid on to Yuma had they not got their clocks stopped."

"The one taking Harper Centrila to start serving out his sentence?" Sam asked, interested.

"Yep, that's the one," said White. He gave Sam a look. "See why I'm a little more concerned than usual?" he said.

Sam nodded. "I know their trail route. I'll ride out and follow it, soon as I water my horse and get something to eat along the way."

"Obliged, Ranger," White said. "I'll get a couple of men and get these off the street." He gave a slight shrug. "Who knows? Could be the wagon shows up before you've gone five miles."

"Let's hope so, Oscar," Sam said. "I'm getting more than my fill of the Centrilas lately."

Three hours later the Ranger sat atop a blaze-faced bay looking out through a telescope across rugged desert terrain. He rode the livery bay in order to let his dun rest at the end of the short lead rope he held in his gloved hand. The dun sidled up close to him on the narrow cliff and looked out as if searching the land with him. This was the third time he'd stopped and searched for the wagon. The other two times he'd seen no sign of it.

But this time he saw three wagon horses still hitched together, a splintered wagon shaft and part of a broken doubletree hanging between them. A few yards away a fourth horse stood with hitch rings and a short chain dangling down its sides. In the distance behind the horses he saw two buzzards circling high overhead.

"Bad news," Sam murmured.

Lowering the lens from his eye, he closed the telescope and put it away. He picked up the lead rope from his lap, turned both horses around from the cliff's edge and rode away. He followed the trail down and across a narrow valley. Across the valley he took another winding trail upward until a half hour later he found the wagon horses standing facing him as they grazed on clumps of pale desert wild grass.

"Easy, boys," he said quietly to the horses, stopping

a few yards back and stepping down from his saddle. As he walked to the three horses, the fourth horse clopped up at a slow gait and stood beside the others. Sam used both hands to rub the horses' muzzles as he looked at the path of hoofprints stretched out along the rock trail behind them.

Clearing the broken team equipment from the horses, he lined and tied the animals in a horse string along with his dun. Then he mounted the bay and led the string back along the rail until he came to the bodies of the guard and the driver lying where the gunmen had left them. Three buzzards stood atop the dead.

Rifle in hand, Sam stepped down and walked forward swinging the Winchester back and forth until the reluctant buzzards finally lifted up grudgingly in a hard batting of wings. The big greasy-looking birds flew only a few yards away and landed and screeched at him. The Ranger ignored them as he forced himself to look at the gruesome remains of Ernest Shule and Curly Ed Townsend. He looked all around and down the steep hillside as the screeching buzzards settled.

He saw the strange meandering tracks of the wagon leading up and over the edge of the trail. He surveyed the tangled, twisted bars, broken planks and scraps of wagon parts strewn down the hillside. In the broken pine tops and among the rocks below, he saw what was left of the rig after making the final plunge. He let out a breath and looked back down at the two bodies, the scattering of horses' hooves surrounding them.

"You deserved better, Ernest. . . . You too, Curly Ed," he said softly.

As he looked down at Shule's mangled, picked-over corpse, he saw where the old Ranger's shirt had been ripped away by the buzzards. Around his neck hung a strip of rawhide with two keys on it. Sam stooped and slipped the rawhide off and stood with the keys in his hand.

Cuff keys, he told himself, recognizing the familiar items to be the same as the key he carried in his trouser pocket. Off the side of the trail he noted the footprints both booted and bare in the loose dirt, on and among the hillside rock.

"Obliged, Ernest. You stalled them as long as you could," he said down to the dead, mangled body. "I'll take it from here," he whispered. Gripping the keys in his gloved hand, he looked off in the direction of the hoofprints riding down the trail in the direction of the nearest border village.

Mejores Amigos, he said to himself. *To get rid of their shackles and cuffs.*

Wasting no time, he dragged both bodies off the trail and covered them with rocks to foil the buzzards' dinner plans. When he made his way back to Fort Hamlin, he'd make it a point to send someone out and have the bodies brought in and buried proper. For now this would have to do, he thought to himself. Being lawmen most of their lives, Ernest Shule and Curly Ed would understand.

With the four wagon horses and the dun on a lead rope, he looked over his shoulder at the trail site as he rode away. Two of the buzzards had flown away. A third stood staring at the rocks as if pondering the unfairness of life. Turning forward in his saddle, he gave a tug on the lead rope and batted his knees to the bay's sides.

And he rode on.

Sam realized there was a chance the prisoners had found a way to get rid of their cuffs and shackles, but the fact that their tracks led toward Mejores Amigos convinced him otherwise. He was convinced that Ernest Shule had thrown something out among the rocks and told the gunmen it was the keys to the prisoners' restraints. It was something a wagon guard would know to do given the circumstances. While it had started as a hunch when he found the keys around Shule's neck, the more he thought about it, the more strongly he believed it. Following their horses' hoofprints only made him believe it more.

The riders had headed for the little border village so quickly that they paid no heed to hiding their tracks. Old Ernest had played his hand right up to the very end, he told himself, riding the last two miles to the little desert town.

As he drew nearer, he saw two old men get up from where they had been sitting watching him. They walked away slowly and disappeared into a row of ancient crumbling adobes. Yet when he rode up moments later, they had returned with a third man joining them. The three stood watching him with dark, worried expressions. Even the sight of the badge on his chest did not serve to loosen the tightening concern from their weathered faces.

"*Hola,*" the Ranger called out, continuing in Spanish, "*Puedo hacerle algunas preguntas, por favor?*" He kept a respectful distance of fifteen feet between them and gestured a hand down at the hoofprints he'd followed across the stretch of sand flats. The same collection of hoofprints led away from the small village back into the desert.

"Hello," one of the men replied in stiff border English. "Yes, we will answer any questions that we can for you."

The Ranger noted a wariness in the three men. Why? And why was he spoken to in English, having let them know he could speak their language? But he sat still, the team horses and his dun gathered up beside him, and he glanced around the small village with its many alleyways and crumbling adobes.

"*Gracias,*" he said. He wasn't going to ask *if* the men had come there—that part was a foregone conclusion. Instead he would ask how long ago? What was their condition? Did they get the chains removed? "I'm following the prisoners who came here looking for someone to remove their chains."

The three Mexicans shook their heads as one.

"No one has come here to our village wearing chains, *señor,*" a thin elderly man said.

The Ranger stared at him for a moment. In the sand he saw both boot and barefoot prints. He even saw what looked like the imprint of a shackle chain. But he would make no mention of it. Instead he raised his Winchester from across his lap and kept his thumb over the hammer, ready to cock it.

"I understand," he said. "May I water my horses at your well? Then I'll be on my way. I have money to pay you."

"Our well is very low and full of mud and grit, *señor*," the same thin Mexican said. "Perhaps you go to the water hole." He gestured toward a rise of sand in the distance.

Sam nodded. He was familiar with the water hole.

"That's what I'll do, then," he said. Without another word he turned the horses and rode away. As soon as he was back onto the path of the hoofprints he'd followed to Mejores Amigos, he nudged the bay up into a hard gallop, let the slack out on his lead rope and led the dun and team horses directly behind him.

Watching the Ranger ride away, the three Mexicans looked at each other with stark trepidation.

"Stirs up a lot of dust, don't he?" said Crazy Bill Seadon, walking up behind them, Bennie Eads only a step behind.

"I don't trust this one damn bit," Eads said, staring out at the roiling dust.

"You don't have to, I do," Seadon said sharply. White-hot madness danced in his eyes. He held the woman, Dafne, against his side, her arm twisted up behind her back. The woman's tattooed face was covered with welts and bruises that had come from Seadon's hands. Seadon himself didn't look much better, owing to the trouncing the Mexican wrestler, Paco Herera, had given him several times before Harper Centrila had brought the show to an end.

"I'm just being cautious, is all," Eads put in quickly,

trying not to upset Crazy Bill. He pictured Paco's body now lying in a drainage gutter behind a goat pen. He'd watched Seadon deliver a forceful blow and sink the blade of the ax that had helped remove the prisoners' chains into the top of the wrestler's skull, no sooner than Harper and the others had left Mejores Amigos.

"Careful, *wagon guard*," Seadon warned him. "Remember the old saying 'Curiosity killed the Quaker.'" He turned, Dafne's arm in hand, and glared at Eads. "So watch your step with me," he said with a sneer.

Curiosity? The Quaker . . . ?

Eads just stared; he didn't know what to say to that. He hadn't mentioned *curiosity* or *Quakers*. Not that it mattered, apparently, he decided. Crazy Bill's warped brain had a way of twisting things to suit his own thinking. Eads stepped over beside Seadon and the woman and stared out as the Ranger and the string of horses disappeared up over the distant rise toward the water hole. A thick cloud of dust loomed in his wake.

"He fell for it!" Seadon laughed. "The stupid fool fell for it like a fish for a bowl of stew!" He continued to laugh loudly. Eads just stared; the three Mexicans gave each other confused looks and stood rigidly watching for whatever came next from this lunatic.

"Don't worry, ol' greasers," Seadon said, "you did a good job lying for us."

The Mexicans looked relieved. The thin one ventured a step forward.

"Then you will let Dafne go, and not kill us, *señor*?" he asked meekly.

"I wouldn't go so far as to say that," said Seadon, his

continence darkening. He eased his grip on the woman and turned to Eads. "Now, you, Bennie," he said as if having serious thought about Eads.

Bennie Eads fidgeted in place under Seadon's cold, insane stare.

"What . . . ?" he said after an uncomfortable moment.

"What *what*?" Seadon countered, raising the Colt that hung loosely in his hand.

Eads shrugged and tried to look at ease.

"We did what we were told. I expect we can ride on now," he offered. "Get up behind the Ranger and chop him down, like Harper said?"

"I don't see how I can trust you," Seadon said to Eads, letting go of the woman's arm but keeping her near him with a hand on her shoulder. "You heard Harper tell me not to kill the wrestler, or this *puta*." He shook Dafne by her shoulder. "I split the wrestler's noggin. I'm getting ready to kill this one too." He shook his head and said, "I can't have you telling Harper about it, *huh-uh*. Mama Lori never raised no fools."

"I'm not going to say anything to Harper about it, Bill," said Eads, feeling a nervous sickness down deep in his guts. "You've got my word on it!"

"Your word, *ha!*" said Seadon. He leveled the Colt at Eads and pushed the woman away. "I don't trust none of you! Every one of you is going to hell today. Starting with you, Bennie—!"

"Drop the gun, Crazy Bill," said the Ranger, stepping out from behind an adobe wall.

The Mexicans, the woman and Eads all froze in

place, seeing the cocked rifle in the Ranger's hands. Seadon kept his Colt leveled at Eads but turned his head, facing the Ranger.

"So you saw through us, law dog," he said. "What was it gave us away?"

What gave us away? Sam thought about the tracks left in the sand, so clear that nobody could have missed them. The imprint of the chain. The fear in the old Mexicans' eyes . . .

"I'm not going to talk to you, Crazy Bill," Sam said quietly. "I wouldn't know how. Drop the gun and I won't kill you. That's all you get here."

"Let me tell you a couple of things," said Seadon. "First off, nobody calls me Crazy and lives to tell about it."

Sam just looked at him.

"Seadon," the Ranger said quietly, "everybody calls you Crazy Bill. It's all I've ever heard you called."

"Not to my face, they don't!" Seadon shouted. "Second, I am not dropping this gun!"

Sam could see that the wild-eyed gunman was on the verge of making a play of some sort. He waited, ready, poised, his finger on the trigger of his rifle.

"Third!" Seadon shouted. "This right here is none of your business. You've got no business even being down here, pushing around ol' boys like me."

"That's three things, Crazy Bill," Sam reminded him.

"Number *four*, any killing done here, I'll do it, Ranger," said Seadon. He cackled with crazy laughter and pulled the trigger on his leveled Colt. The bullet hit Bennie Eads dead center and sent him flying backward.

Still laughing, Crazy Bill swung the Colt toward the woman, who had already turned and started running for cover.

The Winchester barked in the Ranger's hands. Seadon fell backward as Sam levered a fresh round. Seadon rose onto his knees and tried to take aim, but the Ranger's second shot nailed him in the chest and sent him flat onto his back as the Colt fired straight up in the air. The Mexicans watched as the Ranger walked forward and looked down at the dead gunman and kicked his Colt away just in case.

"He—he said if we told you he was here, he would kill us!" the thin Mexican said.

Smoked curled from Sam's rifle barrel as he turned and walked to where Eads lay on the ground clutching his wounded chest. "Don't worry," Sam said to the thin Mexican. "You told me he was here. That's what brought me back."

Chapter 11

"Smart trick, Ranger," Eads said grudgingly, nodding off toward the rise of dust stretching toward the distant water hole. He lay against a low rock wall circling a tall saguaro cactus where the old Mexicans had dragged him out of the harsh sunlight. The Ranger stooped beside him and held out a gourd full of water. The old Mexicans and the woman stood off to the side watching, listening. Other villagers watched from farther away.

"No trick," the Ranger said, watching him take a sip of the tepid water. "All I did was turn them loose and cut away under the dust. They always head for water out here."

"That's . . . *real* good to know," Eads said painfully. "I'll pass that along . . ." There was a dark wry irony in his voice that the Ranger had come to recognize in dying men—men who had played their hand out against the law, only to lose everything. Blood formed at the corners of his mouth. His head drooped; his eyes began to close.

"Look at me, Eads," Sam said firmly, getting his attention. "You need to talk to me before you go."

Eads' eyes opened. He looked at the Ranger closely.

"Why," he said, "so everybody knows what a foul man I've become?" He coughed and tried to give a thin, weak smile. "You can tell them all about me. Make it up, far as I care. . . ."

The Ranger ignored his bitter words.

"Who came to you, who brought you in on this?" he said, jostling Eads' shoulder a little. "How many am I following?" He already had a good idea of their numbers. But it never hurt to ask.

"There was ten of us," Eads said brokenly. "Now there'll be eight. Charlie Knapp . . . came to me. Said old man Centrila wanted his boy sprung." He coughed, gripping his bloody chest; blood trickled from his lips. "I needed the money." He shook his head a little. "Turns out I never even got paid. Can you beat that?"

Sam considered it as he listened. Edsel Centrila had given money to Sheriff Stone to bribe Territorial Judge Albert Long for keeping his son, Harper, from going to prison. Instead of offering the bribe money, Stone had gone to the judge and initiated a charge of bribery against the wily old cattleman. Centrila had now resorted to breaking his son out of custody. Bennie Eads had been greedy enough and fool enough to fall for it. *Simple enough. . . .*

"All you did by taking Centrila's deal was get two good men killed," Sam said. "Not to mention yourself. Why would they give you money when a bullet would settle the account?"

Eads' head drooped again. A string of red saliva hung from his lips. His voice weakened even more, like that of a man drifting farther out to sea.

"I know that *now* . . . ," he murmured, his breath leaving his chest for the last time.

Sam stood and looked down at the dead guard turned outlaw. He stood for a moment pondering Bennie Eads' situation—his grasp for quick and easy money, and where it had taken him.

"Señor Ranger . . . ?" whispered the thin old Mexican who had walked up and stood at his elbow. "*Por favor*, tell us what you would like us to do about the dead. We can dig for them some graves, if that is what you wish."

Sam turned to face him, the empty gourd still in his hand. The Mexican took the gourd and waved in another Mexican, who took it and hurried to a large clay urn, poured water into it and put a lid over it.

"Take care of them for me, *por favor*," Sam said flatly, already knowing some money would have to change hands to bring it about. He fished a gold coin from his vest pocket and placed it on the old man's upturned palm.

"*Sí*, we will take care of them," the old man said. "Do you wish for me to decide how—so you can be on your way?"

"Yes, you decide," Sam said. "I have horses waiting at the water hole."

"Do you wish us to put up markers?" the old man asked. He closed his thin fist over the coin.

Noting something curious in the man's voice, the Ranger eyed him closely.

"How bad have things been in Mejores Amigos?" he asked, putting the question of grave markers aside.

"Very bad," the old Mexican said. He gestured a hand at a sparse flock of skinny chickens scratching in the dirt. "As you can see we are very poor. Even our animals go without—those which cannot forage for themselves."

Sam looked around again and back at the old Mexican. He saw a secretive glint in the old man's eyes.

"I understand," he said. He turned to the bay that a thin elderly woman led in from where he'd hitched it out of sight behind a dilapidated barn. "Markers would be good. But I don't see family ever coming to visit. Do what's best for all concerned."

"*Sí*, that is what I will do," said the old man.

The Ranger stepped into his saddle, adjusted his reins and looked down at the dead outlaws.

Two down, eight to go. . . .

He turned the bay and touched the brim of his sombrero toward the villagers. The old Mexican stood watching him ride away as the old men gathered around him.

"Did you explain to him?" one old man asked quietly.

"No, I did not," the old Mexican said. "I did not have to. He knows." He stood staring at the fresh rise of dust in the bay's wake, headed out toward the water hole.

"How do you know he knows?" the same old man
asked.

"Enough of this," another old man cut in. "If he says
the Ranger knows, then he knows. *Sí*, Miguel?" he
turned his question to the thin old Mexican.

"*Sí*," the old Mexican replied without taking his
eyes off the Ranger, who grew smaller crossing the
stretch of sand flats. "We will do what is best for all
concerned. If he comes back to Mejores Amigos, he will
not ask." He paused and murmured to himself, "Because he knows. . . ."

The Mexicans looked at each other and nodded.
They turned in pairs and gathered the bodies of Seadon
and Eads between them and carried them away toward
the far edge of the village. As they reached an open
wallow of dust, they heard loud squeals and grunts
and saw the dust-covered snouts of the few village
hogs probing toward them. They dropped the bodies,
removed their boots and clothes quickly. The half-feral
animals whirled and bounced in a wild frenzy. The
men rolled the bodies down the side of the wallow
among the squealing hogs, then crossed themselves
and turned and walked away.

It was near evening when the Ranger gathered the string
of team horses and the copper dun at the water hole.
The first thing he did was strip the saddle and bridle
from the bay and let it drink while he tossed the saddle
atop the dun and untied it from the string. He checked
the rested dun over good, then stood with its head in the
crook of his arm and rubbed its muzzle. The horse still

chewed on a wad of pale wild grass from the far side of the water hole.

"I suppose you kept these wagon pullers in line while I was gone?" he said. The dun blew out a breath and nudged its nose against him. The team horses stood nearby and watched with their eyes caged against the red lowering sun.

Sam looked off in the direction the riders had taken and considered his move as he continued rubbing the dun's muzzle.

Eight gunmen were a lot to be following, he told himself, especially when they knew it wouldn't be long before someone came after them. But the number didn't stop him. They were headed into good fighting land for him. Southwest, in both the wide-open Mexican desert flats and hill lines, with a good long-range rifle, he knew he could start trimming the number down quick enough. He looked at the tracks leading away southwest into Mexico.

If that's where they're headed, he said to himself. He had a nagging doubt that they weren't.

He turned loose of the dun and walked to the water's edge, where he sank two canteens and looked away southwest again as they filled. Ernest Shule had thrown the outlaws off their plans when he forced them to ride to Mejores Amigos to slip their chains. They had ridden straight and hard across the soft sandy flats to get there, so straight that they had been careless and paid no regard to hiding their tracks among any rock paths or higher hill trails.

He picked up the filled canteens and carried them to

the dun. Now that the prisoners' chains were off, they would be more careful, he told himself. Yet, careful or not, he couldn't see Harper Centrila headed deep into Mexico. No, as soon as the younger gunman thought it safe, he'd ride onto the rocky hills, swing wide and circle back to the territory. The Centrilas had paybacks to settle with Sheriff Stone. That was where he and his men would be headed.

"Us too," Sam said aloud, thinking about Sheriff Stone there by himself—not even a deputy to watch his back.

He hooked the canteen straps over his saddle horn and looked at the dun, who upon hearing his voice had turned its head toward him and was giving him a curious look.

"Just thinking out loud, Copper," he said, taking up the reins draped over the dun's withers. "You ever do that?"

The dun only pricked its ear a little and scraped a hoof on the sandy ground.

"No, huh?" the Ranger said. He pulled on his gloves as the spoke. "Do you ever see things before they happen?"

The dun chuffed out a puff of breath and stood looking at him.

"I didn't think so," Sam said quietly. He let the bay finish watering and tied it into the string with the team animals. Then he gathered the rope to the string and stepped into his saddle and rode on. He watched as far as he could on either side for fresh tracks leading back toward the border.

He rode until the desert darkness swallowed the land. By the time a strong three-quarter moon had risen and a sky full of stars came forward out of the endless dark, he had made a dark camp at the bottom of a rising hillside. He slept the night wrapped in a blanket against a sunken waist-high boulder, and was back on the trail before dawn.

He followed the same group of hoofprints until he started up a higher trail and stopped when he looked to his left and saw the same fresh tracks on a thin trail below him headed back down toward the flatlands.

Backtracking. . . .

"Looks like we were right, Copper," he said to the dun. "They've made their run, and now they're going home." He turned the team horses and the bay and rode down the way he'd come. "At least we saved ourselves climbing this hill."

At the bottom of the hill line, he rode along its sloping bottom edge until a mile to his right he found where the thin trail met the desert floor. There the hoofprints spilled onto the sand and led back in the direction of the border. By midday as the white sunlight performed its daily ritual of scorching the land and its inhabitants, he brought the horses to a halt under the shadowed edge of a cliff overhanging a deep dry wash.

Here he rested the sweaty animals out of the worst part of the day's heat. There was no great hurry now. It was time to pull back some. They would be checking their back trail the way men on the run always did. He had the hoofprints well in his sights. He would not lose them.

Anyway, he told himself, gazing out across the endless swirl of heat and burning sand, *even if you did, you know where they're headed.*

Harper Centrila set his horse's sore hoof back on the ground and dusted his hands. Charlie Knapp sat atop his horse looking out along the thin desert trail they'd followed back toward the border.

"What's it look like?" Knapp asked without looking down.

"He's done for," said Harper.

"Too bad," said Knapp. "There's a Mexican relay station not ten miles from here. You can double up with somebody until we get there."

Double up? Not hardly.

"Look at me when we're talking, Charlie," Harper said. The mounted gunman brought his gaze around from the rugged desert terrain. Harper went on. "I don't ride double with *nobody*. What are you looking for back there anyway? It's too soon for somebody to be on our trail."

"Just being cautious," Knapp said. He looked the young man up and down. Harper thought he saw contempt in the steely eyes of the older gunman.

"There's such a thing as being too cautious," he said. "If anybody was already back there dogging us, we'd've seen them by now." He gestured a hand toward endless miles of white desert sand broken by hill lines spaced as if to deliberately expose the hunter to the hunted.

"Not if they didn't want us to see them," Knapp replied. "Apache have been hiding here a hundred years. Sometimes the army rides right past them."

"Good for them," Harper said. He looked back at the empty trail and swirling heat looming on the desert floor. "We might want to get something straight here and now, Charlie. I know you take orders from my papa, Edsel. But now that I'm out and ol' Papa Edsel ain't here, guess who you take orders from?"

Knapp just stared at him for a moment and let his blood simmer before answering. Finally he kept himself in check and said, "All right, Harper, what's your *order*?"

"None right now," Harper said. "I'm just making things clear so we'll understand each other. *Comprende?*"

"Yeah, I've got it," Knapp said.

"Good," said Harper. He drew the Colt from his waist, cocked it and turned and fired a bullet between the lame horse's eyes. The horse crumbled to the sand and onto its side. Knapp cursed under his breath, looking back into the dust and heat, certain the shot could be heard for miles.

The six other men had stopped their horses and sat watching from the shade of a deep cut bank along a dry creek bed. Harper walked straight to Lyle Cady, his Colt cocking in his hand. Without a word he jerked Lyle's boot from his stirrup and flipped him from his saddle.

"*Jesus!*" Ignacio Cady said aloud, having to keep his horse settled as his brother landed and stirred up dust beside him.

"I'm taking this horse," Harper declared. He grabbed the loose reins to Lyle's horse. "You *Cady brothers* got anything to say about it?"

Lyle scrambled to his feet but made sure he kept his hand away from his holstered revolver.

"This ain't right, Harper—!" he managed to say before Harper's thumb and fingers clamped tightly on his nose and yanked him forward.

"*Ain't right?*" Harper sneered. "I'll tell you what *ain't right*! My horse coming up lame *ain't right*!" He squeezed Lyle's already sore and damaged nose and shook his head back and forth roughly. "Me having to be broke out of a jail wagon *ain't right*!"

"Please!" Lyle said with a nasal twang. Even in his pain he kept himself from going for his gun. That didn't keep Harper from raising his Colt and poking the hard tip of the barrel against the side of Lyle's head.

"Are you going to squawk about getting up there with your brother and riding double until we get to the relay station?"

"Huh-uh, I'm not," said Lyle nasally, trying to shake his head.

Harper let go of Lyle's nose and shoved him away. He kept his Colt raised and looked at the men who sat watching atop their horses.

"They're brothers. It's the only natural way to do this," he said, justifying himself. A cruel grin came to his lips. "Besides, these Cady brothers sooner ride double with somebody any chance they get."

Humiliated by both Harper's action and the men's round of laughter, Ignacio reached a hand down and helped lift his bother up behind him.

Seeing the end to the incident, Knapp sidled his

horse over near Harper, who was now seated atop Lyle's mount.

"We need to get moving," he said. "That shot was heard by every white man and red heathen in the Sonora."

Harper glared angrily at him for a moment. But then he caught himself and nodded and turned the horse and spoke over his shoulder.

"Let's get moving, amigos," he said, mocking Knapp. "That shot was heard by every white man and red heathen in the Sonora." He gave Knapp a devilish loweredbrow stare and rode away.

Chapter 12

It was late evening when the Ranger found the dead horse lying in the dry wash with a bullet hole in its head. He had heard the faint report of the gunshot earlier as he and the horses waited out the heat. Now, seated atop the dun above the edge of the dry wash, he looked at the hoofprints leading off up the rocky creek bed. Their tracks had been leading almost straight to the border. Yet now, as before, their direction had to be altered to fit their need.

Someone among them was without a horse, he told himself. It would have to be replaced. Riding double was the last desperate form of travel for a gang of outlaws on the run. He thought of the Mexican relay station, and nudged the dun forward, the team horses sidling around him curiously, as if enjoying their desert adventure here without the restraint of wagon and human cargo strapped to their backs. One of the big horses pranced boldly, high-hoofed, and craned its neck out and nipped the bay on its rump as if to speed it up. Having none of it, the bay kicked its hind feet, barely missing the team horse's muzzle. The team horse tried to bite again.

"Here, that's enough of that," the Ranger reprimanded, jerking the lead rope. "Set an example," he said, eying the bay tied in front of the string. The bay galloped on, giving the big horse behind it little regard as all the horses settled and went back to negotiating the sand stirring beneath their hooves.

"That's more like it," Sam said sidelong to the string. He raised his bandanna up over the bridge of his nose against the fine roiling sand.

It was near midnight when Sam pulled the bandanna down again and stopped the horses atop a rise of moonlit sand. He looked down the dune into a wide basin at a dimmed lantern light glowing on a guide pole. The guide pole stood over twenty feet high out in front of the relay station to signal any Mexican land coaches lost on the endless sea of rock and sand.

Knowing the gunmen had ridden here to replace their dead horse, he first thought he would leave the string of horses here atop the dune. But knowing the reputation of the desert wolves in this area, he wasn't going to risk it. He looked at the string in the shadowy moonlight. They stood tired, sweaty and quiet, done in from the day's heat and the hard ride.

Here we go.

He nudged the dun forward, his Winchester across his lap, and led the string all the way up to an iron hitch rail beside a corral twenty yards from the plank and adobe building. Here he hitched the horse string and his dun as well. The tired horses lowered their heads as if knowing what was expected of them. Sam rubbed the dun's muzzle and looked into the corral where two horses stood staring out at him and his hoofed charges. On the corral rail stood two well-worn saddles with empty rifle boots.

Interesting. . . .

He turned and walked away stealthily in the darkness, to where the glow of a single candle showed dimly through an open window. He heard a drunken voice from inside the open window as he drew nearer. Lowering into a crouch, he continued on until he stood beneath the window ledge, listening.

"I'll tell you where it all went to hell," said the thick drunken voice. "We both shoulda made a stand when Knapp killed poor ol' Seamus Gore. I never saw a man take any guff but what he had to take it from then on—else until he split a skull or two."

"Forget all the skull splitting, Coco. It's too late," said another drunken voice, its owner equally liquored up, "Have you noted that we still ain't been paid one dollar, not even for bringing the horses?"

"*Noted* it?" said the first voice. "I have noted it, Jake. I have not only *noted* it, I've been able to think of little else."

There came a silent pause as Sam pictured a bottle being raised, swigged and lowered. A whiskey hiss followed. "Now it's us getting blamed every time one of these cayuse plugs falters out on us," the first voice concluded.

Sam ran the names they'd used, Jake, Coco and Seamus Gore, through his mind. Coco was not a commonly used name. Coco Bour was all he could come up with. Which made sense, he decided, knowing Coco Bour rode with a mean-tempered brawler gunman named Seamus Gore. *Jake . . . ?* He wasn't sure of him. But he was ready to find out.

He had started to raise himself up to the window ledge when he froze, feeling someone grip his leg. Looking down slowly, he saw the sleeve of a Mexican *federale* uniform. He heard a raspy whisper.

"*Señor, por favor . . . ,*" the voice said, fading away. Sam stooped down and saw a wounded soldier lying between the wall and a large rain barrel. Hearing the soldier try to speak again, he quickly clamped a hand over his mouth, reached in and dragged him fifteen feet away from the building. He leaned the bloody man against a water trough and stooped down again. The man's dark eyes tried to focus on the badge on Sam's chest.

"They took . . . all of our horses," he said in the weak pained voice. "They killed me. . . ."

"Shh, take it easy," Sam said, opening the soldier's tunic and shirt and seeing the bloody belly wound. "You're hit, but you're going to be all right." He took a wide bandanna from around the wounded man's neck, wadded it and placed it against the bullet hole, adjusting the soldier so his hand lay on top of it.

"Be *all right . . . ?*" he said, sounding as if the possibility hadn't occurred to him. He looked down at the bandanna, then back at the Ranger. "Who are you, *señor?*"

"I'm Ranger Sam Burrack," Sam said. "I'm tracking these men. Who all is in there?"

"Two of them," the soldier said, his voice sounding strengthened by hope, no matter how slim. "A hostler, his daughter, *y su nieto.*" He reverted to his native tongue.

"A hostler, his daughter and grandson," Sam translated. "Anybody else?" He glanced back at the window as one drunken voice shouted, and both voices laughed raucously.

The soldier only shook his bowed head. He started coughing deeply. Sam tried to quiet him, but it was too late.

"The hell's that?" a drunken voice said inside. "I hope that greaser you shot and threw out ain't still alive."

"Not a chance," the other voice said. "If the bullet didn't kill him, I threw him far enough to break his neck."

Sam laid the soldier flat out of sight and hurried back to the building. He slid to a halt beneath the open window. He huddled low, hearing boots walk across a wooden floor to the window. He looked up and saw a man lean forward out the window and stare straight down at him.

"Who—!" He tried to speak, but before he could, Sam sprang up, grabbed him by his beard and yanked him down out of the window. The gunman hit the ground hard, his breath blasting from his chest. But there was more coming. As he tried to right himself, catch his breath and push up to his feet, the Ranger's rifle butt swung around hard and knocked his head sidelong. The man's head slung back and forth with the impact as if on oiled hinges. Then he fell flat and didn't move.

"Coco, what're you doing? What's going on out there?" the other voice called out.

Sam heard the sound of a rifle levering. Thinking of the hostler, his daughter and his grandson inside, he hurried away from the knocked-out gunman and quickly circled the building toward the front door. As he jerked the door open, he heard the gunman inside call out through the window.

"Coco? Hey, Coco? Who's out there?" Jake Testa shouted out into the night. "Somebody better tell me something here. I'm going to start shooting!"

Standing in the open doorway, the Ranger saw the gunman leaning out the window the same as his partner had done. Looking around quickly, Sam saw the frightened eyes of a young woman holding a child tight against her. An elderly man reached out and wrapped his arms around both of them and pulled them away to a far corner, seeing what was about to happen.

Sam drew his Colt and cocked it. He held his rifle in his left hand now, taking it out of play here in these close quarters.

The gunman in the window turned around, angry and cursing for not having received a reply from outside.

"Son of a bi—" he said, his words stopping short as he saw the Ranger standing with the big Colt out, cocked and pointed at him.

"Jake," Sam said quietly, hoping not to have a shooting break out around the three innocent people in the dark corner. "I figured that was you."

"Me *what*?" Jake asked, in a drunken belligerent tone. He raised his gun, ready to do battle.

But Sam saw it coming and brought it to a quick ending. His Colt barked three times before Jake could get a shot off. Each bullet pounded Jake in his chest, shoved him backward until the third shot sent him flying out the window. Before he hit the ground his gun blazed a wild shot into the darkness. Sam stood poised and ready, smelling the burnt powder wafting around him in the small room, hearing the echo of the shots fall away off the edge of the earth. A tight silence wrapped around him. Breaking the silence, he turned to the three people huddled in the corner.

"Everybody all right?" he asked quietly.

"*Sí*, we are, with many thanks to you for making it so," said the old hostler.

"Good," said the Ranger. "There's a soldier outside that needs lots of help if he's going to live."

"Jorge is still alive?" The young woman gasped as if in disbelief. She and the young boy hurried out to the yard.

"He was here to see my daughter when these men arrived," said the old hostler.

"Can you get him somewhere for medical treatment?" the Ranger asked. "He needs to ride flat, in a wagon."

"They take all of our wagon horses," the old hostler said. He looked worried for the young soldier.

"I can help you there," Sam said. "I have four wagon horses with me, rested and ready to go."

The old man looked astonished.

"Come, help me," Sam said. "We've got plenty to do before daylight."

In the silver-gray hour before dawn, the Ranger and the old holster, who told the Ranger his name was Metosso, had rolled a spare land coach out of a barn and hitched the four team horses to it. Sam walked into the building and brought Coco Bour out with his hands cuffed in front of him. Bour staggered to the land coach, still not recovered from the hard blow he'd taken from the rifle butt.

"You'll never . . . take me alive," he said, half-drunk, half in a knockout stupor.

"Careful what you say, Coco," Sam said. "I can fix that with one shot." He righted the gunman and nudged him toward the coach as Bour started to wander off course.

"You—you killed my pard, Jake Testa?" Coco asked, thick-mouthed.

"I did," Sam said. *Two more down, six to go,* he reminded himself.

"Well, don't go thinking that bothers me any," said Coco Bour, taking on a tough tone. "Far as I'm concerned, you can kill all of them—two of them are the Cady brothers. No loss to anybody there."

"We'll see how it goes," Sam said. He gestured toward the ground at the edge of the corral rail. "Sit down there while we get this rig ready to roll."

The old hostler busily hitched the four wagon horses to the ornately fringed and decorated Mexican land coach.

"You ain't riding me in that whorehouse *hearse*, are you?" Coco asked, eying the coach critically.

"No," Sam said, "the couch is headed a different direction. You and I are riding to Fort Hamlin."

"Riding on *what*, might I ask?" Coco asked in a drunken huff, the whiskey finally overtaking the blow to his head. He jerked his sore head toward the two horses in the corral. "Those cayuses of mine and Jake are done for. That's why we got left here."

"I've got a good horse for you," the Ranger said, referring to the rested bay.

"You do?" Coco asked, amazed. Upon hearing Sam, the old hostler looked around too, he himself a little surprised at the Ranger's ample resources.

"You *provide transportation* these days?" Coco Bour asked. "Had Jake known that, like as not he might still be alive. We figured we were stuck here. Do you happen to carry a change of socks?"

"Don't push it, Coco," Sam said. "If I didn't have to fool with taking you to Fort Hamlin, I'd be right back on their trail this morning."

Coco's voice turned crafty; he offered a thin smile, even as he held a cuffed hand to his throbbing head.

"Oh . . . ," he said. "Well, what if I told you a few things you *need to know*, and in turn you just slip these ol' cuffs off and send me on my way?"

"Things I need to know, like what?" Sam asked.

"Huh-uh," said Coco, "first tell me if we have a deal."

"Like what, Coco?" the Ranger insisted. "I'm not going to ask you again."

"Okay, then. Like who hired Jake and me to help spring Harper—" Coco said.

"That would be Charlie Knapp," Sam said, almost before the gunman got the words out. "Charlie Knapp is Edsel Centrila's top hired gun, so that means Centrila is behind it."

That stopped Bour. He stalled for a second.

"Oh yeah . . . ? But where is it they're *going*?" he asked, undeterred.

"To Big Silver," Sam replied quickly, without having to give the matter so much as a thought. "My hunch is, the Centrilas both want Sheriff Stone dead."

"They do?" Bour replied, looking genuinely surprised and curious. "Why is that?"

Sam just looked at him.

"Do you have information I can use, or not?" he asked. "I'm not wasting time with you."

"Well, pardon the hell out of me, Ranger," Bour said with contempt. "Here's something I *guaran-damn-tee* you *don't* know! I once threw a man off a bridge in Missouri. Nobody—I mean *nobody*—has ever known that but me! How's that for information?"

"That's good, Coco," Sam said. "It's not something I can use, but I'll pass it along, make sure the judge hears about it. Anything else you want to confess?"

"*Confess!*" said Coco, rising to his feet. "I wasn't confessing nothing! I'm trying to trade information—get you to turn me loose, is all!"

"I'm not turning you loose, Coco," Sam said. "Keep talking, though. Confession's good for the soul. You'll likely hang as it is, for killing Ernest Shule and Curly Ed Townsend."

Bour looked ill and sank back to the ground.

"Try to help a law dog, this is the thanks . . . ," he mumbled to himself, shaking his sore head.

Sam took one of the saddles down from the corral rail for the bay. He turned to the old hostler. Two revolvers stuck up from the old man's waist, one that belonged to Jake Testa, the other, Coco Bour.

"Are you folks going to be all right getting Jorge to the mission?" he asked.

"*Sí*, we will be," said Metosso. He patted one of the revolver butts. "And so will Jorge."

"All right, then," Sam said. "I'll tell them at Fort Hamlin that you'll be bringing their horses when you're done."

The Mexican nodded.

"They know me at Fort Hamlin. Tell them I will be there straightaway, *por favor*."

"I'll tell them," Sam said. He stepped back, the saddle on his shoulder, and said to Coco Bour, "On your feet." He watched Bour struggle to his feet and stand weaving in place. Then he gave him a starting nudge toward the bay and the dun standing hitched inside the corral rails. "Any other confessions you want to make, you can do so while we're riding," he said. "Otherwise keep your mouth shut."

Bour walked on in silence, his cuffed hands dangling at his waist.

Chapter 13

Oscar White stepped off the boardwalk out in front of his barred office when he saw the Ranger ride out of the wavering desert heat onto the street. Townsfolk began to gather. They stood watching as the Ranger and his copper dun followed Coco Bour on the bay. Both horses were sweaty and white-frothed from their trek across the last stretch of sand flats leading to Fort Hamlin.

"I'll be skint, Ranger," White murmured to himself. "You sure draw a crowd."

As the Ranger and his prisoner drew closer, White stepped forward into the street as if to direct both horses to the hitch rail.

"I see you managed to bring one who is sitting straight up," he said. He looked up at Coco Bour and said, "Howdy, Coco. I figured you'd show up here soon enough."

"Howdy, White, you old curd," Bour said sourly. He looked at the barred adobe. "This rat trap won't hold me for long," he added in a tough tone.

"It's not supposed to, Coco," said White. "This is only a temporary jail." He grinned through his beard. "Consider it just a stop on your long road to *rehabilitation*." He took the bay's reins and spun them around the hitch rail. He turned to the Ranger as the dun stepped over to the rail. "What's the news on our jail wagon, Ranger?" he asked.

"Bad news, Oscar," Sam said. "The wagon was ambushed. Shule and Townsend are dead. The prisoners are gone. I tracked them a ways but had to break off and bring Coco in. I know where they're headed, though."

White lowered his head and shook it slowly.

"I figured something bad happened when it started taking so long for you get back here," he said. He jerked a nod toward Bour. "Did this one have anything to do with it?"

"Him and Jake Testa were both in on it," Sam said. "They even brought horses for Harper and some of his jail pals."

White just stared coldly at Bour for a moment. Bour got nervous; he fidgeted in his saddle.

"Step down, Coco," Sam said, his rifle standing on his thigh.

"I never shot those guards, though, and that's the truth," Bour said to White. He swung down from atop the bay.

Oscar glanced around at the gathering townsfolk, then looked back at Bour.

"You can tell me all about it, Coco," he said in a low menacing tone, "tonight, when there's nobody watching." He shoved Bour toward the boardwalk as Sam swung down from his saddle and followed. "You can tell me about the ambush, and I'll tell you how good a pal I was with Shule and Townsend. Fair enough?" He shoved Bour across the boardwalk to the open door of the barred adobe building. Once inside, the Ranger touched the brim of his sombrero to the townsfolk and closed the door behind them.

"I found the horses," Sam said. "I lent them to the old hostler at the Mexican relay station. He got hit by the same bunch. They took his horses. He needed to get a wounded soldier to the mission hospital—said he'd bring them back soon as he can."

"That's Metosso," said White. "He's good as gold." He locked the cell and took the handcuffs from Bour's wrists as Bour held his hands up to the bars. He gave the Ranger his handcuffs, walked behind a battered oak desk and pulled out a two-handed blackthorn cudgel. He hefted the fierce-looking club and tapped it on his open palm as he stared at Bour through the cell bars.

"I'll be riding on, White," Sam said, "soon as I get my horses watered and grained."

"I'll help you with your horses, Ranger," White said. He laid the gruesome club down in full sight atop his desk and turned to the Ranger. Bour stood watching from his cell with a sick expression as the two turned and walked out onto the boardwalk. Watching the townsfolk start to disperse, the Ranger gave a faint wry smile.

"Have you ever hit anybody with that mauler?" Sam asked, nodding toward the door behind them.

"I've never had to," White said. "I'm going to leave it lying there and pick it up every now and then, let Coco see it and think about it. I owe Ernest and Curly Ed that much."

The two stepped off the boardwalk and unhitched the horses. As they led the tired animals to the livery barn a block away, Sam said quietly, "I'll get the ones who killed them, Oscar."

"I already figured you would, Ranger," White replied as they walked on.

Charlie Knapp and Harper Centrila rode a few feet ahead of the Cady brothers, Lon Bartow and Three-toed Delbert Swank. They had ridden sand flats, hill lines and rocky valleys for three days, carefully back-tracking time and again to throw off any pursuers now that they were headed up into a remote hideout that Knapp and Edsel Centrila had scouted out weeks earlier.

"The Mexs call this place Cambio," he said. "It means Turnaround in Spanish—I expect that's a warning."

Harper Centrila nodded, looking all around at the wild desolate terrain. Above the stone walls reaching skyward around them, an eagle glided in a wide circle, adrift on an updraft of air.

"You and the old man done good finding this place, Charlie," he commented.

Knapp nodded too and looked up and around with him.

"I almost wish somebody would try to take us on up

here," he said. "It's not often you find a place this good. The trail narrows through a pass up ahead between two stone bluffs. Your pa will have a couple of riflemen lying up there watching us. They've likely already spotted us climbing these switchbacks by now."

"I take it we're less than a day's ride from here to Big Silver," Harper said.

"That's right," said Knapp. "Your pa wants to be close to his new business."

"My pa wants to be close to Sheriff Stone, so we can gig him some before we kill him," Harper said bluntly. He nudged his horse's pace up a little and rode ahead. Knapp put his horse forward too and caught up. Behind them, the other men followed suit.

Two miles farther along the rock trail, they rounded a turn and saw the steep stone bluffs standing before them like giant centurions. No sooner had they slowed to a halt beneath the stone monoliths than a flash of sunlight beamed down from the highest edge and moved back and forth on Knapp's and Harper's faces.

"And there the riflemen are," said Knapp, "just like I said they'd be." He raised his hat and waved it up at the top edge on the bluffs. "See what I mean about this place?" He lowered his hat and nudged his horse forward. Harper stayed right beside him.

"Who you figure the riflemen are?" he asked Knapp, nodding up at the top of the bluffs.

"Most likely, Bob Remick and his cousin, Trent. Your pa's brought in some new guns. Fact is I believe he's ready for all-out war if the law tries to get you back and take you to prison."

"So am I," Harper said loudly enough for the others to hear him. He looked around at them as if to make sure. "What about you, Lon? Swank? You two want to go back to cuffs and chains?"

"Not me," Lon Bartow said.

"Me neither," said Three-toed Delbert Swank. "Only way I'll go back is in a box or on a board."

The Cady brothers looked at each other.

"That's Lyle and me too," Ignacio said. "Nobody's taking us alive."

"Taking you *alive*, ha." Swank sneered.

"What's that supposed to mean?" Lyle asked in a prickly tone.

"It means whatever you want it to mean," Swank said. He spat at the ground and gave them both a cold stare. The other men only glanced at the brothers with contempt, then looked away. Harper shook his head.

"What did the old man mean, hiring those two idiots?" he asked Knapp.

"Your pa never explains his hiring practices to me," Knapp said as they rode on.

Ten minutes later they turned their horses off the trail and led them down through a stand of pine and into a clearing behind a jagged wall of huge broken boulders. There they found a weathered cabin constructed of split pine timber taken from the hillside. On a wide front porch Edsel Centrila sat on a blanket-covered swing hanging by chains from the ceiling. He stood up when the six horsemen rode into the rocky dirt yard.

"Finally here comes some good news, Silas," he said

sidelong to Rudabaugh, who had ridden in from Big Silver earlier in the day. He gave a guarded smile and puffed on his cigar. His gentleman business suit and derby hat had been replaced by a black stockman's-style Stetson and clothes more suitable to the rugged terrain.

"Yes, sir, this is good news," Rudabaugh replied, smoking the cigar Centrila had given him. His rifle hung from his left hand. He picked up a bottle of bourbon from a small table and stepped forward with Centrila as the riders lined their horses along a hitch rail.

"Harper, my boy!" Edsel Centrila said jubilantly, stepping down to the rail. "I was starting to wonder if we'd ever get you out of that squirrel trap."

Harper swung down from his saddle and stretched his back and looked all around.

"Howdy, Papa Edsel," he said with an air of disinterest. "Who does a man have to shoot to get some whiskey here?"

"Here you are, Harper," said Rudabaugh, stepping in, holding the bottle out to him.

Harper looked Rudabaugh up and down.

"Silas Rudabaugh," he said, pulling the cork from the bottle and swishing the bourbon a little. "What brought you crawling out from under your rock?" He gave a tight half grin, half snarl. "Must be a full moon coming tonight."

Rudabaugh watched Harper take a long, deep, gurgling drink of bourbon.

"Your pa sent for me and Boyle—said he needed some killing done," he said. He reached for the bottle after Harper lowered it from his lips. But Harper passed it on to Swank.

"Clayton Boyle's around here too?" Harper said, looking around for the gunman. "Anybody owns sheep best lock them up for the night."

"Clayton's in Big Silver," Rudabaugh said. "I rode out to see your pa on business."

Harper only nodded; he wiped the back of his hand across his parched lips.

Edsel watched as his bottle of expensive Kentucky bourbon made its rounds among the men. When it made it from hand to hand, he reached out and took it just as Lyle Cady held his hand out to take it from Lon Bartow.

"You Cady brothers take these horses, get them watered and grained," Harper ordered. "Rub them down too."

Ignacio and Lyle looked at each other, but made no protest. They gathered the tired, sweaty horses and led them away toward a rickety barn.

Harper grinned.

"All right, pards, listen to this," he said to Swank and Bartow. "While they kept a boot on my neck awaiting trial, I found out Papa Edsel here went and bought himself a nice fat saloon, complete with whores and everything!" He widened his eyes in excitement and rubbed his palms together. "That's enough to make a good son break out of jail."

"Don't let it get your head spinning, Harper," Edsel Centrila cautioned. "I'm going to own the Palace long enough to put that tin-badge sheriff in the ground." He puffed on his cigar with a look of pride. "How many men ever go that far to settle a payback?"

The men laughed and gave him a cheer. Centrila looked at Rudabaugh and said, "That ought to make any man think twice before promising me he'll do something, then *not doing it*."

Rudabaugh's face reddened a little; he looked away.

"The Ranger's dead first time he sticks his head up. You've still got my word on it," he said.

The men fell silent as Harper cocked his head at Rudabaugh with a puzzled expression.

"What's this about, Papa Edsel?" he asked his father. "Did Silas here take on more than he can handle? Is that the *business* he's come here to tell you about?" He kept his eyes on Rudabaugh as Edsel handed him the bottle and he took another deep swig of bourbon. His eyes had already taken on a sharp bourbon edge from his first long, deep drink. This time he held on to the bottle instead of passing it on.

"I made a *small mistake*," Rudabaugh said. "I sent two men out to ambush the Ranger and they never came back. I figure the Ranger got the drop on them, killed them both."

"A *small mistake*?" said Harper, as if not hearing the rest of it. His face appeared to tighten as he spoke. "Huh-uh. Papa Edsel here allows no *mistakes*. I found that out for myself growing up." He looked at his father. "Tell him what happens to people who make *mistakes*, small or otherwise, Papa Edsel."

"Take it easy, Harper," Centrila said in a warning tone of voice. "You and your pards get washed up. I'll have the Cady brothers cook us some grub." He reached to take the bottle from Harper's hand, but Harper jerked it out of reach.

"In a minute," Harper said. "First I want to hear what you've got to say about ol' Silas here making a *small mistake.*"

"Your pa and I straightened it out, Harper," Rudabaugh put in before Centrila could answer. "That's all you need to know about it." His words had iron in them. So did his hands. He gripped his rifle, letting Harper see him do it.

Harper started to take a step forward, but Edsel moved quick and stepped between the two.

"He's right, Harper," said Edsel. "We straightened it out. As soon as the time is right, we're taking another crack at it. The Ranger is going down, along with Sheppard Stone."

"Straightened out, huh?" Harper stared at his father, his contempt only slightly hidden. "I'm hearing a lot of talk here," he said. "But it's going to take more than *talk* to kill them lawmen, Stone or Burrack, either one." He took a step backward and raised another drink of bourbon. "Don't worry, Papa Edsel, *old man,*" he said to his father. "I'll kill the lawmen. I'll kill them both, and I won't have to buy a saloon to get it done." He glared at Edsel and said to Lon Bartow and Three-toed Delbert Swank, "Come on, jail pards. Let's go finish this bottle and get washed up for dinner."

Edsel, Rudabaugh and Charlie Knapp watched the three younger gunmen walk away.

"He's going to be all right," Edsel said, puffing on

his cigar, putting on a confident face. "He's been in jail cells of one kind or another going on three months now, waiting to go to Yuma. It'll take him a day or two, but he'll get back to his old self."

His old self. . . .

Knapp and Rudabaugh looked at each other. Neither of them had ever seen Harper Centrila act much better than he had done just now. But they knew better than to say anything.

"We know that, boss," said Knapp. "Everybody's a little high-strung right now—we'll all feel a lot better when we get these law dogs in our gun sights."

Part 3

Part 3

Chapter 14

———

Three days later: Big Silver, Arizona Badlands

Sheriff Sheppard Stone had awakened in the night with a sense of terrible dread. He'd been sweaty and shaky and could feel his heart pounding hard in his chest. He'd boiled a pot of strong coffee and drunk it mug upon mug, smoking with it the six cigarettes he'd rolled and laid atop his desk. Something bad was coming—coming soon, he'd told himself. Today even. He'd dressed and pulled on his duster and picked up his rifle, wondering how much of this was real, and how much was whiskey craziness.

Either way . . .

Rifle in hand, he'd walked the dark, silent streets until the sun streaked and glittered along the eastern edge of the planet. As the town awakened behind him, he walked the outer perimeters. He had no idea how far he'd walked. He'd walked and smoked and fed himself cough drops one after another until his shirt pocket was nearly emptied of them. Still the foreboding, the dark premonition, whatever it was. He sighed a long breath.

He stood at the edge of town as daylight broke and watched five horsemen riding in across the sand flats. He watched them as the sun rose stronger, and as the morning heat closed over the desert and left the riders obscured in a wavering veil. He still kept a wary eye out toward the riders as he walked back along the busy street.

Suddenly he stopped and a strange realization struck him. Even though the riders were still only distant images in a swirl of sunlight and sand—too far away to recognize—he knew beyond any doubt or any shred of rationale that when they arrived one of them would be Harper Centrila.

Harper Centrila? Whoa, Sheriff, he cautioned, reminding himself that by now Harper Centrila was looking out from behind bars at Yuma Penitentiary.

Take it easy.

He tried to tell himself this was just the whiskey still playing with his nerves, as it had been throughout the night. But he couldn't shake the belief that the younger gunman was out there on the flats, riding into town this very moment. Here it was again, he told himself, that strange feeling that everything happening had happened before. He rubbed his eyes as if to do so might erase the image from his mind. Yet he saw Harper out there, right down to the dusty blue bib-front shirt he wore—*would be wearing,* he corrected himself. He saw him plain as day.

He walked on, feeling the skin on the back of his

neck crawl. This was not some trick of the mind as the doctor suggested. This was real; this was happening.

He moved the cough drop to the side of his mouth as he walked and tapped his fingers to his gun butt, trying to shake the weirdness that had crept in around him. *All right . . .* , he told himself with resolve. He'd been expecting trouble. Here it came. He'd deal with it.

But first things first.

He walked past the Silver Palace, keeping on the opposite side of the busy street. A block farther, he looked all around to make sure he wasn't being watched. Then he crossed the street, maneuvered around passing freight wagons and buggies and slipped into an alley that ran back behind the Silver Palace. He climbed a long set of wooden stairs and unlocked the rear door with a key no one knew he had, and slipped inside unseen. He walked down an empty hallway and stopped and knocked softly on a large oak door. From downstairs he heard a bartender gathering empty glasses, straightening empty chairs.

Stone removed his hat and parked the cough drop in his jaw as the door opened. He looked at the woman's face in the shadowy morning light.

"Mae Rose," he said in a lowered, almost troubled-sounding voice, "are you alone?"

The door opened some more as the young woman stepped back. She wore soft house slippers, a robe with its sash tied loosely at her narrow waist.

"Yes, Shep, I'm alone," she replied stiffly. She glanced along the hallway, motioned him inside and closed the door behind him. She leaned against the door and studied his face questioningly, then lowered her eyes. "I must look a mess."

"Look at me, Mae Rose," Stone said. He stepped forward and tipped her chin up and gazed into her eyes. "If you were any prettier, I don't think I could stand it."

"Go on with you, Sheriff," she said, giving him a bashful toss-away look. "Besides, you've got some nerve showing up here. I don't see you for a month . . . then I hear that you got drunk, shot up the town, thought you turned into a wolf or some such nonsense?"

"That's right, I thought I was a wolf, Mae Rose," Stone said. "I got drunk and shot up the town. I lost my mind. There, that's my confession, satisfied?" he said. He studied the younger woman's face in the dim morning light, a silver pin holding back long ringlets of her red hair, a trace of freckles sprinkled across her nose.

"It's a start," she said. She let out a breath in exasperation and stepped forward against him. Her arms went around him. "Come here, Sheriff, let me take hold of you." Her voice changed that quick, from surly, inconsolable, to soothing, inviting.

Always at her work. . . .

Stone smiled tightly, returned her embrace, but he spoke down to her as she rested her face against his chest.

"I'm not here for that, Mae Rose," he said softly.

"Oh?" She looked up at him, released him a little. "What about me?" she said coyly. "What if it's something that *I* want, Mr. *Law Hawk*?"

"I'm not here to play around, Mae Rose," he said, knowing the game. He lifted her arms from around him gently and took a step back. He reached inside his duster and took out a leather drawstring pouch. "I've come to bring you this." He jiggled the pouch and saw her eyes brighten at the muffled sound of gold coins.

"Oh my, Sheriff," she said, "I see you still know how to tickle a gal's fun spot." She smiled playfully. But she saw the sheriff's serious expression and settled. "What *is it* you want me to do, for *all that gold*?" she said suggestively. She reached out and stroked the leather pouch as he held it chest high.

"I want you to take it and get headed back to Denver City tonight," Stone said. He held the pouch up.

"Tonight?" said Mae Rose. "Why tonight?"

"Why *not* tonight?" Stone said, jiggling the bulging pouch of gold coins. "Take a horse, go after dark so nobody sees you leave. Ride to Secondary and take the stage north from there. The trail to Secondary is always safe of a night—but watch yourself just the same," he instructed. "There's enough gold here to last you awhile, get you settled in." Seeing the questioning look on her face, he added, "You're always saying you want to go back there. Now that this place has changed hands, I figured I'd stake your trip." He released the pouch to her. "You won't like working for Edsel Centrila. He's a snake."

"Oh?" said Mae Rose, chiding him a little. "*Imagine*, a snake in the saloon and brothel business. What's this world come to?"

Stone's face reddened a little; he smiled thinly.

"Take this serious, Mae Rose," he warned. "Centrila has some dangerous men working for him."

"Okay, I'm serious, Sheriff," she said. She spread the drawstring open and looked down at the glint of gold in the dim light. She looked back up at Stone.

"My goodness, Shep," she said ponderously. She hefted the pouch on both palms. Then she said, "I get set up there, and you'll come join me later—like we've talked about?"

Stone stalled for a second. That thought hadn't occurred to him until she mentioned it.

"Yes," he said finally, "that's my plan. I'll be coming later on."

She looked suspicious.

"You're not a good liar, Sheriff," she said. "You're not planning on coming to Denver City." She jiggled the gold coins in the pouch. "What's this about?"

Stone shook his head.

"I've never seen a woman in your profession have such a hard time taking gold from a man," he said, sounding a little put out by her questions.

"Well, you've seen it now," Mae Rose said in a firm tone. "So tell me," she insisted.

Stone cursed to himself under his breath. His fingers trembled as he took the last cough drop from the small wax paper bag in his shirt pocket. He stuck the cough drop into his mouth and wadded the bag in his hand. He looked around for a place to put the empty bag. Mae Rose reached out and took the wadded bag from him.

"All right," he said, "here it is. You know about the bad blood between Edsel Centrila—your *new boss*—and me?"

Mae Rose shrugged, her hand on her hip, the pouch of gold in her other hand.

"I have heard some things, not enough to hang a hat on," she said. "I heard he gave you some money to do a favor for him . . . but you didn't do it?" She eyed the pouch of gold coins.

"He tried to get me to bribe a judge to get his son, Harper, out of going to Yuma Penitentiary," Stone said. "He's likely going to face charges for it."

"Yes, that is what I heard," she now admitted. "But what's any of this got to do with me?"

"I don't want him getting his hands on anything or anybody that he knows will hurt me," said Stone.

"Oh, that's so sweet," Mae Rose said, half-playful, half-moved by Stone's words. "I mean, you caring what happens to me," she added.

Stone looked a little embarrassed.

"Well, I do," he said a little gruffly. "What of it?"

Mae Rose slipped the pouch of gold coins into her robe pocket and kept her hand around it.

"Nothing *of it*," she said. "I just think it's sweet of you, is all."

Stone just looked at her. Again he saw her demeanor change in the blink of an eye. She went from soft and sentimental, to a little edgy, matter-of-fact.

"Nobody knows about you and me, Sheriff," she said. "Leastwise I've never told anybody. What about you?"

"Nobody," Stone said. "It was nobody's business, I always figured."

"Then you have nothing to worry about, do you?" Mae Rose said, her hand still clutched around the pouch as if he might change his mind and demand that she give it back. But Stone had no such intention.

"It wasn't me I was worrying about, Mae Rose," he said, gravity in his voice.

Mae Rose took a deep breath and let it out slowly.

"I know, Sheriff," she said, "and I'm obliged." She stood running things through her mind.

"Then you'll go to Denver City, like I'm asking you to?" Stone said.

She waited another second before answering. Then she raised her hand from her robe pocket and nodded.

"Yes, I'll go," she said. "Truth is, I'm through with Big Silver. Now that you've given me a way out, I might go there and quit this business altogether."

Stone smiled and started to raise his hat and set it atop his head.

"Can you stay awhile, just talk some, Sheriff?" she asked. "I'll get us some coffee and get right back up." She smiled. "You look like a man who could use some *talk*."

Stone let his hat and his hand drop back to his side.

"I expect I *could* use some talk, Mae Rose," he said, "some coffee too, I'd be obliged." He already knew he wasn't about to tell her about anything going on inside his head. She didn't need to hear any of that, and he didn't need to reveal it. He let out a breath and relaxed. This was good, he told himself—a time-out.

*   *   *

When Stone left through the rear door a half hour later, he walked a block down the alley behind the Silver Palace. He made his way back to the street and crossed it amid the morning wagon and horseback traffic. He continued on to another alleyway, one running beside the undertaker's where a dusty black hearse sat, its brass trimmings gleaming sharply in the midmorning sunlight. Along the alleyway pine coffins stood leaning against the wall of the adobe mortuary building.

Inside the building, the strong smell of chemicals permeated the stall warm air as he walked past the viewing room on his left to an open office door near the rear of the building. Seeing the sheriff at his office door, the town undertaker and tonsorial parlor owner, Braden Goss, stood up and tugged at his black linen vest.

"Morning, Sheriff, do come in," Goss said. Sunlight through a window strategically formed a halo around his shiny bald head.

"Morning, Goss," Stone said quietly. "Don't get up on my account." He raised five gold coins from inside his duster lapel and stood the glistening coins in a short stack atop Goss's desk.

"Oh, I see," Goss said, never quite comfortable around men who carried guns, be they outlaw or lawman.

"That should square us . . . and something extra for yourself," the sheriff said, nodding down at the gold coins.

"Indeed, then," said Goss. He gave a thin, mirthless undertaker's smile. "It's not necessary to offer something extra," he said. "Yet always appreciated," he added quickly as his hand shot out, snagged the stack of coins and made them disappear into his clothing like some practicing magician.

Stone waved a hand slightly at the spot the coins had occupied on the desk.

"I believe that straightens me out?" he said.

"Straightens you out . . . ?" It took the undertaker a second to comprehend, given the sheriff's choice of words on the matter. But he managed to catch up.

"Oh, of course, straighten out your *arrangement account*," he said. "Why, yes, it certainly does." He looked Stone up and down with concern. "I do hope everything is all right with you?"

Stone eyed him.

"Couldn't be better," he said, a little wryly. He realized that like Mae Rose, everybody in Big Silver knew there was trouble of some sort brewing between him and the new owner of the Silver Palace.

"Good, good!" said Goss. He cleared his throat and added, "If I appear a bit *caught off*, Sheriff, I beg your pardon. It's unusual for someone to pay for my services in advance, the way you've been doing."

"I understand," Stone said. "I don't like leaving things loose-ended."

"Yes, I see," said Goss. "I'll prepare a receipt for the entire amount, paid in full. Always pays to keep a receipt, doesn't it?" He sat down, opened a drawer. "In case some question should arise regarding the transaction . . ." His words trailed away as he saw how Stone stared at him.

"Why," Stone said, "won't you remember it?"

Goss closed the drawer, stood up.

"Certainly. Yes, I will *indeed* remember it," he said. Again he tugged at the corners of his vest. "Let me commend you on your prudent nature, Sheriff Stone. Some never give thought to their burial preparations." He paused and added, "Now, what would you like submitted onto your grave marker?"

"Just my name," Stone said, "and the day I went under." He touched his fingers to his hat brim. "Done, then?" he said.

"Yes, I will see to it, should the time ever come, God forbid of course," Goss said.

"Of course," Stone said. He turned and walked out the door, past the standing pine coffins, back onto the street.

Walking back along the busy street across from the Silver Palace, he stopped and stood staring ahead at five dusty sweat-streaked horses standing at the hitch rail out in front of the busy saloon. There it was, he reminded himself, just as he'd seen it earlier. There stood the big bay he'd seen Harper Centrila riding hard across the sand flats.

Explain that, Doctor.

He felt a ring of cold ring of sweat around his hatband. But he knew it wasn't from fear; it was the eeriness surrounding him, clutching him like some cold, bony fist. He stepped back, off the boardwalk into an alleyway, and stood there breathing slowly and evenly until his hands felt calmer, steadier. All right, he reassured himself, it was the whiskey after all. He felt better now, much better—so get on with it.

He raised his Colt from its holster, checked it and slid it into its smooth leather bed. He checked his rifle and left his four fingers inside its lever, his thumb across the hammer, ready to cock it.

Here goes. . . .

Chapter 15

———

Inside the Silver Palace Saloon, the drinkers along the polished wooden bar stood elbow to elbow, in spite of the early hour. Behind the bar, two bartenders busily filled glasses with whiskey, mugs with beer. They pulled up black cigars from a tin and laid them in front of drinkers who'd asked for them. They poured steaming coffee for men who preferred it this time of day. Boiled eggs and pickles dripped from large jars and were laid out on saucers. Men gathered and discussed what changes might be expected now that the place had changed hands.

A piano player had seated himself and already played through one number, and made a few springy passes at "Oh! Susanna," when he noted the talking and clatter behind him had stopped. He stopped along with it and looked around at Sheriff Stone standing inside the open front doors.

"Top of the morning, Sheriff," one of the bartenders called out to Stone. "What might I serve you?" Even as he spoke he noted the sheriff's red, hollow eyes, a tightness to his troubled pale face. A man who needed a drink if ever he'd seen one.

"Coffee," Stone said flatly.

The drinkers melted away, leaving a wide, empty space for him as he walked over and laid his rifle atop the bar. All the while he kept a cold stare on four men seated at a table by a side window. The bartender also stared at the four, as if needing someone's permission in order to serve the red-eyed, haggard-looking lawman.

"Coffee for the sheriff, Phil," said Rudabaugh, who sat at the table with a full view of Stone and the bar. He looked Stone up and down with scrutinizing eyes and gave a chuff. "Better make it good and strong, from the looks of him."

A few customers gave short nervous laughs. Stone quieted them with a sidelong glance. The bartender stepped away, filled a mug with steaming coffee and set it on the bar.

"I came here for Harper Centrila," Stone said.

"Harper Centrila?" said Rudabaugh. He and the other men looked at each other. Rudabaugh gave a thin, faint smile. "Maybe your memory ain't what it should be of late, Stone," he said, "but Harper Centrila is on his way to Yuma, last I heard." He looked around at the others and asked, "Anybody heard anything different?"

"Naw, that's what we all heard," said Boyle, staring hard at Stone.

"Anyway, as you can see, he ain't here," said Rudabaugh. He swung his arm around the saloon as if to make his point. Customers watched in tense silence. "If he is, we can't see him." He leaned slightly and looked under the table. "Harper, are you under there? Come on out. You're upsetting the sheriff."

A nervous ripple of laughter moved across the room, then fell away. Rudabaugh smiled.

"There, you see? No Harper Centrila here," he said with a shrug.

Stone stared, unamused, his rifle lying atop the bar, next to the steaming coffee.

"That's his bay at the rail," Stone said. "I saw him riding in off the flats. Him and four others. I'm guessing two of them were you and Three-toed Delbert there."

Swank looked surprised that the sheriff even knew his name. He straightened in his chair a little, his hand poised at his side near a holstered Remington.

"Sheriff, Sheriff . . . ," Rudabaugh said quietly, shaking his head a little. "You're making the customers nervous, talking this way, seeing things. Maybe you need something stout poured in your coffee. Give it some *bristle and bite*?"

"I saw him. He's here!" Stone demanded. He heard the desperation in his own voice, felt himself starting to boil inside. He didn't like it. This wasn't his way of coming into a gunfight. The men were goading him, taunting him. This was no way to handle himself. He knew how crazy this was starting to look to the customers— the ones who would be witnesses after he blew up and shot it out with these gunmen. *Easy, Sheriff,* he cautioned himself. He could smell the pungent aroma of whiskey, the odor of countless spills of beer soaked into the wooden catwalk behind the bar. *Damn it!* It smelled good to him.

On one side of Rudabaugh sat Donald Ferry. On his other side sat Boyle. Next to him, Garby Dolan, who'd found the bodies of the two riflemen, Marlin Oakley and Monk Barber, whom Rudabaugh had sent to ambush the Ranger. Next to Dolan sat Three-toed Delbert Swank. Stone noted that Rudabaugh and Swank carried a patina of fresh trail dust on their shoulders, their hats, boots. The other three did not.

Rudabaugh watched Stone look confused, as if he suddenly wasn't aware of what he was doing here. He smiled and raised a cigar to his lips, letting the sheriff see him move his hand away from his gun butt. This was what Edsel Centrila wanted, he thought. Centrila wanted him to pick at the old lawman like a kid picking at a sick rattlesnake. He could do that, no problem.

Look at him, Rudabaugh thought. This man was not a threat. Rudabaugh and his men could pick at this old whiskey sop. They could taunt him, jeer at him. When the right moment came, they would drop him dead in his tracks and walk away.

"Sheriff, you all right over there?" he said, with a dark chuckle in his voice. "Looks like you mighta lost your berries."

"Naw," said Boyle, grinning, "he looks like he needs a drink."

Stone wiped the back of his hand across his mouth, not even trying to keep his hand from shaking. At the far end of the bar, a townsman named Bernard Aires had seen enough. He looked ashamed for the washed-out sheriff. He ventured a step closer, wanting to put an end to Stone's humiliation. But Rudabaugh wasn't through, not by a long shot.

"Do you, Stone?" said Rudabaugh. "Want a drink, that is."

Stone didn't answer; he didn't have to. The look on his face said it all. He lowered his eyes, his shoulders slumped as if in defeat.

"Top the sheriff's coffee off for him, Phil," Rudabaugh said to the bartender. "We can't watch a man go dry on us." He smiled and puffed on the cigar.

"Here you are, Sheriff," the bartender said, reaching out with a bottle of rye and pouring a stiff shot into the steaming coffee.

But as soon as he'd poured, Stone's hand clamped down on the rifle stock and swung it hard across the bar top, sending the coffee mug crashing against the wall, barely missing the bartender.

The crowd reared back, a tenseness tightening in the already silent saloon. Rudabaugh and the other men sat poised, their hands ready to grab their guns. But Rudabaugh stopped them with a raised hand, seeing the sheriff's rifle wasn't cocked.

"Easy, men," he said in a lowered tone.

"Damn right, I want a drink," said Sheriff Stone, the rifle still in hand, coffee and whiskey dripping down the wall behind the bar. "But I don't drink weakened whiskey." Without looking at the bartender he banged the rifle barrel on the bar and said, "Give me a bottle, Phil. Hurry it up."

The bartender looked again at Rudabaugh for permission. Down the empty bar, Bernard Aires ventured a step closer; he couldn't watch this. But a hard stare from the table stopped him in his tracks.

"Yeah, sure, why not?" Rudabaugh said to the bartender in a grand sweeping gesture, having fun with Stone's weakness. "Give the sheriff a bottle—it's on the house."

The bartender stood the open bottle in his hand on the bar top and reached around for a full one. When he did, Stone laid his rifle down and corked the open bottle and stuck it down into his deep duster pocket. He stared at Rudabaugh. The bartender, unopened bottle in hand, also looked at Rudabaugh for instruction.

"Make it two bottles, Phil," he said with the same dark chuckle.

The bartender shrugged and stood the fresh bottle on the bar.

"Make it *three*," Stone said in a firm tone.

Rudabaugh gave him a curious look. Then he said to the bartender, "Make it three, Phil. I've got a feeling the sheriff's in for a long night."

Stone shoved the second bottle into his other deep pocket. When the bartender handed him a third, he stuck it up under his arm and started to turn to the front door. Bernard eased toward him again.

"Sheriff," Rudabaugh called out in a loud startling voice. Aires froze; so did Stone. He turned slowly and looked at Rudabaugh.

Rudabaugh grinned, his voice softening.

"Don't forget your rifle," he said cordially.

Amid a burst of long held laughter, Stone lowered his head, turned back and picked up his rifle from the bar top and again headed toward the door.

Aires caught up to him and grabbed his arm.

"Sheriff Stone, don't do this, please," he said, speaking quickly. "You're a better man than this—"

"Get off me," Stone growled. He rounded his arm away from the townsman. "I know what I'm doing!"

Aires stepped back, fearful of what the sheriff might do to him in this state of mind.

At the bar, customers moved back into position as Stone walked out the doors; the piano started again. At the table, the men looked at Rudabaugh.

"There's how you nut a lawman without having to use a knife," he said with a dark chuckle in his voice.

"Damn drunk," Boyle said. He tossed back a drink as he watched Stone cross the street.

"Want us to slip around back, kill him when he walks into his office?" Garby Dolan asked.

"Shame on you, Dolan," Rudabaugh said with a short laugh. "Let the man enjoy his day. I figure by afternoon he'll be facedown on his desk." He looked Dolan up and down. "Didn't I hear you're some kind of expert when it comes to slitting a man's throat?"

"If you did, you heard right," Dolan said proudly.

"Then there we are," Rudabaugh said. "When he's gone under, you and Boyle and Swank here, go take care of it. Nobody has to hear a sound. Edsel will like that." He tossed back his drink and let out a whiskey hiss. The others nodded and followed suit.

*   *   *

At noon, sitting leaned back in chairs on the boardwalk of the Silver Palace, Garby Dolan stropped the blade of his big boot knife on a wide patch of leather lying spread on his knee. Leaning on the front wall beside him, Clayton Boyle straightened as he watched the boy from the restaurant carry a tray of food to the sheriff's office and stand outside the door.

"What have we got here?" Boyle said, craning his neck.

"I don't know," said Dolan, "but it reminds me my belly could use a good filling." He stopped stropping the knife blade, sipped from a mug of beer and set it back down beside him. "Waiting to kill a man always makes me hungry."

"There he goes," said Swank, standing next to Boyle. The boy walked through the opened door and came out a moment later, his hand wrapped in a fist around a small coin. The three men watched the boy hurry back across the dirt street. "Hell," Swank added, "if Stone's eating a good meal, he could last all day."

"So?" said Dolan. "We're not doing much anyway. Have a mug, relax yourself."

"Uh-oh," said Boyle, straightening again as the tray, plate and food came sailing out the sheriff's open office door and landed clattering at the edge of the street. An empty whiskey bottle sailed out behind it. "One down, two to go," he added, eying the empty bottle as it stopped rolling.

"Looks like Stone has plumb lost his appetite!" Swank laughed and looked at the other two for further comment.

"Good rye will do that to you," Dolan said with a nod. "Hope he don't go turning *wolf* on us, like I hear he's prone to do."

"Maybe this won't take so long after all." Boyle grinned and licked his dry lips. "I think I will have that beer, Delbert. Bring me one," he said over his shoulder as Swank walked inside. "Tell Rudabaugh that our *good Sheriff* Stone is well on his way to goosing butterflies."

Swank walked inside, up to the bar, where he pushed his way in through the drinkers and ordered two mugs of beer. When he got them, he walked to a table by the window where Rudabaugh sat dealing himself a hand of solitaire. Rudabaugh took the cigar from between his teeth and without looking up said, "How's our drunken lawman doing?"

"He's doing fine, Silas," Swank replied. He stood holding both mugs of beer in one hand. Thick froth oozed down the mugs and dripped onto the toes on his boots. "Boyle said to tell you he's on his way to *goosing butterflies*—whatever that means."

Rudabaugh started to try to explain, but he caught himself and let out a breath.

"Never mind," he said. He turned over a card and laid it in place, almost ignoring Swank.

"We had one rye empty bottle fly out the door," Swank said with a flat grin. "It looks like he'll be ready for the taking any time now."

"Good," said Rudabaugh, "keep me advised." He turned over another card as Swank moved away toward the door.

*   *   *

An hour and a half later, a dark-haired English dove who went by the name Rita Spool handed Rudabaugh his hat at the top of the long stairs reaching up to the second floor.

"Why, thank you, darling Rita," Rudabaugh said politely, taking the hat. "Even though everything here is free for me, being the manager and all, I want you to know that I'm going to tell Edsel Centrila what a wonderful gal you are." He grinned and bit down on his fresh cigar. The dove only gave a half curtsy and walked away down the long hallway.

Down in the saloon Rudabaugh's table by the window sat empty with a deck of cards half-scattered across it. The saloon was still busy, but less than it had been earlier in the day. Afternoon sunlight streaked in long from the west in the waning heat of evening. Rudabaugh met Delbert Swank as Swank turned away from the empty table and saw him coming down the stairs.

"Yeah, what is it, Delbert?" Rudabaugh said, tired of waiting for Stone to get drunk enough to kill quietly.

"Boyle says to tell you another empty bottle just flew out the door," Swank said. His words ended as he fought back a beer belch.

"Jesus, it's about time," said Rudabaugh. "I was about ready to say just charge the place—shoot him full of holes in broad daylight."

"Sounds good to me," Swank said with a slight beer slur in his voice. He started to turn toward the door. Rudabaugh grabbed his arm, stopping him.

"Whoa, hold on," said Rudabaugh. "I said I was *about to say it*, but I *didn't* say it, did I?"

Swank gave a bleary-eyed grin.

"No, you did not," he said.

"Tell Boyle I said stay with it a little while longer," said Rudabaugh. "I think Edsel will get a kick out of us killing Stone this way."

Swank gazed over at the stairs and up to the second-floor landing.

"Is Harper still up there cooling his jangles?" he asked with a half chuckle.

"No, him and Ferry and Bartow rode off a while ago," said Rudabaugh. He reflected for a second and said, "I still don't understand how Stone could have recognized him riding in that time of morning."

Swank gave his beer-smeared grin.

"Good thing you convinced Stone that he *didn't* see him," he said.

"Yeah, I did good," Rudabaugh said, blowing out stream of cigar smoke. Then he straightened and said in a no-nonsense tone, "You men aren't getting drunk, are you?"

"On *beer*?" said Swank. "Phew, whoever heard of that?"

"Good," said Rudabaugh. "Get back out there, keep me informed. Soon as it's good and dark, we're done with Stone for once and for all."

Chapter 16

The evening had darkened to a shadowy purple; the street had emptied of the day's traffic and trade. Lantern light spilled out the open front doors of the Silver Palace where Dolan and Boyle sat watching Delbert Swank walk toward them from the direction of the darkened sheriff's office. A row of empty beer mugs stood along the bottom of the front wall of the saloon beside empty chairs, the men having abandoned the chairs and moved down to sprawl on the edge of the dirty plank boardwalk. Laughter and piano music resounded.

"What'd you learn?" Boyle asked Swank as he walked back to them with his slight limp. "Why's it so dark? Is he too drunk to light up a lamp?"

"I don't know, maybe," said Swank.

"Is he passed out?" Garby Dolan asked, his sharpened boot knife standing beside him stuck into the boardwalk beside a half-full mug of beer.

"Naw, he's not passed out," Swank said. "The drunken fool is singing—talking to himself too." He stopped and took his mug of beer when Boyle held it up to him. "You ain't going to believe this, but his gun belt's lying out front in the dirt by the hitch rail! I saw him throw it, gun and all!"

That caught Dolan and Boyle by surprise. They fell silent for a second. Finally Boyle cleared his throat and spoke as if in wonderment.

"You mean, the sheriff's gun belt is . . . ?" His words trailed in disbelief.

"Lying in the dirt out front," Swank said, finishing his words for him. "That's right," he added, shaking his head with a beer-induced laugh. "I never seen nothing like it."

"Neither have I," said Boyle. "It makes no sense." He stood and dusted the seat of his trousers.

"No human being can drink two bottles of rye and still be up and around singing out loud!" Dolan said. He pulled his knife from the boardwalk and stood up beside Boyle. The three looked down the empty street. Even in the moonlit darkness they saw the door open at the sheriff's office. They saw the third empty bottle fly out and crash in the dirt against one of the other empties.

"All right, I've had enough of this," Boyle growled. "We're going in guns blazing—killing this old peckerwood."

"But I already sharpened this pigsticker real good," said Dolan.

"Tough knuckles," said Boyle. "You can cut him some when we're finished. Let's go!" He hiked up his gun belt and started walking.

"What about telling Rudabaugh?" said Swank.

"Last beers I went in and got, he was headed up the stairs again," said Dolan, catching up to Boyle, walking alongside him.

"Jesus, *again*?" said Swank. "He must be part jack-rabbit."

"Yeah, maybe," said Boyle. "You feel like interrupting him, go ahead. Not me."

They walked to the alleyway alongside the sheriff's office and stepped off the street. With their guns drawn they lined along the wall and listened intently for any sound inside.

"Why's it dark in there?" Boyle whispered to Swank.

"He's probably thinks he sounds better in the dark," Swank said with a beer chuckle. "Look, there's his gun belt, like I told you." He gestured toward the holstered gun lying in the dirt beneath the hitch rail out front.

Boyle looked at the gun in the dirt, then turned his gaze back at Swank and Dolan.

"I don't hear no singing going on," he said in a suspicious whisper.

"I don't hear *nothing* at all," Dolan put in, also in a whisper.

"Maybe he's drunk his fool self to death and saved us the trouble," Swank said. He stifled a little beer laugh.

"That's *real* funny, Delbert," Boyle said with sarcasm. He jerked his head toward the darkened office. "Get your laughing ass up to the front window and see what he's doing. I'm getting sick of all this."

"I don't like doing this," Swank said, peeping around the front corner of the building.

"Nobody cares what you like or don't like," said Boyle. "Get moving. We've got you covered."

Dolan and Boyles loomed at the corner of the building while Swank eased up onto the boardwalk and crept to the small window beside the front door. He crouched and looked inside under the bottom edge of a short curtain, then turned and slipped back to the alley.

"Well?" Boyle asked. "What's he doing?"

"Nothing," Swank whispered. "The fool is just sitting in the dark at his desk, with his head bowed."

"Sitting with his head bowed . . . ?" Boyle said, contemplating the matter.

"Yep," said Swank, "with his head bowed. So, he's either praying or he's knocked-out drunk. Take your pick," he concluded.

"We've spent too long on this fool. Let's get this done," said Boyle, running a hand across his dry lips, "I've got a beer waiting."

The three rushed around the corner of the building and stormed the office, guns drawn, cocked and ready, Dolan with his big knife also in hand. Boyle shouldered the door open as he twisted the handle and lunged inside, Dolan and Swank behind him, but spreading out once inside the door. They stood crouched, their guns out at arm's length pointed at the slump-shouldered character seated behind the desk.

"Wake up and die, *Sheriff*!" shouted Boyle. He aimed at the top of the sheriff's hat crown, Stone's head bowed toward them.

But the still figure at the desk didn't so much as stir

at the sound of the loud voice. Boyle gave the other two a quick nervous glance. They stepped forward as one in the purple darkness.

"What's wrong with him?" Boyle asked.

"How the hell do I—" Swank's voice stopped. The three heard the floor creak behind them. They spun toward the sound in time to see the black hatless silhouette in the open doorway. Before they could shoot, they saw the small office light up in a flash of blue-orange explosions as both of the sheriff's shotgun barrels fired at once.

One blast sent Boyle and Swank flying backward over the desk, knocking out the chair that the sheriff had draped his hat and duster over. The other blast bounced Dolan off the bars of a cell and launched him forward, his face and chest filled with buckshot and iron scraps. He staggered dead on his feet. His upper half crashed through the front window and hung there. Boyle lay dead on the other side of Stone's deck. Swank, badly wounded, dragged himself frantically toward the open door.

"Don't shoot! Don't shoot!" he screamed.

Too late. . . .

Stone had tossed the shotgun aside and drawn his Colt from his waist. He cocked it at Swank as the dying man made it half out the open door. Along the dark street, lamps had come on in windows and doorways. Drinkers stepped out of the saloon onto the boardwalk and the street. All over the waking town, faces looked toward the sheriff's office in dread. They flinched as three revolver shots exploded, causing more blue-orange flashes from the open door of the small darkened office.

"Poor fool's drunk, shooting up the town again," Bernard Aires said under his breath. He turned and shook his head and walked back inside his house at the far end of the street. From the open front window above the Silver Palace, Silas Rudabaugh leaned out and craned his neck to see what was going on. All he could see was a drift of burnt powder looming in the purple darkness above Stone's office. On the street below, townsmen moved toward the office with caution.

"Three dead, Rudabaugh," Stone's voice called out. "Come on down here. Make it an even number."

Three dead? Jesus!

Rudabaugh quickly did the math. If there were three dead, he was the only one left here. He saw the townsmen dash for cover as the sheriff hollered out the invitation. *Huh-uh*, this was no place to be right now, he told himself. Damn Harper and the other two for riding back out to the hideout. Damn Boyle for making a move without telling him first. Rudabaugh jerked his head back inside the window and started snatching his clothes from a chair where he'd laid them.

"What's going on? What was the shooting?" the English dove, Rita Spool asked, sitting up in the bed with a sheet pulled across her breasts.

"Nothing's going on—what shooting?" Rudabaugh said in a hurry, yanking his trousers up, stuffing his shirt down into the waist.

"I heard shooting," Rita said firmly, not to be put off.

"Okay, the sheriff shot some fellows, it sounds like—"

"Rudabaugh . . . ," the sheriff's voice called out again. "Don't be shy. I'll do all the work."

"That son of a bitch," Rudabaugh growled, yanking on one boot, then another. He stamped them into place and threw on his dusty black linen suit coat.

"He's talking to you, isn't he, then?" Rita said, cocking her head curiously.

"Yeah, sort of," said Rudabaugh. He grabbed his gun belt hanging on the bedpost. He started to swing it around his waist, then changed his mind and threw it up onto his shoulder. "Look, I've got to—got some business to take care of."

"Are you going down there like he said?" she asked.

"Probably, maybe, I haven't decided yet," he said, grabbing his hat. He stopped and took a deep breath. "Don't ask so damn many questions. I'll be back real soon."

"I can hardly wait," Rita said, sounding a little insincere. She'd spent most of the afternoon with him—hadn't made a dime for herself. The house charged for her services and paid her half—in Rudabaugh's case it was half of *nothing*, so far.

"Neither can I," Rudabaugh said on his way out the door.

Bounding down the stairs and toward the rear door, he looked over at the two bartenders who stared at him from behind the empty bar, the customers having left to investigate the shooting.

"Look after this place until I get back, Phil," he

shouted, crossing the floor. "You're both doing a fine job." He slung the rear door open, looked back and added, "Keep up the good work."

The good work . . . ?

The head bartender, Phillip Jones, and his younger brother, Ellis, looked at each other.

"I've never seen a man fall apart so fast," Phil said. As he spoke he took out a pencil stub and pocket notebook. "He's like a kid turned loose in a candy store." He scribbled something into the notebook and closed it and put it in his hip pocket.

"We need to get our own place," said Ellis. "That's all there is to it."

Mae Rose had heard the gunshots as she tied her two carpetbags together and threw them up over the rump of the big speckled gray, a rented horse she'd arranged for earlier with the livery hostler. The shotgun and following pistol explosions caused her to hurry. Stone had told her to keep going and not look back—all right, she would do just that.

She'd rented the horse earlier from the livery hostler and paid extra to have it returned to Big Silver when the opportunity presented itself. She had changed out of her brothel attire and put on some no-nonsense trail clothes. She carried a .36 caliber Navy Colt shoved down in her waist that Stone had given her for protection a year ago. The trail to Secondary was known as nothing more than barren sand, rock and dry washes, but she wasn't taking a chance on coming across a stray panther or a wolf in the moonlit night.

She hurriedly tied the bags down with some short lengths of rope and had started to lead the horse from the barn when she halted, seeing Silas Rudabaugh run in through the open doors.

"Everything's all right, miss," he said, seeing the frightened look on her face. He held up a hand as if it would reassure her. "Some trouble on the street. Nothing to worry about." He took hold of the gray's bridle and held on to it.

"Turn loose of my horse," Mae Rose said flatly. She jerked on the horse's reins, but Rudabaugh held firm. She thought about the Colt shoved down in her waist, but she decided against grabbing for it. If she pulled it she knew she'd have to use it, and this wasn't the time or place.

"Hey, you're one of our Silver Palace gals," Rudabaugh said, finally recognizing her in the faded trail clothes. "Where are you going?" He looked suspicious of her.

"Back to Denver City," Mae Rose said. "My mother is ill. I'll be gone a month, maybe longer."

"Yeah?" said Rudabaugh. "I've never met a dove yet who really had a mother—least not one aboveground." He nodded at the bulging carpetbags. "Looks like you're taking everything you own."

"Maybe I am, what of it?" said Mae Rose. "Turn loose of my horse."

"Huh-uh, not just yet," said Rudabaugh. "You're not leaving here until I see that your account is settled. Can't have you running off owing the Palace money, can we?"

"I don't owe the Palace anything," Mae Rose said. "My account was clear when Edsel Centrila bought the place—go check for yourself."

"Oh, I will," said Rudabaugh. He added with a stiff grin, "In my own sweet time." He stepped in closer and said, "You're one of the couple of gals I haven't managed to get *well acquainted* with the past couple of days."

"I know," said Mae Rose, settling down, seeing she would have to deal with him. "I've seen so much of you in the hall I thought you were wallpaper." She smiled coyly. "My feelings were getting hurt that you hadn't come to visit me yet."

"We don't want your feelings hurt, do we?" said Rudabaugh.

"No, we don't," said Mae Rose. "As soon as I get back, I'm going to come looking for you."

"I'd like that—" Rudabaugh suddenly caught himself and glanced back in the direction of the sheriff's office. "Which way are you headed?" he said. He noted the livery's brand on the gray's rump and knew it was a rental horse.

Mae Rose gave a shrug.

"To Secondary," she said. "I'll take the stage from there."

"I'm going with you," said Rudabaugh. "It so happens I'm headed that way myself," he lied. "I can bring this cayuse back for you."

"I already paid extra to have it brought back," Mae Rose said.

"Look at me, little darling. I'm your boss, in a manner of speaking," said Rudabaugh, moving in toward her. He glanced again in the direction of the sheriff's office, then back at her. "If I say I'm going with you, guess what that means?"

All right. . . . She got it.

She only nodded. She followed him as he led the gray to a stable where his horse stood looking at them over the stall gate. She wasn't about to let her bags—one of them carrying her gold coins in it—get out of her sight.

Rudabaugh tied the gray's reins to the stall rail and gave an extra-hard yank on them to make them more difficult to loosen.

Stay cool, she told herself. She was stuck with this overbearing rube for the time being at least. She would have to settle down and play things out to suit herself. She knew his name, his reputation, having heard of him from Rita and the other doves he'd managed to weasel his way into bed with. She watched him step inside the stall and hurriedly saddle his horse, a dark blaze-faced bay. Every now and then, she'd see him looking warily out the open door in the direction of the main street of Big Silver.

"So, what was the gunfire I heard out there?" she asked as he slipped the bridle up onto his horse's muzzle.

"Can't say for sure," he said. "I heard some of the townsmen say it was Sheriff Stone, drunk again, shooting at anything that got in front of him." He looked around and gave her a grin. "I expect somebody might have stopped his clock by now. I hope so anyway," he added. "Stone and I don't get along very well."

"You don't say so," said Mae Rose. He had his back to her now. She knew this was her best chance to draw the Colt and shoot him. But she decided against it. Maybe riding along with him wasn't a bad idea. She could handle him; she was certain.

"I sure do say so," Rudabaugh replied. "Lucky for him he hasn't caught me in a cross mood. I'm a professional stock detective. I'd put a bad hurting on him." He turned to her and gave what she thought he considered a dashing grin.

"Oh my, I believe you would," she said. "I've heard you detectives are not to be messed with."

"You heard right, ma'am—Mae Rose, is it?"

"Yes, it is," she said. She reached and playfully slapped his arm. "There, you see? You even know my name and still haven't come to my suite."

"I am nothing but sorry for that, Mae Rose," Rudabaugh said.

"That's okay," she said, noting that he was quick to warm up to any show of affection. "We'll make up for it when I get back."

"You can count on it," Rudabaugh said. Again the attempt at a dashing grin. "Another thing they say about us detectives is that we are all born women pleasers."

"I already knew *that*," she said with a wide sparkling smile of her own. *Bang!* she said to herself, envisioning drawing the small Colt and firing a round into his spine when he turned his back on her again.

"Ready when you are, Mae Rose," he said in a cavalier gesture, pulling his horse forward from the stall.

Mae Rose only smiled and gestured for him to loosen the gray's tightly tied reins from the railing.

He loosened the reins, but instead of handing them to her, he nodded toward his horse and said, "Why don't you ride my horse a ways, just until we see how hard this rented horse is to handle?

She thought about her pouch of gold lying inside one of the carpetbags. She started to object, but something told her it would do no good—probably only make him suspicious of her belongings.

"Why, thank you," she said sweetly. "That's most considerate of you." She took the reins to his horse; he assisted her up into the saddle.

"After you, then," he said, stepping back as she put the horse forward at a walk. He mounted the gray and left the barn right behind her.

Chapter 17

As a thin ribbon of light mantled the hill lines in the east, the Ranger rode onto the main street of Big Silver and brought his dun to a walk toward the sheriff's office. Three townsmen standing at the corner of a building stepped into the street. They looked up at Sam and waved him to a halt. Sam looked all around, his rifle lying across his lap. Several men stood out in front of the Silver Palace; more yet were scattered here and there in the grainy morning light.

"Ranger, thank God you're here," one of the men said barely above a whisper. "It's Sheriff Stone. He's gone back to drinking, crazy as the last time you had to come settle his hash."

Sam looked at the body lying half out the open door of Stone's office. He saw the other body hanging down out the broken front window.

"They're men who work for Edsel Centrila, Ranger," the same man said. "We knew there's bad blood between Centrila and the sheriff, but we weren't expecting this."

"He hasn't come out of there since this happened," another man said. "Lucky for us you're here."

"I was camped nearby," Sam said, eying the situation, the darkened sheriff's office, the two bodies, broken glass. "I heard the gunfire."

"Are you going to need our help?" a man asked, slipping in off the street with a rifle in his hands.

Sam looked at him, saw the long, pointed sleeping cap hanging down to his shoulders.

"No," he said firmly, "everybody stay back." He swung down from his saddle and struck his rifle down into its boot. The townsmen moved away as he led the dun closer to the darkened adobe building and hitched it out in front of a mercantile store twenty yards away.

He walked to the middle of the street in front of Stone's office and raised his gloved hands chest high. He saw someone move inside the broken window. He caught a glimpse of a shotgun barrel.

"Don't shoot, Sheriff Stone. It's me, Sam Burrack," he called out to the open doorway. "Can I come in?"

There was a silent pause, but only for a moment.

"Of course you can come in, Ranger," Stone called out in a friendly tone of voice. "You can lower your hands too, unless you think your gloves will fall off."

"They're good," Sam said, lowering his hands. He took a deep breath and walked toward the open doorway, seeing Stone appear and step over the dead gunman. The shotgun still hung loosely from his hand, but he'd reloaded it earlier.

"Are you drinking, Sheriff?" the Ranger asked. He

stooped and picked up the gun and gun belt from under the hitch rail on his way.

"What kind of question is that, Ranger?" Stone asked. "Do I look like I'm drinking? Do I sound like it?"

"No, you don't," Sam said, relieved. "But what about all these empty rye bottles?"

"I just needed two or three of them to help me do my job," Stone said.

"I see," Sam said.

He slipped the revolver up from its holster enough to see it was a battered unloaded relic. He shook his head, shoved it back in its holster and stopped only a few feet from the open door. Handing Stone the gun belt and range pistol, he looked all around and sniffed the air. "It smells like a distillery here."

"I know it does. It's driving me crazy. Come on inside," Stone said, looking back and forth along the grainy lit street as he stepped backward inside the dark office. "I'm expecting Silas Rudabaugh any time, soon as he gets his bark on."

"What happened here, Sheriff?" Sam asked, stepping over the body of Three-toed Delbert Swank.

Stone gave him a look.

"This is that trouble you seemed to think I was *imagining* with Centrila," Stone said.

The Ranger only nodded.

Stone said, "I saw it coming. I even saw Harper Centrila riding this way early yesterday morning."

"Hold it," said Sam. "It's likely you *did* see Harper."

"That's what I just said," Stone replied flatly.

"His father's men broke him out," Sam said.

Stone nodded.

"That figures," he said. "I saw a fight coming. I tried taking it to Rudabaugh and some other Centrila gunmen at the saloon. But they saw the shape I'm in and tried to rattle me, goad me out—try to cause me to make mistakes. So I decided if I couldn't take the fight to them, I'd best make them bring the fight to me." He swept a hand about the blood and the bodies. "You can see it worked out better this way."

As Sam watched, Stone picked up a wooden bucket full of rye and walked it to the rear door. He opened the door and swung the bucket, emptying it into the alley.

"It breaks my heart doing that," he said, turning, setting the empty bucket down. "I sat here smelling rye all night, singing out loud, making them think I was drunk and crazy. Bad as I wanted a drink, I never took one."

"That's good, Sheriff," Sam said.

"Now, then," Stone said as if settling things in his mind. "Next time I tell you Centrila is out for payback, are you going to believe me?"

"I believed you all along, Sheriff," Sam said. "I just needed to see it start to play out some." He looked around at the blood, at the dead still waiting to be removed. He shook his head.

"All this just to even a score?" he said. "Judge Long hasn't even brought the bribery charge forward yet. We don't even know that he will. Neither does Centrila."

"It doesn't matter to Edsel Centrila, Ranger," Stone said. "He thinks I crossed him. He wants even. Never stopped to think I was just a lawman doing my job. Anybody doesn't do what he wants is his enemy."

"No chance he'll hear what happened here and back away?" Sam asked.

"No chance in the world," said Stone. He toed a bloody buckshot-riddled chair out of their way. "This is only the start, Ranger," he said, gesturing a hand at the dead. "If I know Centrila, it's going to get a whole lot bloodier before it's over."

Sam gave the matter some thought. He walked around the office to a blood-splattered woodstove and held his hand near the stove's cold belly. He raised the lid of a blackened coffeepot, looked inside and set it back down. Watching him, Stone gave a thin smile.

"Had I known you were coming, I'd have boiled a fresh pot," he said.

Sam nodded.

"How long are you willing to wait for Silas Rudabaugh to show up?" he asked.

"As long as it takes," Stone said.

"And if he doesn't show?" Sam asked.

"Then I'll be very disappointed," Stone said.

"I'll get some fresh water and boil us a pot," Sam said, picking up the cold coffeepot.

"You don't have to wait here with me, Ranger," said Stone.

"I know I don't," Sam replied. He turned and walked out the front door.

Rudabaugh kept Mae Rose riding in front of him across the flats and up onto the hillsides trails. They rode in silence as morning sunlight gathered its strength and began to scorch the rugged terrain. After leaving Big Silver they'd ridden in almost total silence until they reached a fork in the trail, where to their right lay the trail toward Secondary. Without looking around, Mae Rose turned the horse at the fork, only to hear Rudabaugh sidle up close to her and take a hold on the horse's bridle, keeping it going straight ahead.

"Change of plans," he said firmly as Mae Rose turned her head quickly and looked at him.

"What are you talking about?" she said, trying to keep her voice calm and level. "I'm going to Secondary. I'm taking the stage from there. You knew that—"

"I did," said Rudabaugh with a sly little grin. "But like I said, 'change of plans.'" He held up the leather pouch of gold he'd taken from one of her bags and jiggled it in his hand.

"You—you went through my things?" she stammered. "You had no right to do that." She tried jerking the horse free of his hand, but even as she did so she realized that she couldn't make a run for it, not while he was holding all of her money.

Rudabaugh gave a wider grin. "Yeah, I went through your things, so what? I'm your boss, remember?"

Mae Rose only stared at him, smoldering.

"You see, little darling," he continued, "being your boss, I've got every right to know how you managed to squirrel up so much money."

"What do you care how I managed to get it?" said Mae Rose. "It's not Edsel Centrila's money, it's mine."

She tried to make a swipe at grabbing the pouch. But Rudabaugh jerked it out of her reach.

"Try that again I'll smack you cockeyed," he threatened. "We're going to find us some shade somewhere and you can do whatever it takes to convince me that this is your money." He paused and added, "If your story's good enough, maybe I won't have to turn this over to Centrila. You and I might split it up between us and keep our mouths shut. Fair enough?"

That's it, she told herself. He wanted her; he wanted her money; he wanted everything. She knew the type. When he was through using her, never mind splitting the money, he'd take *all* the money and leave her lying dead in a dry wash somewhere. There was no way he would take part of the money when he could have it all.

This pig!

She let him see her take a deep breath and let it out as if in submission. She even gave a suggestive smile.

"Let's find that shade, then," she said. "We'll see what I can do to convince you."

"That's the kind of attitude I like," Rudabaugh said. He turned loose of the horse's bridle and looked off along the trail in search of a suitable place to spread a blanket. As soon as he looked away, Mae Rose reached up under the tails of her blouse, jerked out the Navy Colt from her waist and started shooting.

Rudabaugh heard the gun cock and turned and grabbed for it just as the first shot exploded. The bullet tore through the palm of his outstretched hand and dug into his forearm, streaking along the bone until it blew out a ragged hole at his elbow. Her second shot went through his ribs and out his back, missing his lungs.

As she fired, the horse beneath her backed away, nervously. Rudabaugh, unable to reach her, blood flying from his chest and his arm, grabbed his big revolver up from its holster as another bullet exploded from the .36 caliber Navy Colt. This one sliced along his jawline and clipped off the upper half of his left ear.

Crazy whore!

He raised and cocked his Remington quickly; Mae Rose jerked the horse around to try to put some distance between them. She fired again, but the shot went wild and skipped off a rock on the other side of Rudabaugh. The Remington bucked in the wounded gunman's hand. The shot hit Mae Rose high in her right shoulder and sent her flipping sidelong from the saddle. She hit the ground flat on her back and didn't move. The Navy Colt flew from her hand and landed among the rocks at the edge of the trail.

Rudabaugh cupped a hand to his maimed ear; blood ran down his wounded side, his wounded arm. He swung down from the gray and let its reins hang to the ground. Stepping over to Mae Rose, he tried to wake her by rolling her face back and forth with his boot.

"Wake up!" he said. When the woman only lay there, limp, he nudged her wounded shoulder with his boot toe. "You brought this on yourself, you know," he said. "You made me shoot you."

Mae Rose moaned and stirred slightly at the pain in her shoulder. She opened her eyes and saw him standing over her. But in her addled condition, she closed her eyes against the glare of white sunlight and drifted as his voice grew further away.

Rudabaugh looked all around as he untied the bandanna from around his neck, wadded it and pressed it to his half-missing ear. This was no good, he told himself. He stooped down and loosened the scarf from Mae Rose's neck and tied it around his elbow, using his teeth to tighten it.

"Sheriff . . . help me," Mae Rose murmured mindlessly under her breath.

"Oh," said Rudabaugh, "you want to sic the law on me? Then you better do it quick. When I get you off this trail, you're dead."

He rummaged through Mae Rose's bags behind the rented gray's saddle and pulled out a checkered cotton blouse. Tearing it in half, he folded it into two makeshift bandages and used them to stop the bleeding from his other wounds.

"Come on, whore, take your last ride," he said. In spite of the pain in his wounds, he dragged Mae Rose to the rented gray, raised her enough to shove her up over the saddle. He saw blood on the back of her head where she'd landed on a fist-sized rock.

Mounting his own horse, he led the gray a half mile up the hillside trail where the land on either side had turned less sandy, more rocky, better hidden. This would do, he told himself, swinging down from his saddle. He pulled Mae Rose off the gray's back and dragged her over between two large rocks, out of sight. With plenty of smaller rocks to cover her, he thought. *Perfect.*

He drew his Remington and reached out arm's

length and cocked the hammer, the tip of the barrel only inches from her forehead.

"Too bad you never got to know me, whore," he said in a lowered tone. He started to squeeze the trigger. But before he did, he glanced up and saw Harper Centrila and Lon Bartow easing their horses into sight down the hill trail toward him. They both had rifles raised and ready.

"The hell is going on with you, Silas?" Harper called out less than forty yards away. "We heard shooting a while ago."

Damn it!

Rudabaugh turned loose of his knotted shirttails and wiped a bloody hand across his sweaty brow.

"Nothing's going on with me," he said, trying to play off his surprise. He lied, saying, "I heard horses—I'm glad it's you all. You won't believe the time I've had."

"You better *hope* I do," Harper chuckled darkly. "Who are you fixing to shoot there?"

"*Shoot?*" said Rudabaugh as if surprised. "I wasn't fixing to shoot anybody." Realizing he'd been seen too clearly about to pull a trigger, he hastened to add, "Leastwise I was hoping I wouldn't have to." He gestured Harper and Bartow down to him. "Come look what I've got here." He backed away from the knocked-out woman and lowered his Remington to his side.

"Whoa," Harper said as he and Bartow stepped their horses over and looked down at Mae Rose lying limp between the two rocks.

"That's one of your pa's saloon gals," Bartow said. "I saw her there when we was in town."

"So did I," said Harper. He and Bartow both stepped down from their saddles. He looked from Mae Rose to Rudabaugh, looking him up and down, his bloody chest, his arm, his blood-soaked bandaging. "What's the story here, Silas?" he asked.

"I caught her a mile back," Rudabaugh said. "She ambushed me. Look at me."

Harper and Bartow looked at his closer.

"You *caught* her?" Harper questioned him skeptically. "So you were out here *trapping whores*?" He and Bartow gave a slight chuckle.

"That's real funny, Harper," Rudabaugh said flatly, not sharing their humor.

"Funny?" Harper's expression darkened. "Here's something not so *funny*. You and your pals were supposed to be in Big Silver, taking care of Stone." He cocked his head a little. "Anything funny to say about that?"

"Things went bad," Rudabaugh said, deciding it was time to come as clean as he could about the gold coins, in case it was brothel money. "I was out here headed to report in to Edsel. I ran into her. She tried to kill me. She's carrying a lot of gold coins. I figured she might be stealing from us." As he spoke he raised the pouch from his duster pocket and held it up for Harper to see.

Harper looked at him suspiciously.

"Thought you said she was carrying it?" he said. "Ain't that what he said, Lon?" he asked Bartow.

"Yep, he did," Bartow said. "I heard him say it."

"Let me get this straight," Harper said. "You're out here, coming to report to Papa Edsel? You get ambushed by a whore who's robbed the brothel—?"

"I'll answer to Edsel," Rudabaugh said firmly, the Remington still in his hand.

"Where are Boyle and the others?" Harper said.

"Dead, is where they are," said Rudabaugh. His hand tightened around the butt of his Remington. "But I don't want to talk about it."

"They're dead, but you don't want to talk about it?" Harper said as if in disbelief. "Excuse the hell out of me. But I think you need to tell me what the hell—"

"Like I said, I'll answer to Edsel Centrila—*my boss*," said Rudabaugh. "Nobody else."

Harper stared at him a moment longer, then said to Bartow, "Lon, help him get this woman patched up some and up into her saddle. I bet she can help Silas here tell us his story, if we can keep her alive, that is."

"That suits me right enough," Rudabaugh said. He stepped over with Bartow; the two of them raised the wounded woman from the dirt and leaned her against one of the rocks where Rudabaugh had intended for her to die.

"Get her some water, Silas," Harper said to Rudabaugh. "And get something to plug that bullet hole."

Mae Rose slumped against the rock. She could hear them now. She could make out what they were doing. But she wasn't going to open her eyes, not now, not yet. It was time to lie back and figure out her next move. This desert was too eager, too inviting to men like these. If she answered all their questions and they saw no reason to keep her alive, she would still die out here.

Chapter 18

———

Mae Rose rode with her wrists tied together around Harper Centrila's waist. She awakened on and off, but remained slumped against Harper's back. At a water hole in the early afternoon, she allowed herself to look revived long enough for Lon Bartow to seat her at the water's edge and wipe dried blood from the large welt on the back of her head. She wobbled in place as Harper and Rudabaugh looked on.

"Wha—what's going on . . . ?" she murmured dreamily. She reached a hand out and gripped Bartow's forearm for support.

"That's what *we* want to know," Harper replied, making sure he gave Rudabaugh a cold stare. "But our *pard* here will only speak to *his* boss, Papa Edsel Centrila." He gave him a sour look up and down. "Ain't that right, Silas?"

Rudabaugh looked away. He'd kept his hand resting on the butt of the big Remington all morning long.

"I didn't want to have to tell what happened in Big Silver more than once," he said.

"Afraid you can't remember well enough to tell it twice?" Harper said, half goading the older gunman.

"Hell no," said Rudabaugh. "I can tell it all day long. It won't change, because it's the truth."

Harper grinned.

"The *truth*!" Harper called out to Bartow. "What is it they say, Lon—?" he called out to Bartow. *"The truth shall set you free?"*

Bartow stopped holding the cloth against the back of Mae Rose's head.

"Huh-uh," he disagreed. "Where I come from they say *the truth shall get you shot.*"

Harper chuckled and shook his head. He drew his Colt and spun it on his finger, as if making a point.

"Lon says the damnedest things," he said to Rudabaugh. "But most times he makes good sense if you listen to him." He called out to Bartow, "Ain't that right, Lon?"

Rudabaugh was tempted to yank his Remington up and let fly. But he breathed deep and calmed himself. Even if he killed them both, the woman too, he would still have to face Edsel Centrila and go through all of this again.

"Yep, I make good sense if you listen to me," Bartow agreed. He grinned, a wide, flat grin that made no change in his surly expression.

Mae Rose kept her eyes closed and her head slumped as Bartow continued holding the wet cloth on her sore knotted head, listening.

"All right, Harper," Rudabaugh said, getting tired of the constant suspicion, "I'm going to tell you what happened, but then I'm done with it until I get to where we're going."

Harper and Bartow looked at each other, then at Rudabaugh.

"Let's have it, Silas," Harper said. His Colt stopped spinning on his finger and hung there, loosely pointed at Rudabaugh's already bloody chest.

Rudabaugh glanced at the woman sitting slumped by the water, then wiped a hand across his forehead. He knew he needed to get as close to the truth as he could without putting himself on the spot.

"I told Boyle and the others to not make a move without me giving them the go-ahead," he said. "But while I was off taking care of some business, they took it on their own to go kill Sheriff Stone—"

"Hold up right there," said Harper, waggling the barrel of his Colt. "This 'business' you were off 'taking care of.' Did it require any of the Silver Palace doves keeping their ankles in the air while you 'took care' of it?"

Bartow stifled a laugh; Rudabaugh's face reddened with mortification and rage.

"No! It did not!" he barked, shooting a cold stare at Bartow. "I was going over the day's take, making sure the Jones brothers don't rob the place blind. I am the manager, you know."

Harper stared at him curiously for a moment.

"No, I *didn't* know you were the manager of the Silver Palace," he said. "Papa Edsel must've forgot to mention it." He gave Rudabaugh a skeptical look.

"Well, I am the manager," said Rudabaugh. "Edsel told me so." He amended his words quickly, adding,

"Not in so many words, but he told me so, in his own way."

Harper continued staring at him.

"Go on," he said.

"As far as the doves go," said Rudabaugh, "I won't deny, I like women. I like them a *lot*."

Harper nodded at Mae Rose, who sat slumped and bloody.

"I can see you do," he said.

Bartow stifled another laugh. Rudabaugh fumed and ignored Harper's remark.

"Anyway," he continued, "soon as I heard that Stone had killed Boyle, Swank and Dolan, I figured Edsel needed to hear about it right away. I skint out of there. Got to the fork in the trail and this one jumped up and started shooting at me." He looked back and forth between the two gunmen, gauging their belief of his story. "I figure she stole the brothel money and thought I was on her trail." He stopped, satisfied with his loosely woven tale.

After a pause for consideration, Harper spun his revolver again, this time landing it expertly into its holster.

"That's a good one," he said. "Ain't that a good one, Lon?"

"It's a good one," Bartow agreed.

"And it's the damn truth," said Rudabaugh. "I won't be called a liar."

"I never said you were lying, Silas," Harper replied. "I just said it's a *good one*. Didn't I, Lon?"

"That's what you said, sure enough," Bartow replied.

"There, you see?" Harper said to Rudabaugh. He gave a short shrug of dismissal. "What's it matter what I think? It what's Papa Edsel thinks that counts." He gave a smug half smile. "I reckon we'll know what he thinks soon enough."

The Ranger and Sheriff Stone walked along the wide dirt street of Big Silver under the scrutinizing eyes of wary townsfolk. Halfway to the livery barn, Stone took off his hat and waved it back and forth all around as they walked.

"Don't worry, folks. Your sheriff is sober," he called out amiably. "I'm sober now. I'll be sober the next time you see me. Three gunmen came to kill me in the night, but as you can see, the law was kept."

The peopled studied him for a moment, and then a short round of applause rose among them.

"I knew you were sober, Sheriff," a man's voice called out from the doorway of a saddle maker's shop.

"Bless your heart, Winslow," Stone called out without looking around. Under his breath he gave a low growl like that of a wolf. Then he looked at the Ranger with a wry smile. "Just joking, Ranger," he said.

The Ranger nodded. They had waited as long as they needed to for Silas Rudabaugh to show up. Now that he hadn't shown up, they needed to find out if he or any of Centrila's men were still around, lurking somewhere, ready to ambush the sheriff as he walked the streets.

They walked down an alleyway back to the town livery barn and along the straw-covered floor as Stone looked all around for Rudabaugh's dark blaze-faced bay.

"He's gone," Stone concluded, sounding a little disappointed with his findings. He gave a last close look all around. Before they turned, a short bowlegged hostler walked in through the front door with a hay rake in his hand.

"What can I do for you, Sheriff?" he asked. He waddled forward between the two rows of stalls.

"I'm looking for the dark bay," Stone said, "but I see it's gone."

"Silas Rudabaugh's horse," the hostler said. "Yep, he left here right after the shooting last night."

"Really?" said Stone, he and the Ranger looking at each other, a little surprised. "He sure turned out a bit shy for a big bold stock detective," he added.

"I wouldn't call him shy," said the hostler. "I heard some miners say they couldn't get to the doves for him being stuck there tighter than a door wedge."

"Is that a fact?" said Stone. He and the Ranger started to turn and leave.

"Yep, he rode out of here with one last night," the hostler said. "I expect he's one of them whose ma slapped him away from the tit too soon."

Stone stopped with a jolt and looked at the man.

"What did you say?" he asked in an almost menacing tone.

The hostler looked frightened.

"I didn't mean nothing, Sheriff," he said. "I heard some men had mamas do them the same way, they come up just fine. Some men just don't grow out of it—"

"Stop!" Stone said, almost shouted. "I mean the dove he was with. Who was she?"

"It was Mae Rose, the one with the little freckles across her nose."

"Are you sure?" Stone asked, reaching a hand out to steady himself on a stall rail.

"Sure as I can be," said the hostler. "I rented her a horse earlier. She came back for it and they rode away together, except she rode his bay and he rode the rental."

Sam saw the affect this was having on Stone. He watched and listened closely.

"Did you hear them talking?" Stone asked, his face suddenly grim and ashen.

"No, I never heard them say a word," the hostler replied with a shrug. "They were riding out the back door when I came in the side door from the corral—but I saw them, sure enough."

Stone lowered his head and shook it slowly.

"Of all damnedest things," he murmured under his breath.

"Can I do something for him?" the hostler asked, looking at Sam.

Sam only nodded him toward the door. The bow-legged man took the hint and turned and waddled away.

"All right, Sheriff, what's going on?" he said to Stone.

"This woman. Mae Rose is a personal friend of mine, Ranger," Stone said. "She wouldn't have gone off with Rudabaugh unless he forced her to."

Here we go, Sam told himself, knowing how hard it could be getting information out of Stone.

"Why would he force her to go with him?" he asked, sensing there was more to the story.

"You heard the hostler. Rudabaugh thinks he's a stud. Probably doesn't know it's all make-believe to these doves. He might have saw her traveling alone and moved in like a panther—gets her out there alone and does whatever suits him."

Sam studied his face, seeing there was more to it.

"There's more, Sheriff," he pressed. "What is it?"

Stone cleared his mind with a deep breath.

"I gave her some money to get out of here before the fighting started. If Centrila finds out she's a friend of mine, he'll use her to get to me. She don't deserve that."

Sam considered it for a moment.

"Just how close a *friend* is she?" he asked.

Stone gave him a cool gaze.

"I need to ask, Sheriff," Sam said. "I remember how it was riding with you and Sheriff Deluna hunting down Bo Anson and his bunch. I don't like learning things a drop at a time. So tell me everything right now. I don't want a surprise around every turn."

Stone thought about it and nodded.

"You're right, Ranger," he said. "I'm bad about letting out information—but I'm getting better at it." He fished a cough drop from a fresh pack in his shirt pocket and popped it into his mouth. "Mae Rose and I are just good friends," he lied. "You remember Sheriff Maynard Rossi, used to be over in Tumbling Creek?"

"Sort of," Sam said. "He got killed about the time I came into law work."

"Well, he was a friend of mine," Stone said. "Mae Rose Rossi is his daughter."

Sam just looked at him, not knowing what to say.

Stone eyed Sam.

"It's the truth," he said. "She showed up here over a year ago, working as a dove. I hadn't seen her since she was a child. I couldn't talk her out of the sporting life, so I've tried to look out for her any way I can—hoped someday she'd come to her senses."

"And that's all?" Sam asked. "She's Maynard Rossi's daughter, a friend and nothing else."

"That's the whole of it, Ranger," Stone said. He pulled a match from his shirt pocket, struck it and lit the cigarette. "Satisfied?" he asked.

"Satisfied," Sam said. He walked to the open rear door and searched the layers of hoofprints in the dirt. As he did so, Stone walked to the side door and summoned the hostler back inside.

"Are all your rental horses still wearing Star Brand shoes?" he asked.

"Yes, they are," the hostler said. "That way we can track them down by that raised star emblem if we have to." He turned and took a dusty horseshoe down from a nail on the wall and handed it to Stone. The sheriff only glanced at it and pitched it to Sam as he turned from the door and walked back inside. "Here's who we're looking for," he said.

"I know," said Sam. He examined the horseshoe and looked at the ground inside the door, seeing the deeper imprint of a star, the same as the raised star on the shoe in his hand. "These same prints are heading out to the hill trails." He gestured toward the sand flats, and beyond toward the distant hill lines.

"You know I've got to find her," Stone said. "Rudabaugh will find that money on her—it's just his detective nature. He'll take it from her and kill her. That's his nature too. I don't have to see the future to know that."

"I understand," Sam said quietly. "I'm riding with you."

The two gathered their horses and left without delay, filling their canteens from a wooden bucket of fresh water. They rode at a gallop, in a silence of dread for the first three miles, following the two horses' tracks across the sand flats. They only slowed the animals enough to pay respect to the steep dangerous trail as the animals climbed upward in the heat of the day.

At the fork in the trail, they stopped and looked down, seeing the hoofprints lead on up into the rugged hills.

"This is bad," Stone said, studying the trail ahead. "She was headed to Secondary to catch a stage."

Sam saw boot prints on the ground and swung down to take a closer look. He saw the trace of blood on the fist-sized rock and stooped and picked it up for Stone to see. Stone's jaw tightened in anger.

Sam saw the glint of metal in the rocks off the trail and walked over to find the Navy Colt. He walked back toward Sheriff Stone, dusting it off.

"I gave her that gun, Ranger," Stone said. He took the gun and noted it had been fired four times. "That's my gal," he said in a tortured voice. "She must've fought him till the end."

His gal?

"Don't give up hope, Sheriff," Sam said. "There's a chance she's alive."

"I know," Stone said. He shoved the Navy Colt down behind his belt and stepped up into his saddle. "Ranger, I lied to you earlier," he said in a lowered tone. "Mae Rose and I are a lot closer than friends."

"You mean the two of you . . . ?" Sam let his words trail.

"Yep, that's what I mean. She's my gal," said Stone, gazing away as he spoke. "I didn't realize it until I heard myself say it. But she is. She wanted me to go away with her—I turned her down." He paused, then said, "I should be ashamed of myself, at my age . . . her being my friend Maynard Rossi's daughter." He shook his head. "I'm a damn fool, ain't I?"

"You're full of surprises," Sam said, "I'll give you that. As for being a fool, yes, probably so."

Stone cocked his head toward him.

"She's your gal and you care about her. What else is there to consider? If you're bothered by what Maynard Rossi would think, ask yourself if he'd be happier knowing that his daughter's a dove than knowing that she's with you."

Stone let out a breath.

"He wouldn't be, would he?" he said.

"If he would, he'd be the fool, not you," Sam said as

the two turned their horses to the trail. "Anything else you want to tell me, Sheriff?" he said sidelong to Stone.

"No," Stone said, "I believe that about squares us up, Ranger. If I think of anything else I'll let you know." He stared straight ahead.

"Obliged," Sam said, also staring straight ahead beside him. They nudged their horses up into a gallop.

And they rode on.

Part 4

Part 4

Chapter 19

Harper Centrila and Lon Bartow rode into the stony front yard of the hideout with Silas Rudabaugh riding in front of them. Bartow led the gray rental horse beside him. Harper still had the woman riding slumped on his back, her wrists tied around his waist. Seeing them ride in, Edsel Centrila stood up from the blanket-covered porch swing and stepped forward. He spread his hands and leaned on the porch rail. A cigar stood clenched in his teeth.

"The hell are you doing, Harper?" he said as the Cady brothers and the other gunmen gathered in the yard. "You know better than to ever bring anybody here."

"Take it easy, Papa Edsel," Harper said. "This gal has been knocked out all day. If you see the back of her head, you'll know why."

Edsel leaned and looked the woman up and down as best he could, able to see part of the bloody bandage on her right shoulder.

"What happened to her?" No sooner had he asked

than he looked at Rudabaugh and saw his bloody bandages too. Rudabaugh still held a blood-blackened bandanna against his half an ear. "What happened to you?" he said.

"They done this to each other, the best we can find out," Harper said. "Silas shot her, said she shot him first." He shrugged. "It could have been a lovers' spat. She's one of your doves. He was getting ready to head-pop her when Lon and I rode up to them on a hillside. Ain't that right, Lon?" he said over his shoulder.

"Right as rain," Bartow put in. He grinned; Edsel Centrila just looked at him sourly.

"A lovers' spat? With one of my doves?" Edsel said in a raised voice. He jerked the cigar from his mouth, giving Rudabaugh a cold, stiff look. "What're you doing diddling one of my doves in the desert? Have you and your men taken care of Sheppard Stone yet?"

Harper looked down, shook his head and gave a little chuff at his father's question. Rudabaugh mumbled something inaudible and looked down at his saddle horn.

Edsel jerked his head back toward Harper.

"Did I say something *funny* here?" Edsel snapped at his son.

"No, sir, Papa Edsel, you surely did not," Harper said. He raised a boot from his stirrup and pulled a knife from its well. "Go on and answer him, Silas," he said to Rudabaugh. "Papa Edsel might make some sense of it. I sure didn't." He gestured the Cady brothers to him, then stuck the knife blade under the rope holding the woman against him and sliced through it.

Ignacio Cady rushed in just in time, reached up and eased Mae Rose down into his arms. He turned and carried her toward the house, his brother, Lyle, right beside him.

Edsel stared at Rudabaugh.

"Where's the others?" he demanded.

"They're dead, Edsel," Rudabaugh said, shamefaced. "They acted outside my orders. There was a big shooting. The sheriff killed them, all three."

All three dead?

Edsel stared at him for a moment as if in disbelief.

"Get down and get over here, Silas," he finally demanded. "I want to know what's been going on."

Feeling all eyes on him, Silas Rudabaugh swung down from his saddle and walked up onto the porch.

Charlie Knapp, who'd been standing listening, looked down at the hoofprints leading into the yard. As Rudabaugh stepped onto the porch with his bandanna against his maimed ear, Knapp cursed under his breath.

"Edsel, you might want to take a look at this," he called out to the porch. He stepped over to the gray, lifted its front hoof and inspected its shoe. The men gathered around. Bartow and Harper stepped down from their saddles and also looked at the gray's upturned shoe.

"Jesus," said Harper as his father walked over quickly from the front porch. He looked down at the clearly marked hoofprints in the dirt, then back at the raised star on the horse's shoe.

"Damn it, damn it, *damn it to hell*!" shouted Edsel, shoving his way through the men to the horse's side.

He glared at Harper. "You might as well have raised a flag!"

Harper gritted his teeth, staring at the telltale hoof-prints leading out to the trail and beyond, all the way back to the fork along the rocky hillside.

"This is Silas' doings, Papa Edsel," he said, glaring at Rudabaugh still standing up on the porch, holding the bandanna to his half an ear. "He brought this to us."

"It doesn't matter whose fault it is now," Edsel said. "The fact is anybody who comes looking for you can track this cayuse to your doorstep! I didn't get you broke out to see you hang." He looked at the gray, then all around. "Everybody gather their rolls. We're riding out of here."

"To where?" said Harper. "For how long?"

"To Big Silver," said Edsel. "For as long as it takes to find out what kind of shenanigans this fool has pulled." He pointed at Rudabaugh, who hung his head in shame. "And to get Sheriff Stone dead and in the ground," Edsel added.

"I was part of this," Harper said. "For the time being Lon and I can't be seen in town anyway with this jail-break hanging over us." He nodded at the prints in the dirt. "We'll stick here and ride out come morning, drag some brush over the hoofprints. We'll sweep the trail clean."

"You two do that, Harper," said Edsel, without having to give it any thought. "Then sit still here until we get all this settled." He raised a finger for emphasis. "*Do not* ride into town again. You're lucky you made it out last time."

"You've got it, Papa Edsel," said Harper.

The men moved away toward their gear and horses; Edsel walked briskly to the porch and bounded up the short steps. Rudabaugh stood beside the swing, waiting for him.

"All right, Silas, give it to me," Edsel said in an impatient tone. "Who's the dove and what were you two doing out on the desert?"

"Her name is Mae Rose, I learned from the gals upstairs. I caught her with a lot of gold coins on her. I figured she stole the money from the brothel. We got in a fight over it."

"Hold it," said Edsel. "How much time were you spending with the *gals upstairs*?"

"Not a lot," said Rudabaugh. Hoping to edge away from the subject, he said, "I was mostly too busy keeping an eye on the bartenders, making sure they don't rob you blind."

"Rob me blind, Phil and Ellis Jones?" said Edsel. "Listen to me, you damn washed-out stock detective. The Joneses are two of the most trusted bartenders this side of Salt Lake City. They're instructed to keep tabs on every dollar that comes in or goes out of the Silver Palace. They can tell me how many times you raised a glass to your lips, how many times you went up those stairs, and with whom." Cigar in hand, he poked his finger into Rudabaugh's chest. Ashes fell to the toes of the worried gunman's boots.

"I—I figured drinks were on the house, me being the manager so to speak," Rudabaugh said, not about to mention all the times he'd spent with the doves.

"Manager . . . so to speak?" said Edsel, squinting, having a hard time even comprehending such a ridiculous notion. "I never said the word *manager*. You must have gotten that in your head all on your own. I told you to keep an eye on the place—meant, *don't let the crowd get too rowdy*." He paused and stared hard at Rudabaugh. "How bad is it going to look when the Jones brothers show me your saloon tab?" he asked in a low, menacing tone.

"Well . . ." Rudabaugh swallowed a knot in his throat. "Had I realized you didn't mean I was the manager, so to speak, I would have done different—"

"Wait," said Edsel, holding up a hand, stopping him. "Don't tell me now. I've got too much on my mind. Get yourself cleaned up." He jerked his head toward the weathered house. "I want to get to town and hear from the Joneses."

As Rudabaugh walked inside, Charlie Knapp led his and Edsel's horses around from a rope corral.

"Charlie, didn't you tell me you know of a game path down from here without using the main trail?" he asked.

"Yep, I do," Knapp said. "It's steep and skittish." He studied Edsel's face as he spoke. "But it'll get us down to the sand flats without anybody knowing we were here."

"Good work, Charlie," Edsel said. "That's just the way I want it." He puffed on his cigar and blew out a stream of smoke. "You know, I'm mulling it over," he added with a reflective expression. "I'm glad Silas and the others didn't kill Sheppard Stone after all. I'm thinking now that that's something I want to carry out on my own, you know . . . just to watch him die?" He gave a cruel, dark grin and chuckled under his breath. "They say no payback ever feels as good as one you make for yourself."

"I hear you, Edsel," Knapp said boldly. "But you might want me around when you do it, just in case." He patted the big Colt holstered on his hip.

"Yes, of course, Charlie," Edsel said. "I believe that goes without saying." He lifted two glasses from the table beside the swing, handed one to Knapp and filled them both from a bottle of bourbon. "To killing Sheppard Stone," he said, the two lifting their glasses in a toast.

The Ranger and Sheriff Stone had followed the two sets of tracks to the fork in the trail. They stopped when they saw that the set of hooves wearing Star Brand shoes turned away to the right in the direction of Secondary. The other hoofprints seemed to vanish altogether.

"She was headed for Secondary," Stone said as the two stepped down from their saddles to rest their horses. "Rudabaugh must've gotten that out of her."

Sam nodded, looking all around, and at the clear, clean trail ahead of them up the hillside.

"He must've figured it out about the raised star," he said quietly. "Wonder if he thought we wouldn't notice the other horse disappeared?" He stooped and examined the star hoofprints closer, laying his fingertips in the indentation as if measuring their depth. Then he followed the tracks with his eyes as they led away to the right of the fork. "There's no rider on this horse," he said almost to himself.

"What? Let me see," said Stone, stooping down beside him as Sam raised his fingertips from the hoofprint. "You've got a tracker's eye, Ranger," Stone said.

Sam didn't appear to hear him as he stood up and walked a few steps along the upward trail. He stopped and looked down at the clear, undisturbed dirt.

Stone caught up and stood beside him.

"Nice try," Sam murmured toward the distant hilltops above them.

"You figure he swept this trail?" Stone said, looking up the rock trail with him.

"Not a doubt in my mind, somebody did," the Ranger said. He turned and walked back to the horses, reconstructing the event as Stone walked alongside him. "I'm speculating there's a place up there somebody doesn't want to be found. The rental horse was sent on its way down the trail toward Secondary to throw off anybody following that raised star on its shoes."

"Yeah, I agree," Stone said.

"I'm figuring the rental horse won't go far on its own," Sam said, the two of them stepping back up into their saddles. "It's used to riding with other horses. Let's follow its trail a little ways just in case we're being watched from up there. We'll find a path somewhere and cut back farther up."

"Sounds right to me," Stone said.

The two turned their horses to the right in the direction of Secondary. Yet they had only ridden a mile or less when they spotted the gray rental horse plodding toward them at a slow walk, its head lowered.

"Good call, Ranger," Stone said. He looked Sam up and down and said, "You're not starting to see things before they happen, are you?"

Sam just looked at him.

Stone gave a dark little chuckle as the gray drew nearer. When it was close enough, he reached out and picked its reins up from where they had been wrapped loosely around its saddle horn. With the gray in tow, the two lawmen veered off the trail and rode along the lower scrub and sand sloops until they found a slim rocky path leading back up to a higher point along the main trail.

Riding upward, they passed two dust-covered bundles of dry brush that had been cast aside. They saw two sets of hoofprints appear as if out of nowhere and lead upward toward the two large rocks towering above the hill trails.

"We're getting onto something up there," Sam said sidelong to the sheriff, without taking his eyes off the towering rocks. "Do you want the trail or the rocks?"

Leading the gray, Stone said, "You go ahead. I'll keep this trail covered."

Atop one of the tall rocks above the trail, Lon Bartow lay prone, looking down at Sheriff Stone through a telescope as the lawman rode into sight, leading the rental horse beside him. On the other side of the rock behind him, Harper Centrila sat reloading his rifle, having just given it a good cleaning.

"Here comes Sheriff Sheppard Stone himself," Bartow said over his shoulder. "Looks like he didn't fall for our ruse with the rental horse."

Harper finished loading the rifle quickly and hurried forward in a low crouch.

"Damn it," he said, "after all the work we did sweeping this trail?" He looked back and forth, then down at Stone with his naked eyes. The sheriff looked small and unclear from such a distance. "I don't want to let him up into our hideout."

"He's going to be a long, hard shot from up here," Bartow said in a cautioning tone. "We only get one shot. If we miss he can clear out—come back to call on us any time he pleases." With that said, he laid down his telescope down and started to pick up his rifle lying beside him.

"Huh-uh, hold up, Lon," Harper said, stopping him. "Keep him in your lens. I'll go down close and make that one shot count. I've been wanting to kill this knothead for a long time for all the trouble he's caused me."

"You sure about this?" Bartow asked. "Don't get in range of his Colt. He knows how to make it bite."

"I've got him, Lon," said Harper. "Follow him up in your lens, then come on down if you want to see it up close."

"Don't mind if I do," Bartow said, raising his telescope back up to his eye, adjusting it onto the sheriff. "I always enjoy watching good rifle work."

"Suit yourself," Harper said. He moved backward across the top of the rock and slid down ten feet to where the rock stood stuck deep into the hillside. Then he moved quickly and quietly down through a maze of rock and brush. After twenty minutes of working his way downward, he reached a point where he could see Stone at a distance of three hundred yards. He dropped down behind a rock and lay waiting, watching, clean rifle in hand.

But when Stone left his sight at a wide turn in the trail and didn't come back out, he looked all around. On the rocky hillside behind him he looked up as a small rock broke loose and bounced down a few yards and stopped.

"Over here, Lon," he said, keeping his voice down. "Get on down here. When he gets back in sight, we'll both shoot him at once."

"Not today," said a voice behind him. Harper jerked his head around quickly and saw the Ranger standing atop a rock less than thirty feet away, his big Colt raised, cocked and pointed at him.

"Well . . . Ranger," Harper said, trying to gain his composure, hoping to stall for a second, then swing his rifle into play. "I have to say, I'm surprised to see—"

The loud blast of the Ranger's Colt cut him short. The bullet hammered him high in the right side of his chest and sent him rolling and bouncing backward down the rocky hillside, almost into Sheriff Stone's arms. Stone stepped out, rifle in hand, from behind a rock as Sam's single shot resounded. He looked down at Harper lying sprawled on the dusty trail. Then he looked up at the Ranger and nodded.

"Anybody else up there?" he asked the Ranger.

"Lonnie Bartow, another jailbreaker," Sam said,

picking his footing, stepping down among the rocks. "He's cuffed around a scrub pine—it'll be a while before he knows it, though."

They stood looking down at Harper, who lay writhing and moaning in the dirt.

"I'm riding on up there," Stone said, staring up the trail, "see if Mae Rose is there." He pitched a pair of cuffs to the Ranger and started walking toward his horse and gray that he'd hidden out of sight.

"She's . . . not up there," Harper said to the Ranger when the sheriff was out of sight.

"Where is she, then?" Sam asked offhandedly, not making it sound too important. He bent over Harper and drew his wrists together and cuffed him.

"She's with . . . Papa Edsel," he said. "Her and Rudabaugh tried to kill each other. She took a bullet . . . put three in him."

"Good for her. How's she doing?" Sam asked.

"She's okay," said Harper. "She won't be working her trade for a few days."

"Where are they headed?" Sam asked.

"You figure it out," Harper said in defiance.

"I will, once we get you behind bars," Sam said.

"You might think I'm done," Harper said. "But I'm not. . . . Ranger, you'll see." His voice was strong but pain-filled. "One gunshot don't slow me down."

"Keep talking, Harper," Sam said. "I'll shoot you again. Those dead wagon guards were friends of mine."

When he'd dragged Harper over beside the trail, he heard Stone's horse coming back down toward them at a gallop. Seeing the look on the sheriff's face as he slid his horse to a halt, Sam stepped in and kept him from going straight to where Harper sat in the dirt.

"Out of my way, Ranger. Mae Rose is not up there. I'm going to start chopping pieces off him till he tells me where she is—"

"Easy, Stone," Sam cautioned him, keeping his voice lowered so Harper wouldn't hear them. "She's with his pa and his men. He just told me everything."

"He did?" Stone gave him a puzzled look. "Then he doesn't know Mae Rose and I are . . . ?" He let his words trail.

"No, he doesn't know it," Sam said. "And let's hope Edsel Centrila doesn't find out. He'll use her to get Harper set free."

"I *will* set him free before I'll let something happen to Mae Rose," Stone said. "I'll let you know that straight up, Ranger."

Sam nodded. He studied the hard resolve in the sheriff's face as if considering his reply.

"I understand," he said finally.

"What kind of shape is she in?" Stone asked.

"Harper told me she's got a bullet wound, but nothing too serious," Sam said. "Let's keep everything to ourselves and get on to town. I've got a feeling that's where they've taken her."

Chapter 20

The day-drinking crowd had fallen off a little at the Silver Palace until shopkeepers, tradesmen and businessmen caught sight of Edsel Centrila and his band of gunmen riding into town. Riding between Edsel and Charlie Knapp, Mae Rose Rossi sat atop Lyle Cady's horse. Behind the rest of the men the Cady brothers sat double on Ignacio's horse. Rudabaugh and Donald Ferry rode side by side, but had nothing to say to each other. Behind them rode Bob Remick and his cousin, Trent Baye, the two riflemen who'd guarded the hideout from the towering rocks above the trail.

At the hitch rail out in front of the saloon, Edsel stepped down and handed his reins to Ellis Jones, who'd seen them coming and rushed out onto the boardwalk to greet the new owner.

"Welcome to *your* Silver Palace, Mr. Centrila," the younger of the Jones brothers called out, spreading his arms wide. His black hair had been well oiled and had a severe part down the center of his head. "And welcome one and all!" he said to the others, as well as to the townsmen who now came to join the crowd. He turned his arms as if to sweep the men inside. "Is there anything I can do for you, sir?" he asked.

Edsel jerked his head toward Charlie Knapp and Mae Rose as Knapp helped her down from the saddle.

"Yeah, help my man get this woman inside," he said. Then he asked, "She is one of ours, isn't she?"

"Yes, she is indeed, Mr. Centrila," Ellis said, already stepping over to assist Knapp with the woman. Mae Rose tried to brush them both away. But Ellis stepped in close and supported her arm and said close to her ear, "What are you doing leaving without even telling anybody?"

Mae Rose just stared at him.

Ellis noted the bandaging on her shoulder.

"What's happened to you anyway?" he asked. "You're a mess. Look at you!"

Mae Rose didn't answer. She looked past him in the direction of the sheriff's office.

"Do you know where her room is?" Edsel asked the young bartender.

"Yes, I do," Ellis said, he and Knapp both supporting her, one at each arm.

"Take her up there," said Edsel. "Keep her there while I talk to your brother. I'll be on up." He gave a proud smile as he stretched his back and looked all around and said, "Now, then, let me take a look at my new saloon." He inspected the newly painted facade, the striking new signs hanging high above the doors.

While Ellis Jones and Charlie Knapp accompanied Mae Rose inside the saloon and up the stairs, the Cady brothers, along with Bob Remick and Trent Baye, stayed close around Edsel Centrila as he walked back and forth admiring his new business interest.

"What do you want me to do, boss?" Rudabaugh asked, standing off to the side.

The smile faded from Edsel's face. He walked briskly past Rudabaugh into the saloon.

"Follow me," he said gruffly.

Remick and Baye gave Rudabaugh a thin, smug grin.

"After you, Silas," said Remick. They allowed him in front of them as they followed their leader inside the Silver Palace. Instead of walking to the crowded bar where all eyes had turned toward him, Centrila lifted his hat in a salute and walked to the table at the side window.

"Everybody gets a drink on me, Phil," he called out to the bar where Phillip Jones stood busily filling glasses and beer mugs.

"Yes, sir, Mr. Centrila!" the bartender called out amid the cheers and applause of the drinkers.

On the stairs, Ellis Jones bounded down and hurried over to the window table. At the top of the stairs, Rita Spool and five other doves stood lined along the banister, poising seductively for the new owner and the drinkers at the bar. Rudabaugh looked down as if trying not to be seen.

"What may I serve you, Mr. Centrila?" Ellis asked, his hands folded at his abdomen. Black garters rounded his white shirtsleeves at the elbows. Sweat made the shirt cling to his chest, his shoulders and back.

"Go take over the bar for Phil," Centrila said, taking quick charge of the place. "Tell Phil to bring his pocket ledger over here—have him bring a couple bottles of rye and some glasses."

"Yes, sir," said Ellis, "right away." He turned sharply on his heel and hurried over behind the bar.

The gunmen against the wall on either side of the window looked at Rudabaugh, who stood on the opposite side of the table from Centrila. Rudabaugh swallowed a tight knot in his throat and stood in silence; Edsel sat sprawled, cigar in hand, staring intently at him.

In only a moment, Phil the bartender set a tray with two fresh bottles of rye and several clean shot glasses on it. He quickly opened the first bottle and filled glasses all around. Rough hands reached in and claimed the glasses and raised them. Centrila raised a glass of his own. Rudabaugh took a glass of rye but only held it to his chest.

Phil Jones stood back as the men took their drink.

"Now, then, Phil," said Edsel, "let's take a look at what kind of tab Silas here has run up for himself." He stared at Rudabaugh as he spoke.

"Here we are, sir," said Phil. He produced a small leather-bound pad from his hip pocket and flipped it open and laid it in front of Edsel Centrila. The new owner studied the page regarding the brothel and studied the figures for a moment. Satisfied, he turned to a page and half of amounts listed under Rudabaugh's name. He let out a low whistle. The gunmen gave each other a look and masked their elation. Rudabaugh slumped and looked worried.

"Silas . . . Silas," Centrila shook his head. "You've managed to run up a drinking and sporting tab of seven hundred and forty-seven dollars—most of it on *sporting*," he added, giving a nod toward the women lined along the upstairs banister. "I'm amazed you're able to walk upright."

The men stifled a dark laugh.

"Holy Joseph," Rudabaugh whispered. He swallowed hard again; he raised his glass to his lips and drained it. When he set it down he said, "Edsel, I'm going to pay you. I swear I am."

"Of course you are," Centrila said. He closed the pocket ledger and slid it to Phillip Jones. Then he stood and walked across the saloon and started up the stairs. He summoned Ellis Jones from behind the bar to join him. Ellis and the gunmen hurried to catch up to him. They followed him up the stairs and down the long hallway to where Charlie Knapp motioned them to Mae Rose's room. Rudabaugh kept his face down as the doves stared coldly at him.

"You're going to be working for me the next three years for *free*, Silas," Centrila said over his shoulder. The men held their laughter to themselves.

Mae Rose sat slumped on a wooden straight-back chair in the middle of the floor. Charlie Knapp stood beside her, his rifle held loosely across his chest. As Edsel and the men walked in and Lyle Cady closed the door behind them, Knapp reached over with his rifle butt and lifted Mae Rose's lowered face.

"Look at Mr. Centrila when he talks to you," Knapp said harshly.

Mae Rose stared up at Edsel from the wooden edge of the rifle butt. Knapp took the butt away when Centrila pitched the pouch of gold coins onto her lap. Ellis Jones stood beside Edsel, unsure of what was going on.

"I see there's no money missing from the brothel," Edsel said to Mae Rose. "Whose money is this?"

Centrila studied her eyes for a moment.

"What were you doing out there with Silas Rudabaugh?" he asked. He gave Rudabaugh a dark look. Rudabaugh avoided his eyes.

"I was *with him* out there because he forced me to leave here with him," Mae Rose said. "I was headed for Secondary. He made me go with him—stole my money." She turned a cold stare to Rudabaugh. "I knew he was going to try to kill me. I tried to get away. He shot me and I hit my head on a rock. I woke up and found that Harper and Lon Bartow came along. I figure they saved my life."

Centrila continued staring at her, unable to find any holes in her story.

"And you had nothing to do with Rudabaugh before that?" he asked.

"No, never," said Mae Rose. "I'm only sorry I didn't blow his brains out instead of shooting his ear off."

Edsel looked at Rudabaugh with contempt and nodded toward the door.

"Get out of here, Silas," he growled over the cigar in his teeth. "Go somewhere and figure out how you're ever going to pay my money back."

Rudabaugh left the room with his head lowered. Lyle Cady opened the door and closed it behind him.

Centrila looked back at Mae Rose.

"Now, then, what about the money?" he said. He leaned in close and stared her squarely in the eyes.

"It's mine," Mae Rose insisted. "I squirreled it away a little at a time—"

"Huh-uh," said Edsel, cutting her off. "You didn't squirrel that much money away—unless you were bedding customers on the sly and not turning in the money."

"No, I didn't do that," Mae Rose said. "I've always been straight with this brothel. Ask the last owner. That money belongs to me, nobody else."

Edsel gave Ellis Jones a questioning sidelong look.

"Phil has had me watching this upstairs like a hawk, Mr. Centrila," Ellis said. "I've never seen anything untoward out of Mae Rose. She handles her share of business and keeps to herself. Some of the miners call her *the lady*, she's so straight up." He paused, then said, "I expect she reminds them of their gal back home."

"*The lady*, huh . . . ?" Edsel looked all around the room.

"I'm not lying to you," Mae Rose said, staring squarely at Centrila. "That money is mine."

"Of course you're lying to me, *lady*," Centrila said matter-of-factly. "All doves lie. . . ." He let his words trail as he continued looking around the room.

He singled out a large oak wardrobe in a corner and stepped over to it. He pulled both doors open and looked inside. A few dresses she'd left behind hung there. On a shelf he picked up an almost empty bag of

Blue Cut chopped tobacco, looked at it and turned with it in his hand. On a bedside table the wadded-up wax paper lining of a cough drop carton caught his eye. He picked it up, unfolded it and sniffed it.

"Um, cherry flavored," he said with a slight grin. "Have a cough, do you, *lady*?" he said, as if concerned.

"I—I did have," Mae Rose said. "I'm over it now."

"Might have been brought on from your smoke fixings," he said flatly. "Blue Cut's about as strong as smoking hemp rope." He pitched the tobacco bag onto her lap and picked up the pouch of coins. He stepped back. As he did he spotted another wadded-up wax paper lining lying just under the edge of her bed. "Get that, Ellis, if you please," he said.

Ellis picked up the wax paper and laid it in Centrila's outstretched hand.

"My, my, looks like the maid missed this," he said with a slight grin. He unwadded the lining and sniffed it. "I'm thinking you're a cherry-flavor gal."

Mae Rose sat staring, turning rigid in the chair, sensing things could turn ugly any moment. Beside Centrila, Ellis nervously wiped his fingertips on his trousers, sensing the same thing, gauging the darkening look on his boss' face.

"You've been in Big Silver awhile, bartender," he said to Ellis without taking his menacing stare from Mae Rose. "Who sucks cherry cough drops and smokes Blue Cut tobacco?"

"Well, now . . . ," said the young bartender. For Mae Rose's sake, Ellis tried to stall. He cleared his throat.

"Before you answer me, young man," Centrila said

to Ellis, still staring at Mae Rose, "remind yourself there's a good possibility that I might *already know*."

"Yes, sir, I understand," said Ellis. His jaw tightened with the realization of what he had to do. "The truth is, Sheriff Stone is the only man I can think of." He added quickly, "But I have to say I've never seen him come up here—"

"Oh, he's been up here, bartender," the saloon owner said, cutting him off.

"Mr. Centrila, I *do* want to say that this woman has never been a problem—no dope of any kind, only drinks a little, enough to keep—"

"That'll be all for now, Ellis," Centrila said, still staring straight ahead at Mae Rose. "Get on downstairs— take those doves with you. Give them a drink on me. Tell the piano player I want to hear him hammering that ivory."

"Yes, sir, Mr. Centrila," said Ellis, backing away.

"You men go down too. Keep those doves entertained for a while. Charlie and I are going to have a talk with *the lady*."

As the men filed out behind the bartender, Lyle Cady glanced at Knapp and saw him lean his rifle against his leg and pull on a tight leather trail glove. Knapp grinned to himself a little as he opened and closed his gloved fist.

Outside in the hall, Lyle closed the door and whispered to his brother, "I would not want to be standing in that woman's shoes today, *huh-uh*," he said.

Ignacio gave his brother a curious look.

"Why do you want to wear her shoes anyway?" he said.

"Whoa, Iggy! I *don't mean* I want to wear her shoes," said Lyle. "It's just a figure of speech."

Ignacio shook his head and walked away.

"It worries me the way you talk sometimes, Lyle," he said over his shoulder.

Chapter 21

In the saloon Lyle and Ignacio Cady sat at the window table sipping shots of rye and drawing swigs of frothy beer from tall mugs. The other gunmen, excluding Silas Rudabaugh, lounged around the table with the Cadys. Some of them sat with brothel doves perched on their laps like exotic birds. The piano player pounded on the keys like a man driving nails with his fingertips. Gaming wheels clicked and turned at green-felted tables; a roulette wheel chattered and spun amid the din of the day-drinking crowd.

Around the table, eyes of gunmen and doves alike turned toward the upstairs hallway, but only for a quick glance, then they moved away.

Silas Rudabaugh had left the saloon and prowled the back alleys in the afternoon heat like some whipped dog. His unbridled indulgence of drinking and sleeping with brothel women had plunged him over seven hundred dollars in debt to Edsel Centrila. Clearly he had to pay his tab at the Silver Palace. Just as important, he needed to redeem himself in his employer's eyes.

As he leaned against a pole considering his situation, touching his bloody bandages, especially the one covering his half-severed ear, he peered down the far end of the alley. He saw the Ranger and Sheriff Stone leading Harper Centrila and Lon Bartow to the rear door of the jail.

Holy—!

He straightened sharply, watching them step down from their horses. He batted his eyes in a double take and stepped back quickly into the shadows to keep from being seen.

All right, here it is! he told himself, settling down, ready to seize this opportunity that had fallen into his lap. He drew his revolver from his holster, checked it and kept it in hand. He wished he'd brought his rifle, but this would have to do. He just needed to get a little closer.

Raising his revolver at elbow level, cocking it, he moved along the alleyway, pressed against the back of buildings like some stalking predator of the wilds. At fifteen yards he stopped and watched the sheriff and the Ranger hitch their horses, the horses of the two prisoners and the gray rental horse to a rail. He saw the lawmen motion for Harper and Bartow to step down from their saddles. He wanted to get closer, but this was the best he could do.

He stood tensed, ready, watching as Harper and Bartow started toward the door, the Ranger and Stone behind them, in the open.

Now! he told himself. He stepped out away from the building behind him and took quick aim, seeing Sheriff Stone's back in his pistol sights.

"Hey! The hell are you doing?" a drunken voice shouted from a loose stack of firewood and debris piled against the building behind him. Rudabaugh swung toward the sound of the voice, catching a glimpse of the Ranger and the sheriff turning toward it as well.

Damn it!

A ragged drunken derelict staggered out of the shadows and pawed at his face with filthy hands. Before Rudabaugh could get a shot off, a grimy palm shoved the gun barrel away so hard that Rudabaugh lost his grip. The revolver fell to the dirt.

Damn it to hell! As Rudabaugh bent and tried to grab the gun, the derelict pawed at his back, kicked at him, fell against him. Rudabaugh struggled to keep from going down beneath the drunken man's weight.

"It's Rudabaugh!" Stone said. His Colt streaked up from its holster. But he held his shot, seeing the derelict grappling half atop the bowed gunman.

Rudabaugh saw the sheriff's raised Colt. He saw the Ranger raise his rifle. Knowing his plan had gone awry, he managed to fling the drunkard from his back, turn in a crouch and run stumbling away down the alley.

"Wait. Don't shoot," Sam said sidelong to the sheriff. "Let him go."

"I wasn't going to shoot," said Stone, "unless he got that smoker up and shot at us first. I want to hear what he's done with Mae Rose." He relaxed his big Colt and lowered it. The two stood watching as the derelict stood with his feet spread, weaving unsteadily over the gun on the ground. He stared down at the big revolver wide-eyed as if it had fallen from the sky.

"Leave it be, Darby," Stone called out to the ragged, filthy drunkard.

"Hey, I don't want it, Sheriff," the man called back to him with a loose drunken shrug. "Did I save your life, or what?" The man bent to reach for the gun.

Sam moved in quick, picked up the revolver and stepped back. "You *might have* saved our lives," he said. "We're obliged."

"Think nothing of it," the man said, still weaving in place. He took his hand from inside his trousers and fumbled with the fly buttons again. "Remember when you and me got drunk, Sheriff?" he said. "You told me I could turn into a wolf—tried and tried. Far as I ever got was a coyote."

"Is that a fact?" Stone said, looking a little embarrassed.

Watching from the rear door of the jail, Harper shook his head and said to the Ranger, "If you're smart, you'll turn us loose before Papa Edsel finds out we're here."

Sam just stared at him. Up the alley Stone helped the drunkard back to the woodpile where he'd been sitting.

"Ranger, this never had anything to do with you. It's all between Stone and my pa," Harper continued. "You need to get out of it while you can. Ain't that right, Lon?" he said over his shoulder.

"You're *right*, that's right," Bartow said. A welt from the Ranger's rifle butt stood out on the side of his head.

"Save yourself, Ranger," said Harper. "No jury will convict me for killing those jail wagon guards." He gave a shrug. "I was in the wagon cuffed, unarmed."

"Save your breath," Sam said. "It's not my job to say who hangs. My job ends at the jailhouse door." He stepped back as Stone walked up holding the key to the rear door.

"Still running their mouths, huh?" Stone said. He unlocked the rear door and swung it open for them.

Sam followed the two prisoners inside.

At the cell door, he and the prisoners stopped and waited while Stone unlocked the barred cell door and swung it open.

"Welcome home," he said as the two walked into the cell and turned to have their cuffs unlocked.

"Okay," Harper said, letting out a breath, "what's it going to take?" He looked all around at the iron bars, the stone and adobe walls, a rear window—now repaired—where Boomer Phipps had ripped the bars away, iron frame and all. "I learned from Papa Edsel that every lawman has his price." He gave a sly little grin. "So, tell me yours—let's get this thing settled."

Stone and the Ranger stepped back out of the cell without answering. Stone closed the barred door and motioned the two closer so he could reach through to take off their cuffs.

"Hey, don't be like this," Harper said, stepping over to the bars. "This can't be all about you and Papa Edsel taking revenge on each other. This is crazy. Right, Lon? What's it going to take for both of you to get things settled between you?"

"Yep, it's crazy," Bartow said. "Paybacks are always crazy. Anybody thinks payback ever fixed anything is wrong as a—"

"Shut up, Lon. I'm talking here," Harper snapped at him, cutting him off.

"Listen to me, Harper," Stone said, lifting the cuffs through the bars. "Your pa did you no good raising you to think all lawmen can be bought. I'm one who can't. Here's another one." He nodded at the Ranger. "Every move your pa has made trying to fix things for you has only led you one step closer to hanging. Now you're just about there. The best thing you can do is sit down and keep your mouth shut. You'll go to Yuma this time. Whatever your fate is will be there waiting for you."

"You don't know Papa Edsel," Harper said. "It's not likely he'll stand still for any of this."

"Then he'll likely get you killed before you leave here," Stone said.

"*Ha!* Now you're talking out of your head, Sheriff." Harper sneered. "I heard you do that a lot, when you're not turning into a wolf." He grinned smugly. "When you're lying with your guts shot out, don't say I didn't warn you."

Sam expected Stone to explode at the gunman's remarks. He started to step forward in case he needed to keep the sheriff from slinging open the cell door and going inside. To his surprise, Stone stayed calm, perhaps even calmed down more. Sam watched him step back, pull a cough drop from his shirt pocket and put it in his mouth. He looked at Sam as he stepped over to the woodstove.

"Nothing settles the wolf in me like a good cup of coffee, Ranger," he said. He gave a slight grin. "Think we ought to boil us a pot before the storm hits?"

Sam only nodded, glad to see Stone turning steadier, calmer, not allowing himself to be shaken by Harper Centrila's threat or insults.

Before the storm hits . . . ?

Stone thrived on this sort of thing, Sam reminded himself. That was good to know.

With his holster empty, Rudabaugh rushed into the Silver Palace, sped across the floor and bounded up the stairs. Seeing him, Bob Remick and Trent Baye sprang to their feet, dropped two doves from their laps and gave chase. Ferry and the Cady brothers ran right behind them. Halfway up the stairs, Bob Remick raised his Colt out at arm's length and tried to take aim, but Rudabaugh kept running. Hearing the boots pounding along behind him, he beat his fists against the locked door.

"Knapp, Edsel! Let me in! The sheriff's got Harper and Lon Bartow!"

"What?" Edsel shouted on the other side of the door. As the men closed in behind Rudabaugh, a latch dropped on the other side of the big door. Knapp swung it open. "What the hell are you saying, Silas?" he shouted as Rudabaugh hurried inside. The men slid to a halt behind him. Edsel hurried over and looked Rudabaugh up and down quickly, seeing the empty holster. Mae Rose sat slumped in the wooden chair, her face lowered. Blood dripped from her face onto her lap and the floor surrounding the chair.

"It's the truth, Edsel!" said Rudabaugh, out of

breath. "I just saw Stone and the Ranger taking them into the jail through the back door.

"Why didn't you stop them, fool? Where's your gun?" Edsel demanded.

"I *tried* to stop them," Rudabaugh lied. "They had a lookout man hidden in the alley. He jumped me. I barely got away! I lost my gun."

"A lookout man . . . ?" Edsel eyed him skeptically. "You lost your gun?"

"I swear it's true, Edsel," Rudabaugh said.

The gunmen hurried into the room and gathered around Edsel and Rudabaugh. Knapp peeled a blood-smeared glove from his right hand and shoved it behind his gun belt. Seeing the men wince at the sight of Mae Rose, Edsel stepped into their line of vision and blocked her from view.

"Get her out of sight, Charlie," he said to Knapp. He looked back at Rudabaugh as Knapp dragged the beaten woman, chair and all, into a small adjoining room. "How the hell could they have taken Harper and Bartow without a fight?" he said.

"There must've been one," said Rudabaugh. "Harper's got a bandage on his shoulder. Bartow's sporting a welt the size of a goose egg on his head!"

"Damn it!" Edsel slammed a thick fist onto his palm. "I never should have left Harper there."

"What do you want me to do, boss?" said Knapp, walking back in from the other room. He picked his rifle up from against the wall and levered a round into the chamber.

"We're busting Harper out of there," Edsel said. "He's going free if I have to kill every lousy law dog between here and West Texas!" He looked at the men. "Come dark I want the Ranger and Stone both dead! I'm through fooling around here."

Looking around at the men, he noted some were only wearing revolvers. He looked out the window at the distant afternoon sky. "Get rifled up, all of you, and get back here, pronto!" he barked. "Cady brothers," he said to Lyle and Iggy, "go downstairs, bring one of the doves up here. Make sure she gets Mae Rose cleaned up and revived—get this mess wiped up too." He gestured at the blood on the wooden floor planks.

"Let's go, Iggy," Lyle said. The two left the room and bounded down the stairs side by side, ahead of the other three gunmen.

Knapp gave his boss a questioning look as the sound of boots rumbled on the stairs.

"Clean her up?" he said. "Edsel, the woman's beat all to hell. We've got all we're going to get out of her. She admitted she's Sheriff Stone's gal—"

"That's right," Edsel said sharply. "She's Stone's gal. That makes her our ace in the hole." He turned and walked to the window so he could look out in the direction of the sheriff's office.

At the bar, Phil and Ellis Jones and the drinking crowd looked up at the sound of the Cadys and the other three gunmen racing down the stairs. The piano stopped playing.

"Nothing to get excited about, folks," Lyle Cady called out to the drinkers. He and Ignacio grabbed Rita

Spool by her arms and yanked her along with them back up the stairs. The other doves milled and scowled and stared up angrily at the two gunmen.

"I don't know what's going on up there," one said, her hand on her hip.

"I don't know either," another one replied, "but if it's a party starting up, Rita ought to count us all in on it."

Chapter 22

The Ranger bided his time, all the while keeping an eye on the Silver Palace through the gun port of a wooden shutter now closed, covering the broken front window of the sheriff's office. At one point he gripped the iron shutter hinge that stood sunken deep into the thick wooden window frame. He tried shaking the immovable hinge as if testing its strength.

"Getting a little edgy, Ranger?" Stone asked, watching him.

"What? Oh," Sam said, turning loose of the iron hinge, "maybe so."

When he and Stone had finished their coffee and cleaned and loaded their rifles and sidearms, Stone walked to the window himself and looked back and forth along the street, bright from the afternoon sunlight. The piano in the saloon had been silent for the past hour. The day drinkers had left two and three at a time. Few evening drinkers came to replace them. In the cell behind them Harper and Lon Bartow lay dozing on cots.

"It'll be dark soon enough," Stone said over his shoulder. "I'm not waiting any longer—"

Turning around as he spoke, he stopped suddenly, finding himself staring into the barrel of his own Colt, the Ranger holding it aimed at his face. In reflex his hand slapped against his empty holster. Then he raised both hands chest high.

"What's this, Ranger?" he said.

A handcuff slapped shut around his wrist. The Ranger shoved his wrist back to the window and snapped the other cuff around the iron hinge, ratcheting it down tight.

"Sorry, Sheriff," he said. "This is *me* making you listen to reason."

"Listen to *reason*?" said Stone. "I *am* listening to reason!" He jerked against the handcuff. "Turn me loose. I've got to get Mae Rose loose from Centrila and his cutthroats! What the hell has come over you?"

"You said yourself, Sheriff," Sam replied, "that if Edsel wanted to trade Mae Rose for Harper you would do it. I can't allow that."

"That was just me talking, Ranger!" said Stone. "There's no way I'd do it!"

"Too late, Stone," Sam said. "You'll say anything now to get me to take those cuffs off your wrist. I can deal with Centrila coolheaded. But you can't. You're too close to the woman to handle this the way it's got to be handled."

"So help me God, Ranger, if you get her killed," Stone said in a barely controlled rage.

"I won't get her killed, Stone," Sam said, "not if I play this out my own way. Centrila will never believe that you're willing to give up this vendetta between the two of you. He'll be watching every move you make, ready for you to try a double cross."

"You don't know him like I do, Ranger," Stone said. He tugged angrily on the shutter hinge. "Edsel is the king of the double cross. He'll chew you up and spit you out. Turn me loose! Dang it, Ranger!"

Sam pointed a finger close to Stone's face. "See? This is why I cuffed you. If the least little thing went wrong while we stood in front of Centrila and his men, you and he would both blow up and turn it into a blood-bath."

"You can't do this to me, Ranger!" Stone raged.

Sam looked at the sleeping prisoners, seeing that Stone's raised voice hadn't waked them. Then he walked around behind Stone's desk, sat down and slumped for a moment in the sheriff's chair, Stone's big Colt on his lap.

"I don't *like* doing it, Sheriff," he said, "but here's how it is." He laid Stone's gun on the desk and made sure Stone saw him lay the handcuff key beside it. "You cool yourself out some. When you figure out how to get yourself loose, your gun is here waiting for you. By then you'll know I'm right. You won't come barging in once this thing is in play."

"Wait, Ranger. Listen!" Stone said as Sam picked up his Winchester and walked to the door. "All right, I did mean what I said. I would trade Harper for Mae Rose." He was talking fast as Sam opened the door to leave.

"You know why? Because it's the right thing to do!" He saw the door closing behind the Ranger. "Make the trade, Ranger. For God's sakes, *make the trade!*"

Sam listened to the sheriff shout from inside the shuttered front window. But he refused to listen. He leaned against the door for a moment, then straightened and walked across the boardwalk, stepping down onto the street.

Here goes. . . .

He walked purposefully along the middle of the street, wanting to be clearly seen from the Silver Palace— from the upstairs window overlooking the street. On the balcony, Charlie Knapp caught sight of him as soon as he'd stepped away from the sheriff's office.

"Edsel," he said over his shoulder, "the Ranger's coming.

"What? The *Ranger?*" said Centrila. He stepped out onto the balcony beside Knapp and jerked his cigar from his mouth. "Can't he get it through his head this is *personal vengeance,* between Stone and me!"

Knapp gave him a dubious look.

"I don't know," he said wryly. "Him being a lawman, maybe he just figures jailbreak and killing the guards makes it his business?"

Centrila spun a half turn and stared at him.

"Are you being *funny* with me, Charlie?" he growled.

"No, sir, sorry, boss," Knapp said. He lowered his eyes. Behind him the other men stood inside the frontmost room they had taken over. Mae Rose lay on a bed; Rita Spool sat on the bed's edge, touching a wet cloth to her badly bruised and swollen face.

"These pigs didn't have to beat you this way, love," Rita whispered near her ear in her lingering Cockney accent.

"I—I told them everything . . . ," Mae Rose replied in a painful whisper, ". . . about . . . Shep and me."

Shep and me . . . ?

Rita considered her words.

"You and the sheriff?" she said, with surprise.

Mae Rose only nodded slightly.

"My, my. Then," Rita whispered, touching the cloth to Mae Rose's black-purple eyes, "the sheriff is not going to like this one bit."

Behind the two women, Edsel Centrila stepped forward and leaned in close over Rita's shoulder.

"How's our dear little dove doing here?" he asked, inspecting Mae Rose's battered face.

"She's been badly beaten, that's how," Rita said in a crisp tone. She gave Edsel a harsh glance. Behind Edsel, Knapp gave her a flat, menacing grin.

"You can cover most of this with powder and rouge," said Centrila.

"Rouge will only make it look worse," Rita said.

"Nonsense," said Centrila. "My late wife did it all the time."

Late wife . . .

"Did she *indeed*?" Rita said.

"Oh yeah, all the time," said Centrila. "Now you hop around here, prontolike, see what you can come up with." He looked all around. "I know you doves keep lots of stuff like that on hand." He leaned down to Mae Rose. "Honey, don't you worry about nothing here.

Rita will have you looking as sweet as a peach for that sheriff of yours."

"You're bloody *joking!*" Rita said, gesturing toward Mae Rose's swollen, battered face.

Edsel clamped a big hand down on Rita's shoulder and gave a quick hard squeeze.

Mae Rose managed to open her swollen eyes a little and turn them up to Charlie Knapp.

"He . . . was going to . . . slit my throat," she rasped.

"Now, now," Centrila cut in, "let's have none of that kind of unproductive talk." He gave a tight, thin smile. "Anyway, that was hours ago. We're all of the same accord now." He straightened and tugged at his vest and motioned Knapp aside, away from the bed and away from the gathered gunmen.

"I don't like seeing the Ranger come here instead of Stone," he said. "I want to trade this dove for my son, but we've got to get things off on the right foot. This Ranger can't handle me when it comes to negotiating. But I want to establish myself as being in charge from the get go."

Knapp nodded, looking his boss up and down.

"What do you want me to do?" he said.

"You and the men get down there before me," said Centrila, "meet him when he gets here. He's going to want to see me—but don't let him, not right off. Make him think this is more important to him than it is to me." He blew a thin stream of smoke to the ceiling. "That's called taking a winning position," he said with an air of superiority. "It works every time. Keep him waiting, keep turning him down. I'll be listening. At the right time I'll step in and take over. He won't know what hit him."

"You got it, boss," said Knapp, liking the way Centrila handled things.

The Ranger saw the gunmen file out of the Silver Palace onto the boardwalk. The six of them stood in a row facing him. At their center stood Charlie Knapp. Behind them the inside of the saloon looked deserted. The drinkers had seen enough to know that the trouble between Centrila and Sheriff Stone was at full boil. The Ranger walking down the middle of the street, Winchester in hand, only proved it.

"Top of the evening to you, Ranger," Knapp called out, both thumbs hooked behind his gun belt, a rifle hanging over his left forearm. He had planned to tell the Ranger to *stop right there, that's close enough.* But before he got the chance, Sam stopped twenty feet away, looked from one gunman's face to the next, then settled onto the leader's.

"I'm here to see Edsel Centrila," Sam said, no nonsense, no short talk.

"Just like that, huh?" said Knapp. He raised his right hand and snapped his fingers.

"Yes, just like that," Sam said firmly. He offered nothing more on the matter.

"You can't see him," Knapp said, putting him off. "In case you don't know it, Mr. Centrila is a busy man." He waited. Here it came. The Ranger would press, but he'd stall him some more. Knapp gave a thin smile, prepared for a drawn-out situation.

Sam nodded, looked around again.

"I understand," he said quietly. He turned around, started to walk away.

Knapp, taken aback by the Ranger's unexpected reaction, batted his eyes and collected himself quickly.

"Hold on, Ranger," he called out. "What is it you want to see him about? Maybe I can tell him and see what he says—"

"He knows we've got Harper in jail," Sam said, stopping, turning back toward him. He held the rifle in a pistol grip, cocked, ready, his finger on the trigger. "When I get back to the jail, Stone says he's going to shoot him and pitch him into the street," he added calmly. He turned again to walk away.

"*Whoa* there! Ranger Burrack!" Centrila shouted, springing from his listening spot inside the saloon doors. "What's this you're saying?" He skidded to a halt beside Knapp.

Sam stopped and turned back around.

"I left Stone handcuffed to the front window shutter," he said to Centrila. "When I get back I'm cutting him loose. Stone can do what suits him. I'm done with this."

"That's it?" Centrila said, looking stunned. "That's what you came to tell me?" As he spoke he gave Lyle Cady a nod toward the jail. Lyle ran to his horse, jumped atop it and raced off to see if the Ranger was lying.

"That's it," Sam said. Again he started to turn away; again Centrila stopped him.

Lyle Cady bounded across the boardwalk out in

front of the jail, leaped back atop the horse and came racing down the street in a cloud of rising dust.

"He's right, boss," Lyle said. "Stone's standing cuffed to a window shutter. I saw in through a gun port."

Centrila nodded and stared at Sam.

"What about the woman?" he said. "What about a trade? The woman for my son? We can work something out here. I know we can!"

Sam stared at him poker-faced.

"What woman?" he asked flatly.

Centrila stared at him.

"The sheriff's dove, Mae Rose," he said. "We've got her. Don't act like you didn't know."

"I know you've got her," Sam said. "But I didn't come here to trade. I'm here to enforce the law."

"Oh? Enforce the law how?" Centrila said. "By shooting Harper and throwing him into the street?"

"That's the sheriff's call," Sam said. "My job was to bring him to justice for breaking jail and killing the guards. That's done. I'm out of here. Stone will handle the rest of it. I came to tell you how things stand. Nothing else."

"You can't just pull out of this thing, Ranger," Centrila shouted. "Stone will kill my son, just to satisfy his own vengeance!"

"That is a possibility," Sam said. "Especially since you've got his woman."

Centrila spread his hands in a shrug of desperation.

"But I'm willing to trade the woman," he said. "You can have her safe and sound. I just want Harper . . . and

Lonnie Bartow too, of course," he added in after-thought. "Let's make a deal here."

Sam seemed to consider it. The gunmen stood silent, watching, waiting, all except for Bob Remick.

"*Ha!*" Remick scoffed, taking a step forward. "This is all one big bluff! Stone's not going to shoot Harper, and this Ranger ain't going to—"

Sam's rifle bucked and exploded in his hand. The shot hit Remick dead center, hurled him crashing backward through the large glass window of the Silver Palace. Remick landed inside, one boot resting on the window ledge. His boot rocked twice, then slumped onto its side.

The rest of the gunmen tensed, ready to start shooting. So did the Ranger, levering a fresh round into his smoking Winchester. But Centrila raised his hands to his men, stopping them.

"Everybody stand down!" he shouted. "Damn it, *stand down!*" he repeated, seeing Remick's cousin, Trent Baye, ready to leap forward with his rifle raised.

"Edsel, Bob Remick's my cousin," Baye said. "I can't let this go unavenged!"

"I said stand down!" Centrila shouted. He shoved Baye's rifle down at the ground. "Charlie! If he raises his gun, shoot him!" he demanded.

Sam stood with his rifle ready, cocked and poised to fire again. He looked from face to face as if asking who wanted the next round.

"There's no room for bluffing here," he said to everyone listening. "No bluffing, no payback games. I'm here for the law, nothing else."

Centrila turned away from the gunmen and stepped down onto the dirt street, closer to the Ranger.

"You were thinking about it, Ranger, I could tell," he said in a lowered voice, careful not to be heard by his gunmen. "Don't let that idiot spoil everything." He gestured toward Remick's body lying inside the window frame.

Sam took a deep breath and let it out slowly.

"Stone's dove is unharmed?" he asked, as if making up his mind.

"Yes, she's unharmed," Centrila lied. "Fresh as morning dew. You have my word on it."

"Get her," Sam said in a resolved tone. "Bring her to the jail. I want this thing over and done with."

Chapter 23

—————

Dozing in their cell, Lon Bartow and Harper Centrila had awakened moments earlier to the sound of Sheriff Stone shouting at the Ranger, who had just closed the door behind himself. The two prisoners looked at each, at the sheriff standing cuffed to the window shutter, then at the gun and cell key lying on the oak desk.

"You two stay right where you are," Stone said, seeing their intentions in their eyes.

"Yeah, sure, law dog," Harper said over his shoulder. He picked up his wooden-framed cot and slammed it to pieces on the hard plank floor. As it broke, Bartow stooped and stripped the woven rope from among the debris and stretched it out between his hands. Harper found a broken corner piece of the bed frame and tied the rope around it.

Stone looked all around quickly. Seeing nothing else to do, he cursed the Ranger under his breath and stretched out as far as his handcuff would allow. He hooked his boot toe around the short leg of the desk and tried to drag it to him, farther out of the prisoners' reach. But it didn't work. Seeing what he was doing, Harper hurriedly swung the rope out from between the bars and hooked the corner bed piece around the short leg closest to him.

The sheriff and the prisoners played tug-of-war with the desk. The desk bumped up and down from the two opposing forces pulling against it. With so much pressure between the sheriff's boot toe and the prisoner's taut rope, finally the leg broke on the prisoners' end and the desk slammed down six inches to the floor. The weight jarred the entire office; the big gun and the cell key slid off the desktop and bounced and landed less than three feet from the barred cell.

"Yee-hi!" Bartow shouted. He reached through the bars, grabbed the gun and handed it up to Harper.

Turned hefted the gun in his hand and gave Stone a menacing grin.

"Now it's *my* gun," he said calmly. "You stand there like a *good boy*. Keep nice and quiet."

Stone stood rigid, knowing what came next.

"Why?" he said. "What have I got to lose?"

On the cell floor, Bartow snatched the cell key in his fist and stood and held it up for the sheriff to see. He cackled with dark laughter and shuffled his boots on the floor in a strange little dance.

Harper took a deep breath, cocked the big Colt and held it out at arm's length through the bars, aimed at Stone.

"You've got a point there, Sheriff," he said. Bartow stood with his arm already stuck through the bars ready to stick the key into the cell lock. He stopped long enough to watch.

"Shoot him *square in the head*!" he said, a sharp gleam in his widened feral eyes.

"Adios, law dog," Harper said, holding tight aim, his left eye squeezed shut. He pulled the trigger; the hammer fell. Bartow flinched, but the gun only clicked in Harper's hand.

"The *hell . . . ?*" said Bartow.

Stone had tightened his chest for the oncoming blast. Now he released it. He stood staring.

"Damn misfire," Harper said. He looked at the gun, then recocked and reaimed. He pulled the trigger. Still the gun only clicked in his hand.

"Jesus, Harper!" said Bartow, still holding the key ready.

"Shut up, Lon. I've got it," said Harper. He shook the gun as if that might solve the problem. He recocked quickly and pulled the trigger again. "Damn it! *Damn it to hell!*" He tried twice more. Nothing! He slung the gun sideways in his hand and opened the gate, checking it. Bartow looked on intently.

"Son of a . . ." Harper's words trailed.

"Empty," Bartow said. He looked up from the gun and over at Stone. "*Empty . . . ?*" he repeated. "What kind of sheriff *are* you?" he said skeptically.

"Shut up, Lon! Get this door open," Harper ordered. "He'll have bullets in his desk." He and Sheriff Stone stared hard at each other. "You're still dead, law dog," Harper said. "You just don't know it yet."

Bartow stuck the key into the lock and twisted it. But it stopped short and refused to turn all the way.

"Come on, Lon!" said Harper, hurrying him.

"It's stuck!" said Bartow, getting nervous, tense. He twisted the key back and forth madly. Nothing! He jerked the key from the lock and inside the cell. He inspected it.

"Give it here, Lon! Damn it!" Harper raged. He stuck Stone's Colt into his waist and yanked the cell key from Bartow's hand. Bartow watched as he twisted the key wildly back and forth, getting nowhere. Stone watched too, something dawning on him as he did so. The Ranger's words came to mind.

"When you figure how to get yourself loose, your gun is here waiting for you. By then you'll know I'm right."

"Dang you, Ranger," he murmured to himself as the two prisoners dropped their arms to their sides and stood slumped, staring at him. He patted a hand on his shirt pocket and felt the metal object there. He fished his fingers down beside his half bag of tobacco and his near-empty cough drop paper.

The key. . . .

He almost felt like laughing, but it wasn't funny, he told himself. He pulled the handcuff key from his shirt pocket and turned to his fettered wrist. The prisoners watched, puzzled, silent. He felt his face redden; he felt like saying something, but there was no one to say it to. As he turned the small key and let the cuff drop from his wrist, he looked out the window's gun port and saw the Ranger walking back from the Silver Palace.

Harper and Bartow watched the sheriff rub his freed

wrist as he walked over to his badly tilted desk and
jerked a drawer open. He gave them a knowing look
and took out a box of bullets and set it down hard atop
the oak surface. In silence he turned and walked to the
cell. Without a word he looked at Harper and held out
his upturned palm.

Harper pulled the Colt up from his waist, reached
through the bars and laid it on Stone's hand. Behind
Stone a hard, jarring crash caused him to spin around
with the gun up even though it was empty. He saw his
desk leaning forward now, the leg on the other corner
having just broken off. He watched items slide off the
desktop and plop one after the other onto the floor.
The unopened box of bullets slid off into his chair.
Stone turned back to the cell and yanked the key from
the lock where Harper had left it. He looked it over,
recognizing it as the key to the barred door of the ill-
fated jail wagon.

"Figures," he said aloud to himself, pitching the key
over onto his desk chair with the box of bullets.

When the Ranger stepped inside the office, Stone had
just finished loading his big Colt. He stood leaning
back against the edge of the tilted desk, the gun still in
his hand. Sam slowed a step, his rifle in hand. He noted
the short broken desk legs on the floor, the wanted
posters, letters, other items.

"Are we all right?" he asked. He stepped on inside
and reached back and closed the door.

"I don't know how I fell for it." Stone chuffed and
shook his head. "Yeah, we're all right. I couldn't have

looked at Edsel Centrila without blowing his head off."
He paused, then said, "I heard a rifle shot?"

"Yes," Sam said. He picked up the box of bullets and
the key from the chair and slumped down into the
chair. "A gunman by the name of Bob Remick decided
to hurrah everything. I saw it as a good chance to whit-
tle the odds down some." He looked at the two prisoners seated on the remaining unbroken cot looking out
at them. Standing up, he nodded Stone toward the
shuttered front window. Stone straightened and followed him, closing the loading gate on his Colt and
holstering it.

"How does it stand with Mae Rose?" he asked. The
slightest tension in his lowered voice told the Ranger
the woman was his main concern, and rightly so.

"They're bringing her to us," Sam said in the same
lowered voice, rolling a glance out the gun port now
and then toward the Silver Palace.

"What? They're bringing her to *us*?" Stone said, surprise in his lowered voice.

"Yep," Sam said. "Should be here in just a few minutes. Soon as Edsel figures how he can get what he
wants and still manage to kill you." He pulled up a
fresh rifle round from his pocket and shoved it into the
Winchester, replacing the one he'd used on Remick.

"So *you did* make a trade with him?" Stone asked
again.

"Not exactly," Sam said. He switched the subject. "I
had to do what I did to you, the handcuffs . . . ," he
said. "Edsel would never have dealt with you."

"I know," Stone said, "I saw Lyle Cady ride up and

check on me. Anyway, you told me that before you left. I wasn't seeing this thing coolly enough to go face-to-face with a man holding Mae Rose. If he's bringing her to us, it looks like *you was*." He took a deep breath. "I'm obliged, Ranger. I owe you a lot for how you've done this. As wild-eyed as I was, I'd have likely got us both killed, and Mae Rose too."

"It's not done yet, Sheriff," Sam warned. "There's still some twists and turns ahead of us."

"What are you saying, Ranger?"

"Edsel knows Mae Rose is your gal," Sam said. He studied the sheriff's face and asked, "How hard was it to get her to tell him that?"

Stone winced a little. His anger flared in his eyes.

"I'll kill that *lousy, rotten—!*" He caught himself and stopped. He took out a cough drop with trembling fingers and stuck it into his mouth. "All right, at least she's alive," he said. He took another deep breath and calmed himself down. "I'm all right. Tell me what you want me to do."

"I don't want you to do anything, except to cover me from inside here," Sam said.

"Huh-uh," Stone said. "If shooting starts I want to be right out there with you. I can handle my end. You ought to know that by now."

"I do know it, Sheriff," Sam said. "But I need you in here, covering me from the window."

"What about when you make the trade?" Stone said. "What if Edsel crawfishes at the last minute, keeps Mae Rose just to spite me? Don't put it past him, Ranger," he cautioned.

Sam let out a patient breath.

"Listen to me, Sheriff," he said. "I don't put anything past Edsel Centrila. I can't count on anything he says. That's why it's important that I can count on us. He told me Mae Rose hasn't been harmed. I don't believe him. I'm prepared for what she might look like. Are you?"

Sheriff Stone didn't reply, which the Ranger took as a reply in itself.

"That's what I thought," he said flatly. "That's another reason I want you in here, instead of out there."

Stone glanced out the gun port toward the Palace.

"They're forming up, Ranger," he said. He barely saw Mae Rose standing beside Centrila in a long cape, hood up so her face was hidden.

"What's it going to be, Sheriff?" Sam asked. "If you want the woman back alive, I'm going to need you right here by this window, just like you're still cuffed to the shutter."

"All right, you've got it," Stone said. They both looked over at the cell and saw Harper Centrila and Lon Bartow back on their feet, as if sensing trouble in the making.

"Give me your word that you won't come charging through this door if the woman's been badly beaten," Sam insisted.

Stone glanced out the gun port again, then at Sam, and said in a resolved tone of voice, "All right, you've got my word on it, Ranger."

The Ranger nodded; he held the box of bullets out for Stone.

"Here, you might need these," he said.

They shared a look, then peered out the gun port at the Silver Palace. They saw Lyle and Ignacio Cady step down from the boardwalk with the woman between them. Ahead of them Edsel Centrila stood with Charlie Knapp, Silas Rudabaugh, Don Ferry and Trent Baye gathered around him. A few drinkers who had ventured to the saloon in spite of the impending trouble stood inside and stared out through the open doors at Centrila and his men.

Chapter 24

———

"As soon as we make the swap and Harper is safe, chop this Ranger down where he's standing," Centrila said. "Leave this lousy wolf-turning *Sheriff Stone* for me." He paused, seeming to consider the matter, then added, "That is, if it looks like I'm coming out ahead. If I get in trouble, blast him, of course."

"In other words, remember who pays your wages," Knapp put in quietly. The men looked at each other and nodded in agreement. They understood.

Knapp said just between him and Centrila, "What if Stone is still cuffed, like the Ranger said?"

Centrila gave a thin, faint grin.

"That would be his misfortune," he said. Staring toward the sheriff's office, he added, "Besides, I've got a feeling he's not cuffed. That was just a ruse the Ranger came up with." He looked Knapp up and down. "Ready?"

"Ready," Knapp said, Rudabaugh right beside him.

"Let's go, then," Centrila said, staring straight ahead at the sheriff's office.

The gunmen walked forward, the Cady brothers and Mae Rose a step behind. Each of the brothers kept a hand on Mae Rose's arm. On Centrila's right Knapp held a cocked rifle at port arms.

As they neared the front of the adobe-and-plank structure, Knapp gave Ferry and Baye a nod, telling them to spread out. The group of gunmen formed a half circle in the street in front of the sheriff's office with Centrila in the middle. The big erstwhile cattleman turned saloon owner pulled his suit coat back behind a shiny nickel-plated Remington holstered on his right hip. But before he called out, the Ranger opened the door slowly and stepped out onto the boardwalk.

"Here we are, Ranger," Centrila said, "as agreed to." As he spoke he noted that the Ranger's Winchester had been replaced by a short double-barreled shotgun he'd taken from the gun rack. "Now bring out my son and Bartow."

The Ranger only stared at him. He gestured at the woman, the hood of the cape partially hiding her face.

"Let me see if she's Mae Rose Rossi," Sam said.

Edsel reached around and pulled the woman up beside him; the Cadys let go of her arms. He pulled back the hood and revealed a swollen, badly beaten face that rouge and powder had done a poor job concealing.

The Ranger saw the damage and almost tightened his finger on the shotgun hammers, expecting Stone to throw open the door and shoot Centrila on the spot. After a second passed, he lightened his finger on the triggers, grateful that Stone was a man of his word.

"Are you all right, ma'am?" Sam asked.

"I've . . . been better," Mae Rose said through cracked and swollen lips.

"You lied," the Ranger said to Centrila, looking away from the battered woman's face.

Centrila pulled the hood back up onto Mae Rose's head and gave a smug grin.

"I might have lied a little," he said. "You can expect some of that when it comes to *deal-making*, eh—am I right?" Still grinning, he looked around at his men for support. They nodded, agreeing with him. "After all, I understand that Harper has a bullet wound in his shoulder."

"All right," Sam said, as if conceding the matter. He gestured toward the front door. "Send her on in." As he spoke he rested a hand on the door handle.

The Cadys stepped in to take the woman's arms, but Centrila stopped them.

"Wait a minute, what about Harper and Bartow?" he said to Sam.

"I take her in, I bring them out," Sam said.

"Huh-uh, I don't like that," said Centrila.

"Then we're back where we started," Sam said coolly, his hand still on the door handle. "I see I'm out-gunned. I get the woman inside, or you can all go back to your saloon and I'll send Harper and Bartow to you tied over their saddles. I shot him once, I can shoot him again."

"Why, you no-good law dog . . ." Centrila caught himself and let his words trail.

"Easy, boss. I smell a trick in the works here," Knapp said beside him.

"I say we start shooting," Trent Baye put in, giving the Ranger a hard, searing stare. "This cur killed my cousin—"

"Shut up, both of you!" Centrila snapped, trying to get a grip on the situation. "It's not your son in there!" He reached over and pulled the woman forward. "All right, take her inside," he said to the Cadys. "Come out of there with Harper and Lon Bartow, or I will have your hides!"

Have their hides?

The Cady brothers looked at each other, the two of them on the spot all of a sudden. Lyle started to say something, but the look on Centrila's face warned him against it. The two stepped onto the boardwalk and toward the door, the woman between them. Sam turned the door handle, ushered them in, then stepped inside behind them and closed the door.

Harper Centrila and Lon Bartow stood pressed against the bars watching intently, awaiting their release. They saw the Ranger drop a thick iron latch on the door, grab Lyle Cady and shove the short-barreled shotgun into his belly. In reflex Lyle turned the woman loose. She hurried away and huddled against the wall. Ignacio Cady raised his hands chest high, not wanting to see his brother cut in half by a shotgun blast.

"Don't shoot, Ranger!" he shouted.

"It's a double cross, Papa Edsel!" Harper shouted toward the front window. "Get me out of here!"

"Sheriff?" Sam called out. "Sheriff Stone . . . ?" Looking all around quickly, seeing no sign of the sheriff, he lifted both Lyle's and Ignacio's guns from their holsters and pitched them away. He shoved the brothers across the office, back against the cell and cuffed them to the barred door. "Stay back," he warned Harper and Bartow as they tried to move closer, Harper still shouting to his father on the street. Sam heard fists pounding hard on the front door. He looked around once more for Stone, but the sheriff was gone.

"Get away from that door," Sam warned, bracing the shotgun at his side. But the pounding continued a second longer until he heard Stone call out from the street.

"Here I am, Edsel Centrila," the sheriff shouted, from somewhere farther back behind the gunmen.

Hearing the sheriff, Mae Rose started to move away from the wall. But the Ranger raised a hand, stopping her as he hurried to the shuttered front window.

"Stay where you are," he said to her. He looked out through the gun port and saw Sheriff Stone facing off with the gunmen, no rifle, no shotgun, only his big Colt hanging in his hand.

"Here I am, Edsel," Stone repeated, "you son of a bitch. I'm the one you came here for. Stop beating around the bush—let's start killing, just you and me!"

A tight tense silence fell over the street.

"That will suit me fine!" Centrila called out. He walked off the boardwalk back onto the dirt street, seeming to forget that his son, Harper, was still in the cell.

"Papa Edsel! Get me the hell out of here!" Harper shouted. He shook the bars with both hands. The Cady brothers stood helpless, one set of handcuffs looped through the bars, holding each of them by their wrists.

Sam saw the gunmen spread out toward the sheriff.

"Stone, you fool," he said under his breath.

"Ranger, stop him!" Mae Rose shouted, knowing what was about to happen out there.

Without replying, Sam hurried to the door, threw the latch back and swung the door open.

The gunmen looked at him; so did Centrila, who cut his gaze to the Ranger for a quick glance, then back to Stone.

"Stay out of this, Ranger, you double-crossing cur," he warned.

Sam looked at Stone, then at Ferry, Knapp, Rudabaugh and Trent Baye, the four of them ready to kill the lone lawman at Centrila's command.

"Not a chance," he said.

"You don't belong here. Damn you, Ranger!" Centrila shouted, still facing Stone.

Sam gripped the shotgun, ready to fire.

"I'm the law, Centrila," he called out. "You two have a grudge to settle, I'm right in the middle of it."

"Then to hell with the law!" shouted Centrila.

"This is for cousin Bob, Ranger!" Trent Baye shouted suddenly out of the blue. He swung his rifle toward the Ranger as Centrila made his move on Stone. But before he got off a shot, the shotgun bucked in the Ranger's hands, sending a blue-orange streak of smoke and iron scraps through Baye's chest, his face, both shoulders.

Baye's hat flew from his head in a bloody spray of shredded felt and pieces of skull and brain matter. Wasting no time, the Ranger swung the loaded barrel at Charlie Knapp. But Knapp and Rudabaugh had seen the mess the shotgun had made of Baye. They dived for the cover of a water trough.

Centrila's shot hit Stone in his collarbone and sent the sheriff staggering backward, a shot from his big Colt firing down into the dirt. Making the mistake of thinking he'd killed Stone, Centrila swung his aim toward the Ranger, levering a fresh round into his rifle chamber.

Sam threw the shotgun aside and drew his Colt. Out of the corner of his eye, he saw Rudabaugh and Knapp, upon seeing him toss the shotgun away, rise from the water trough and start firing. Sam had to ignore Centrila for now.

"Kill him!" Rudabaugh shouted.

Crouched, the Ranger fired his Colt at Rudabaugh and saw him fall backward as a bullet sliced through his stomach. On his way down, Rudabaugh's rifle flew from his hands. The rifle hit Knapp and sent Knapp's shot flying wild. Before Knapp could recover and reaim, Sam put a bullet in his chest and saw him fall backward. As Knapp fell, Sam saw the front door fly open. Mae Rose ran out toward the fallen sheriff.

"Shep! Shep!" she screamed as she ran, in spite of swollen lips, her battered condition.

"*Look out,*" Sam shouted at her, hearing Centrila's rifle fire, feeling the slice of the bullet rush past his head like an angry hornet. From inside the open door, Sam heard the *ping-ping* whine of the bullet ricochet twice off the iron bars. He heard the Cady brothers shriek in fear. He spun toward Centrila just in time to see Stone rise onto his knee and put a bullet through Centrila's chest. Centrila's rifle fell in the dirt beside him.

Sam looked all around, still crouched, his smoking Colt cocked, guiding him. He saw Donald Ferry's rifle lying abandoned in the dirt, and when he looked up, he saw the scared gunman racing away as fast as his boots could carry him. Heads ventured out of the doors of the Silver Palace. Burnt powder wafted on the air.

"You've killed him, Ranger, you son of a bitch," Sam heard a voice call out from inside the open door. He straightened warily, backed his way to the open door and walked inside. Behind him on the street, Mae Rose helped the bloody sheriff to his feet. Supporting each other, they walked toward the open door.

Inside, Sam stepped over to where Ignacio Cady stood holding his free hand to his brother's bleeding forehead. Lyle's head bobbed limply on his chest, both of them held up by their wrists cuffed through the bars.

"Bullet graze, knocked him cold," Ignacio said.

Sam just looked, his Colt slumped a little.

"Not him, damn you!" Lon Bartow cried out from inside the cell.

Sam looked around and saw Bartow kneeling on the floor, Harper Centrila's head held tight against him, a wadded bandanna pressed against the side of Harper's bloody neck.

"He's dead. He's dead sure enough," Bartow said, rocking back and forth slightly as if comforting a child. "I hope this is enough for you," he said accusingly, "you law-dog son of a bitch."

Sam heard the sheriff and the woman's footsteps and half turned as they walked in. Stone, using Ferry's abandoned rifle as a walking cane, seated Mae Rose in his chair at his badly tilted desk. He stepped over to the Ranger, his left hand cupped to his bloody, broken collarbone, a sliver of white sticking up through the ripped skin.

"You—you shot him?" he asked the Ranger in a lowered voice.

"Huh-uh." The Ranger shook his head and tipped his Colt toward a fresh gash Edsel Centrila's rifle shot had left on the iron bar after grazing Lyle Cady's head. "Ricochet," he said quietly. He nodded out the door at the street where Edsel Centrila lay grappling in the dirt, but going nowhere.

"Lord God!" Stone said. "Edsel killed his own son."

"Yeah," Sam said, still in a lowered tone. "After all the men who've died. After all he went through just to get his payback on you." He shook his head and let out a thin breath. "He ended up killing the person he was trying to protect to begin with."

The two lawmen looked out and watched Centrila push himself up onto his knees. He struggled and raised the shiny Remington from his holster and waved it back and forth.

"Stone, it's not over!" he shouted. "Hell no, it's not! Ranger, send Harper and Bartow out here! You made a deal!"

Stone looked around at Bartow, at Harper's body and shook his head.

"This don't feel as good as it should," he said.

Sam just looked at him. He watched the sheriff take the bandanna from around his neck, wad it and press it carefully onto the broken collarbone. He took his hand down and let the blood soak through and hold it in place for the time being. Rifle in hand, he walked to the open door.

Sam gave him a curious look.

"Will telling him he killed his son make you feel any better, Sheriff?" he said. On the street, Edsel Centrila managed a wheezing broken laugh. He swung the Remington back and forth as if searching for something or someone to kill.

"No, it won't," Stone said over his good shoulder. "Far as I'm concerned, he need never know he did it." With that, he raised the rifle to his good shoulder. With no regard to the pain it caused him, he steadied the front stock, took aim and fired a round that left a red mist looming as Edsel Centrila fell back dead in the street.

Sam stood for a moment, making it right in his mind. For all of the bitter vengeance festering between the two, in the end Sam figured Stone just did the man a favor. He watched Stone lower the rifle and lean it against the wall. He saw him go to where Mae Rose sat watching, the cape gathered at her throat.

"Let me look at you, Mae Rose," Stone said, easing the hood back so it fell to her shoulders.

"Don't look at me, Sheriff," Mae Rose said. "I know I look terrible." She tried to look away, but Stone moved his face with hers.

"Look at me," he said. He carefully tipped her swollen chin up and looked into her blackened, swollen eyes. "If you were any prettier, I don't think I could stand it."

The Ranger looked away and walked to the open

door. Ignacio Cady stood staring. His brother, Lyle, had come around some and stood with his bloody head bobbing on his chest.

"I'll just go get the doctor and bring him back," Sam said. He stepped out across the boardwalk and onto the dirt street. At the Silver Palace, men were venturing out and looking toward the sheriff's office.

"Ranger," Stone called out before Sam had gone fifty feet. When he stopped and looked around, he saw Stone in the open door, cupping his bleeding wound. "I kept my word, you know," he said.

Sam just looked at him.

"I promised not to come out this door, and I didn't, huh?" He gave a thin half smile and touched a finger to the side of his head. A cough drop lay in his cheek.

Sam offered no reply. He only shook his head and gave a toss of a hand back over his shoulder. And he walked on.

Read on for a look at one of
Ralph Cotton's most loved Westerns

WILDFIRE

Available from Signet.

Arizona Territory

Wildfire raged.

The young Ranger, Sam Burrack, sat atop a rust-colored barb on a bald ridge overlooking a wide, rocky chasm. With a battered brass-trimmed telescope, he scanned beyond the buffering walls of boulder and brush. Long, rising hillsides ran slantwise heaven to earth, covered by an endless pine woodlands. He studied the blanketing fire as it billowed and twisted its way north to south along the hill lines. He watched flames the color of hell lick upward hundreds of feet, drifting, blackening the heavens.

Through the circle of the lens, he spotted four wolves sitting next to one another along a rock ledge, winded and panting. Their pink tongues a-loll, they stared back at the wall of smoke and fire as if numbed, overpowered by it.

At the bottom of the hills, where the woodlands came to an end at a chasm, Sam saw a large brown bear stop in its tracks, turn and rise on its hind legs. The large beast stood erect with its forearms and claws spread wide and raged back at the fire, ready to do battle. Yet even so powerful a beast looked helpless and frail beneath that which lay spoil to its domain. At the end of its roar, the bear dropped back onto all fours as if bowing in submission, and loped on.

The Ranger shook his head, noting how little caution the other fleeing woodland creatures paid the large beast as they darted among dry washes and gullies and bounded over brush and rock with no more than a reflex glance in the roaring bear's direction. Even the barb beneath him paid no mind to the bear's warning until a draft of hot smoke swept in behind it. Then the horse skittered sideways and chuffed and scraped a nervous hoof.

"Easy, now . . . ," the Ranger murmured, tightening on the reins and collecting the animal. "We're not going to get you cooked." He patted a gloved hand on the barb's withers. "Me neither, I'm hoping," he added, closing the telescope between his hands. He looked down at the sets of hoofprints he'd been tracking for three days and gave the barb a tap of his bootheels.

But the barb would have none of it. Instead, the animal grumbled and sawed its head and stalled back on its front legs.

The Ranger picked up his Winchester from across his lap. He gave another, firmer tap of his bootheels, this time reaching back with his rifle and lightly striking the barrel on the barb's rump.

"Come on, pard, we know our jobs," he said.

This time he felt the barb take his command and step forward onto the down-winding path toward the rocky land below them. But even as the animal did so, he gave a chuff of protest.

"I know," said Sam. "I don't like it either. . . ."

Four hundred yards down, the meandering dirt trail hardened into rock and left the Ranger with no sign to follow other than the occasional broken pine needles where one of the four men's horses had laid down an iron-ringed hoof. But that gave him no cause for concern—the old overgrown game trail lay down the rocky deep-cut hillside. And now that the fire had moved in across the thick woodlands, there would be no other logical way north at the bottom of the hills except to follow the rock chasm to its end.

He knew the bottom trail would stretch fourteen miles before coming to water—twenty-six miles farther before reaching Bagley's Trading Post. By then, the men he followed would need fresh horses. They wouldn't rest these horses out before riding on. That took too much time, he told himself. Men like Royal Tarpis, Silas "Red" Gantry, Dockery Latin never wasted time when they were on the move. Out in the open this way, these men instinctively moved as if someone was on their trail, whether they knew it to be a fact or not.

Men with blood on their trail . . . , Sam told himself, knowing there was a younger man leading the gang these days. That man was the Cheyenne Kid, and he was known to be ruthless. But now the Kid was wounded, bleeding. He'd shot and killed two men in

Phoebe, a bank teller and the town sheriff. The sheriff had managed to put a bullet in the murdering young outlaw before falling dead in the street. Sam had picked up the men's trail the following day, and he'd been on it ever since.

Sure, they knew someone was coming.

Sam drew the barb to a halt at a break in the trail and looked to his left, across the chasm where the fire roared, smoke filling the sky. He took off his left glove and felt the barb's withers. The horse's coat was dry— hot to his touch. So was his own left cheek, he thought, raising his palm to his face, feeling the prickliness of his beard stubble, noticing the stiff, scorched sensation along his cheek line, the dryness in the corners of his eyes as he squinted them shut for a second, gauging the heat.

Untying the bandanna from around his neck, Sam fashioned a curtain of it beneath the brim of his sombrero and draped it down his left cheek. It would help some, he thought.

"I hope I didn't lie to you, pard," he said to the horse, recalling his earlier words to the animal.

He picked up his canteen hanging from his saddle horn, uncapped it, swished a mouthful of water around in his mouth and spit it out along the left side of horse's neck. He leaned forward in his saddle and poured a thin stream of water down the horse's muzzle and along its left side, taking in his own leg and back along its flank. The horse shuddered and chuffed and reached its tongue around to lick at its side.

"That's all for now," Sam said.

He capped the canteen and rehung it. All right, it was hot, but he'd expected that, he reminded himself. Three miles ahead of him, give or take, he saw the fire had waned on its push southward. In the wake of the billowing inferno stood a few bare and blackened pine skeletons.

But he and the horse were safe. He had calculated the risk before putting the horse forward onto the trail. Had the wind made a sudden shift and blown straight at them before they'd reached the trail's halfway point, he would have turned back and raced to the top again before succumbing to the heat. Halfway down the trail, he'd realized there was an end to the fire a few miles to the north—the direction he was headed in. From that point, had the wind changed suddenly, he would have raced down the trail.

Whichever way, they'd make it.

And oddly enough, he thought, owing to the rise of heat, it had been hotter atop the trail than it was here below. Still, it had been risky, said a cautioning voice that often admonished him at times such as these.

Yes, it had, he admitted. *But . . .* He let out a breath of relief.

" 'Life is naught without its risks,' " he quoted to himself.

Who had said that? He shrugged as he nudged the horse forward. He didn't know. Probably some obscure penny dreadful author who had stood, or *imagined* himself to have stood, on just such a trail as this.

He started forward along the lower end of the trail, where he knew the heat would be less intense. As he rode he shook his head. Leave it to men like these to ride into a wildfire, he thought.

Why had they done that?

But as he asked the question, he had to remind himself that he had followed without hesitation—so closely that he'd had to water both himself and his horse down to keep up his pursuit. What did that say about him? He didn't want to think about it right now.

He rode on.

Four miles farther down along the chasm trail, he felt the heat on his left begin to wane. A mile farther the temperature had subsided enough that he was able to take the bandanna down from his face. Beneath him the rusty barb rode at a stronger gallop. Along their left, beyond the buffer of boulders, dirt and shale, the woodlands lay blackened and ruined, smoke still rising. It was slower now, less intense, but nevertheless engulfed them in a gray, suffocating haze.

Now he had another problem.

He stopped the horse and stepped down from his saddle. He listened to the barb wheeze and choke, its labored breath rattling deep in its lungs.

"Easy, boy," he said, rubbing the horse's muzzle. He stepped back to his saddlebags, rummaged out a shirt and shook it out.

He tied the sleeves up around the horse's head and made a veil of the shirt. The horse resisted a little and whipped its head until the Ranger took the canteen and poured water down the horse's face and threw the shirt onto its parched muzzle. He held the wet shirt in place, letting the animal breathe through it. When the horse felt the good of what the Ranger was doing and settled, Sam took his hand off its muzzle.

"Good boy."

He poured water onto his bandanna and tied it across the bridge of his nose. He led the horse forward by its reins, feeling the thickness of the smoke with every step.

"I make it . . . seven, eight miles to water," he rasped, as if the winded horse understood his words and took comfort in them.

Three miles farther, he noted the smoke had let up, enough that he could make out the blue of the sky. The horse breathed easier; so did he. Stopping, he took down the warm canteen and lifted the shirt from the horse's muzzle. He kneeled in front of the horse and took off his sombrero like a man given to a vigil of prayer.

"You need this worse than I do," he said, pouring the water into the upturned hat.

The horse lowered its muzzle into the sombrero and Sam let the wet shirt fall around the ensemble.

When the horse finished the water and tried chewing at the hat brim for more, Sam stood and pulled his wet sombrero away and placed it atop his head. Canteen in hand, he climbed into the saddle and gave the horse a tap of his heels. On their left, among boulder rocks and dry washes, antelope, deer, coyote and an assortment of smaller creatures still skirted in the same direction, slower now that the threat of death inched farther into the distance.

National bestselling author
RALPH COMPTON

THE MAN FROM NOWHERE
SIXGUNS AND DOUBLE EAGLES
BOUNTY HUNTER
FATAL JUSTICE
STRYKER'S REVENGE
DEATH OF A HANGMAN
NORTH TO THE SALT FORK
DEATH RIDES A CHESTNUT MARE
RUSTED TIN
THE BURNING RANGE
WHISKEY RIVER
THE LAST MANHUNT
THE AMARILLO TRAIL
SKELETON LODE
STRANGER FROM ABILENE
THE SHADOW OF A NOOSE
THE GHOST OF APACHE CREEK
RIDERS OF JUDGMENT
SLAUGHTER CANYON
DEAD MAN'S RANCH
ONE MAN'S FIRE
THE OMAHA TRAIL
DOWN ON GILA RIVER
BRIMSTONE TRAIL
STRAIGHT SHOOTER
THE HUNTED
HARD RIDE TO WICHITA
TUCKER'S RECKONING
CHEYENNE TRAIL
DOUBLE-CROSS RANCH
THE DANGEROUS LAND
VIGILANTE DAWN
THE EVIL MEN DO
STRAIGHT TO THE NOOSE
THE LAW AND THE LAWLESS
BROTHER'S KEEPER

"A writer in the tradition of Louis L'Amour and Zane Grey!" —*Huntsville Times*

Available wherever books are sold or at
penguin.com

S543

No other series packs this much heat!

THE TRAILSMAN

#369: BADLANDS BLOODSPORT
#370: BLIND MAN'S BLUFF
#371: CALIFORNIA KILLERS
#372: MISSOURI MASTERMIND
#373: UTAH TERROR
#374: FORT DEATH
#375: TEXAS SWAMP FEVER
#376: NEW MEXICO MADMAN
#377: BOUNTY HUNT
#378: WYOMING WINTERKILL
#379: HANGTOWN HELLCAT
#380: TEXAS TORNADO
#381: BOWIE'S KNIFE
#382: TERROR TRACKDOWN
#383: HIGH PLAINS MASSACRE
#384: DIABLO DEATH CRY
#385: THUNDERHEAD TRAIL
#386: NEVADA VIPER'S NEST
#387: APACHE VENDETTA
#388: BORDERLAND BLOODBATH
#389: OUTLAW TRACKDOWN
#390: DEVIL'S DEN
#391: NIGHT TERROR
#392: COLORADO CARNAGE
#393: SIX-GUN INFERNO
#394: BURNING BULLETS
#395: BLACK HILLS DEATHBLOW
#396: DEAD MAN'S JOURNEY
#397: RIVERBOAT RECKONING

Available wherever books are sold or at
penguin.com